MW01153469

TWITCH TWITCH

Written by
Lee Love

authorHOUSE®

AuthorHouse™
1663 Liberty Drive
Bloomington, IN 47403
www.authorhouse.com
Phone: 1-800-839-8640

© *2011 Lee Love. All rights reserved.*

No part of this book may be reproduced, stored in a retrieval system, or transmitted by any means without the written permission of the author.

First published by AuthorHouse 5/16/2011

ISBN: 978-1-4567-5616-1 (e)
ISBN: 978-1-4567-5617-8 (hc)
ISBN: 978-1-4567-5618-5 (sc)

Library of Congress Control Number: 2011904448

Printed in the United States of America

Any people depicted in stock imagery provided by Thinkstock are models, and such images are being used for illustrative purposes only. Certain stock imagery © Thinkstock.

This book is printed on acid-free paper.

Because of the dynamic nature of the Internet, any web addresses or links contained in this book may have changed since publication and may no longer be valid. The views expressed in this work are solely those of the author and do not necessarily reflect the views of the publisher, and the publisher hereby disclaims any responsibility for them.

In Loving Memory

Of

Yolanda & Alethea & George

TABLE OF CONTENTS

PART ONE—TYRANTS AND ASSES

CHAPTER 1

YOU HAVE TO PROMISE ME that you won't tell anyone. Please. This is just between us, right? I was told this in the strictest confidence myself, and I'm telling you in the same manner. But stories like this, they just demand to be told. They take on their own lives, don't they? Some things you just can't keep bottled up.

It started with a name ringing out and echoing around the cube farm of Lexhouse Advertising's corporate office: "Le-*teeeee*-shuh!"

Leticia looked up, first in surprise, and then in resignation. She sighed. She hadn't been working at Lexhouse, or for Melba, for long, but it had been long enough.

Melba Grossott stalked out of the Monday morning staff meeting fuming. She was red faced, her eyes narrowed into slits. In her two-and-a-half-inch spiked heel pumps, Melba looked like a scrawny pencil with blond curly hair. Her lips were pressed into such a thin line they looked penciled onto her face. The ugly sneer added decades to her face.

Steam was practically coming out of her ears as she stormed right into her assistant's mouse-sized cubicle. "Leticia." Melba said it so sharply, the three-syllable name seemed to collapse into a single, staccato sound.

"Melba," Leticia responded cautiously. She peered up at her boss. Melba was high strung, self-involved, and quick to anger on the best of days, but the raw anger distorting Melba's features was new to Leticia.

"You stole my money."

Leticia's eyes widened, as large and saucer-like as Melba's lips were compressed. Too shocked to speak, she just shook her head in denial.

"You stole my money!" Melba repeated. Melba rarely used her indoor voice anyway, but by the end of this statement, there was surely not a person in the office who hadn't heard. Indeed, the background office noises had fallen utterly still. Leticia felt her face and neck burn as she flushed under her dark skin. Still, she couldn't quite articulate a response.

"Admit it, you … you … *immigrant!*"

Leticia's mouth, which had been soundlessly trying to form words to deny Melba's outrageous accusation, snapped shut. She returned Melba's glare. "I did no such thing," she said with as much dignity as she could muster. She spoke with a pronounced Jamaican accent, but she always spoke clear, proper English.

"You were the only one who could. You were in the office alone with my purse, and when I checked later, the money was gone, so you did it! Process of elimination! You're a filthy, lying, treacherous little thief! I knew it was a mistake to hire you; I knew it the first minute I laid eyes on you—"

"Melba." The firm voice was perhaps the only one in the office with the impact to stop her in the middle of her rant. Melba's head swung around. Mr. Foles stood a few feet away, gazing steadily at her.

She leapt on her chance. She thrust a long, bony finger in Leticia's face, so close the Jamaican flinched back. "She's a thief, she—"

"I heard you the first time. The whole office heard you, Melba. My office. Now. You too, Leticia." Without waiting for a response, he turned on his heel and walked away. He spoke evenly, not a single syllable betraying any emotion, but only a fool would mistake his irritation at Melba's public disruption.

That fool was Melba, apparently.

"Ha!" she said to Leticia. "Now you'll get what you deserve." And then she, too, marched off in a head-held-high victory parade of one. Leticia stood more slowly, her face hot with humiliation. As she rose, she saw heads all across the office poking above their cube walls, watching the drama unfold in front of them. Leticia's eyes burned with unshed tears of indignation.

She followed Melba and Mr. Foles into his office. She kept her eyes focused straight ahead, blinking rapidly to hold back any tears, too proud—and innocent of the accusation—to look down, but still too embarrassed to meet anyone's gaze.

Leticia walked past Mr. Foles's assistant, Frances, who watched her with a bemused expression. She stepped past Mr. Foles at the entrance to his office. He shut the door behind them and moved to his desk. Leticia sat delicately in the vacant chair.

Melba, already seated, launched immediately into her explanation. She spoke so fast it was hard to understand: "This is what happened: Leticia came into my office this morning so I could give her the receipts to finish my expense report; while she was gathering those, I stepped out to use the ladies' room, leaving my purse in there when I got back—"

"In the ladies' room?" Mr. Foles interrupted.

"What?"

"Did you leave your purse in the ladies' room?"

"No, in my office. I left my purse in my office with Leticia, and when I got back, I went immediately to our staff meeting; while in the meeting, I went through my purse—you remember that, I'm sure—and that's when I realized it was missing." She finally paused to take a breath.

"What was missing?" Mr. Foles asked.

"The money. The money I got from the bank this morning." She turned a dark look on Leticia. "A lot of money. I'm sure it seemed like an irresistible amount to someone like her."

"No, it's not true!" Leticia finally exclaimed.

"Leticia. You'll get your turn. Let Melba finish, please."

"All the cash was gone." Melba turned to Leticia. "You need to get on your banana boat and go back to your island and pick coconuts. You don't belong here." She swiveled to face Mr. Foles again. "She'll be fired, of course."

Mr. Foles's eyes flicked over to the young assistant. "Leticia?"

"It's not true, Mr. Foles! I swear! After Melba left her office, I didn't even realize she'd left her purse behind; I didn't even see it. I love working here; I would never jeopardize—"

"Well, *of course* she would deny it."

Mr. Foles stared at Leticia for a long moment, and then turned back to the older woman. "Melba, you're making a serious accusation against Leticia. Are you *sure* the money is gone? Perhaps it just wasn't where you remembered putting it."

"I think I'd remember where I put two hundred dollars in cash."

"Still, perhaps you could check your purse once again."

Melba didn't move at first, and Leticia wondered if Melba was going to refuse. But then the fake blonde just shook her head and pulled her

Coach bag up into her lap. She started rummaging through its contents, pulling out personal items one by one and banging them onto Mr. Foles's desk. "Really, it's not going to be in here." Her fingers sifted through papers and small packages. "And of course I searched thoroughly in the meeting; surely you noticed."

Her fingers snagged her pocketbook, and she pulled it out. She unsnapped the latch and rifled through its contents. "I'm telling you, I'd hardly let a wad of cash go astray; I'm much too responsible for th—oh." She fell silent.

After a moment, Mr. Foles said, "Melba?"

Without looking up, Melba pulled a bank envelope that had been clipped into a recessed fold in the pocketbook. She opened the envelope, revealing a small stack of crisp twenty-dollar bills.

"Is that the money?" Mr. Foles asked.

"Ah. Yes. Yes, that would be it." She looked up at Mr. Foles with a smile that she probably thought was flirty. Melba laughed in a fake girlish way. "Oh, I'm so sorry, Mr. Foles, for wasting your time like that. It's just one of those Mondays, I guess. False alarm."

Mr. Foles gazed at her, frowning slightly. Leticia found it very difficult to read Mr. Foles's expressions, so she couldn't tell what he was thinking. Leticia herself was fuming.

Melba stood and turned, as if to go, when Mr. Foles's voice caught her again. "Melba."

She looked over her shoulder expectantly.

"I'm not the only one to whom you owe an apology." He nodded at Leticia.

"Oh, yes, of course." She shot a glance in Leticia's general direction. "Sorry, 'Ticia. My mistake." She looked again at Mr. Foles, who nodded almost imperceptibly. Melba left the office without a backward glance. Leticia rose to follow.

"Melba, please step back inside and close the door," said Mr. Foles sharply. "Leticia, please sit down again," he continued. "Melba, please listen closely to what I am about to say. This organization will not tolerate anyone, *anyone*, demeaning anyone's ethnicity. Appropriate action will be taken if that happens. Do you understand me, Melba?"

"Yes," replied the humiliated Melba meekly. Mr. Foles watched as Melba left wordlessly.

Back at her cube, Leticia swiveled some more in her chair and tried to pretend she could see out the window.

From the eighth floor of the Universe Building, smack in the middle of the New York City central business district, the New York branch of Lexhouse Advertising overlooked vast and busy streets below. But none of the eight account representatives took advantage of the view from their office windows. Always on the phone with clients or chattering with each other, slyly trying to worm their way up the corporate ladder, they hardly noticed the wonderful vantage.

Leticia sighed. Naturally, the people who would appreciate the view had no access to it. But then, she probably wouldn't get any work done. Even after months in the city, she still stared in wonder at the thick New York snowfalls that blanketed the city in velvety white. The winterscape never ceased to fascinate her, so alien from the tropical climate of her native Jamaica. Even the burst of foggy breaths on frigid days entranced her. She would stand at the bus stop and stare until she caught herself. Exhalations of smoke, one after the other, and no cigarettes involved. For some reason, it made her think of her favorite Charles Dickens novels.

Leticia's parents had always taught her to do whatever was necessary to succeed. Sometimes, you have to scratch and claw your way to the top, and that's just what it took. She remembered one of her mother's favorite expressions: *"Duppy know who fi frighten."* Ghosts know who to frighten; bullies know who to pick on. If Melba had targeted her, did that mean Leticia wasn't doing everything she could to succeed?

But her father specifically had advised her to "lie low" and just "soak that New York way up." So that's what Leticia had been doing; is that what had made Melba think Leticia was toothless, defenseless?

Leticia got back to work, wondering what Mr. Foles was thinking about the whole sorry situation. When Melba was around him, she always pretended to be a team player and act like a grateful employee, but hopefully, Mr. Foles saw through her act.

And it sure was an act! That Melba was nothing but one giant hypocrite.

Sighing, Leticia swiveled back toward her desk to get back to work.

Later that afternoon, on her way back from the ladies' room, someone grabbed Leticia by the arm. The girl swung her head around but relaxed when she saw it was Evanne, the only coworker Leticia had befriended.

"Girl, that was some drama. I've been dying to hear about it, except that Henry wouldn't let me leave. 'Got to finish these.'" Evanne rolled her eyes, and then focused on Leticia. "So spill, girl, before I die of not knowing."

"Melba accused me of stealing money."

"Well, duh. Everyone heard that bit. What happened in Mr. Foles's office?"

"He made her search her purse again, and she found the money."

Evanne frowned. "Well, that doesn't make any sense then."

"What doesn't?"

"You haven't heard? Oh, I just assumed … because of what happened … that you knew."

But Leticia was frowning in confusion. Evanne grabbed her arm again. "Come on."

Evanne dragged Leticia into the break room. As they moved, Leticia marveled at her friend's wig of the day bouncing in front of her. Each day it was something different: black, brown, auburn, reddish brown, blonde, short, long, curly, even an Afro now and then. Today, the hair was so red it was nearly magenta, and it hung straight down to Evanne's shoulders. Evanne's gaze swept through the break room to make sure they were alone. She pulled Leticia over to the corner by the refrigerator, whose low hum helped masked some of the office noises.

"What is it?" Leticia asked.

Evanne leaned in close. "Melba went to human resources about you!"

Leticia's mouth fell open into a little O. But she was proven innocent! Evanne nodded, eyes wide and serious. "Oh my Lord," Leticia gasped.

Evanne pulled at her lips, staring off into the break room. "What's she up to, you think?"

CHAPTER 2

"M E?" L ETICIA RESPONDED IN SHOCK and amazement.

Evanne continued, "The woman went to HR and asked for you to be her private secretary. Can you believe it? As if she hasn't already made you her personal servant." Evanne nearly spat. "She's upset because the company won't give her her own personal assistant."

"She wants me be her *secretary*? She just accused me of stealing from her! She said I didn't belong here!"

Evanne leveled a look at Leticia. "This is Mega-Maniac Melba we're talking about." Sometimes, Evanne called Melba a megalomaniac, and sometimes just a maniac.

"Oh. Right."

"If she can't defeat you …"

Leticia took several deep breaths, thinking that over. It didn't bode well. Then: "Well, what did HR say?"

"They said no, but according to my source"—Evanne's eyes twinkled, but Leticia guessed it was Evanne's boss, Tim, an easygoing and affable account exec—"she still intends to use you like her own private secretary. As if she doesn't already." She grabbed an apple from a bowl of fruit on the counter. She rubbed it on her shirt, and then took a big, juicy bite.

"Why would she want me as a secretary? I can't do secretarial work!" Another way to get Leticia fired?

Evanne shrugged and took another bite, and then she said with a mouth full of apple, "Melba's trying to make you into her own personal whatever."

Leticia thought furiously for a moment. "Is there anything I can do?" she asked. "I was hired only as a file clerk. My computer skills got me the job, but that's all I know how to do: make sure all the accounts in the computer have the proper documents, and if not, then research, find the problem, and fix it."

"A file clerk?" Evanne asked. She frowned. "I thought you were a document control specialist, like me."

"Well, they have me working as a file clerk. Apparently, that's where the 'company need' is."

"Huh. Well, Melba's been with the company for over ten years, and all she got on her ten-year anniversary was a watch. You know James is going to be out all next week?"

Leticia nodded. She missed Mr. Foles already.

"Well, you pay attention to Melba closely. Note the way she acts, and especially her attitude when James isn't around. She's going to try to take advantage of you, and you can't let her! Keep in mind I'm telling you that HR said no! You were hired as a file clerk, you're being paid as a file clerk, and that is that.

"However, you know she's going to have you do things that a secretary would, but for no extra pay. Don't you do them! Don't you let her exploit you like that!"

But Leticia could only hear part of Evanne's comments around the mouthfuls of apple.

* * *

The next morning, Leticia had barely settled into her desk when she heard a breathless "Leticia!" from behind her.

She turned around and found Melba standing behind her like a proud peacock dressed in her dark business suit, white shirt, and pearl button earrings: the perfect uniform of a complete corporate soldier.

"They don't like me," Melba hissed. "They treat me, oh God! Leticia, they treat me as if I am a cleaning lady. I am a college graduate with over ten years of direct advertising experience." Leticia nodded noncommittally, but Melba paid her no mind. "And all these men that James Foles keeps advancing and giving accounts, tell me why? Those guys can't do any better than me. They can barely manage the accounts they *already* have."

Leticia was surprised Melba didn't start again how her rival account rep *Paul* had *three* assistants, how *Paul* got all the plum accounts, and on and on.

Truth be told, Leticia sympathized with both Mr. Foles, who always had a warm smile and a kind hello for all his charges, and Paul, who was so friendly. And so handsome! Leticia was by no means alone in that assessment. Broad-shouldered and tall, with deep blue eyes and silky blond hair, Paul turned more than a few female—and even male—heads.

With a start, Leticia realized that Melba had stopped speaking and was staring at her as if she were a circus clown out in public in full makeup. Leticia blushed. This was her first job, after all, and she desperately wanted to master the ways of the office. She hadn't forgotten her humiliation at Melba's hands the previous day, but what was the alternative? She didn't want to return to Jamaica because she couldn't last in New York. Her parents would welcome her back with open arms, and they would also be terribly disappointed in her.

Melba finally said, "I can't see any promotion here."

Puzzled, Leticia wondered what Melba meant. Had she been expecting a promotion? Or was she talking about Leticia herself?

Her boss added, "Did you finish those expense reports I gave you?"

Leticia frowned in consternation. "Um, no."

Melba's face darkened. Leticia hastened to add, "I was confused." The assistant pulled out the paperwork and said, "This doesn't make any sense to me." Melba bent over her, and Leticia could smell the woman's cheap perfume covering a musty old-lady smell. And to think Melba claimed to be thirty-five.

"What?" Melba asked, her face scrunching up.

"See here?" she said. She held up a receipt alongside Melba's personal accounting of the expenses from her recent business trip to the BALI headquarters.

"This says forty-five dollars for your lunch." Leticia tapped the personal accounting. "But this, the numbers, they're smudged, but it looks like they say thirty-five dollars."

Melba snatched the receipt from Leticia's hand. She peered closely at it, and then at Leticia, who was watching her expectantly. "It looks like forty-five dollars to me. And anyway, forty-five dollars is what it cost me. So I'm going to get reimbursed forty-five dollars." She shrugged it off.

"They're all like this," Leticia said.

Evanne excitedly walked to Leticia's desk, but Melba either didn't notice Evanne or was just ignoring her. Melba snapped, "Just put down the numbers I gave you. God, how dumb are you? All I want is for you to fill out the damn expense report form and turn it in. Je-*sus*. What about the BALI account numbers?"

Leticia turned away. She didn't want Melba to see her expression. "I'll get started on them now." She did her best to keep her voice even. It was hard.

Melba stared at the papers over Leticia's shoulder, making a soft smacking noise as she sucked on her teeth. "This all seems clear to me. What is it with you and money? You're just bound and determined to make problems for me, aren't you?"

Leticia turned an incredulous expression toward Melba. "Then why did you—" But she stopped herself. She wasn't sure if she was supposed to know the news about Melba going to HR, and she didn't want to get Evanne in trouble. Evanne just looked at a bewildered Leticia and shook her head side to side.

"Look, Leticia, all I'm saying is I'm the boss. You just do what I say, and everything's fine."

And suddenly, Leticia understood. All of Melba's irrational, confusing behavior converged into a single common thread. Melba was trying to put Leticia in her place, to make sure Leticia understood the proper pecking order. She was just doing it in Melba's own peculiar mega-maniac way. But instead of calming or amusing Leticia, this realization enraged her. Treating Leticia as though she were some kind of *peasant*?

But Leticia didn't let her emotion control her. Her parents always said, "Do whatever it takes to succeed. We all have to do things and pretend things we don't like. That's just what it takes."

So Leticia smiled and said, "Of course, Melba, you're absolutely right. You're the boss."

Her boss stared at her for another long moment. "You speak well, for a foreigner, but sometimes your accent is so thick I can't understand a single thing you're saying."

Leticia didn't respond. No one else had that problem. Leticia refrained from educating Melba on her university background.

"You know, we took a corporate cruise a few years back through the Caribbean. It seemed like every island was full of horrible, rude people, all trying to hound us, selling us cheap homemade souvenirs, and taking

10

advantage of us. Are you from one of those islands?" Did Melba not remember Mr. Foles's advice about condescending remarks, or did she feel so powerful that she did not care?

Although Leticia had no idea how to respond to that, she knew Melba well enough to understand her boss was just being bitchy because Leticia had questioned her. "Um …"

"Don't worry, you don't have to say," Melba said in a fake sweet voice. "I wouldn't want to admit it either." And with that, she turned. She froze when she realized Evanne was behind her. "How—how long have you been standing there?" Apparently, Melba was not aware that Evanne overheard the conversation.

"Long enough, Melba," Evanne said coolly. "Just wanted to say good morning."

"Well, good morning!" Melba snarled and stalked out of the cubicle.

At that moment, Mr. Foles, affectionately known as Mr. Head Honcho, approached and paused outside Leticia's cube. Leticia, angry and shaken, took a deep breath and didn't utter a single word. She heard Melba's high-pitched voice carry over the short cubicle walls: "James! That was a great meeting. You've really put together some good teams."

"Thanks, Melba."

Leticia and Evanne rolled their eyes simultaneously. Although why was she surprised to hear such hypocrisy from Melba? She look back to find Melba had returned. Her boss was smiling at Mr. Foles, a wide toothy grin, nodding her head ceaselessly like one of those head-bobbling toys.

"Was there something else, Melba?" Mr. Foles asked. He smiled, too, and his voice was friendly, but his tone left no doubt that unless Melba had further business to discuss, she was to depart.

Her smile disappeared in a flash, replaced by two thin ruby lips pressed together. Melba glanced at Leticia, half angry, half scared. Leticia looked away, confused again—what was up with Melba? She wasn't the most stable or thoughtful person to begin, but today she was going over the top.

Then Melba turned back to Mr. Foles and said, "Not at all. I just gave Leticia several important assignments that should keep her busy the rest of the afternoon. I'll let her get to work." *And you should, too,* she left unsaid.

Mr. Foles nodded sagaciously. After Melba turned her back and strode away, he shook his head a little. He looked at Leticia, and his smile warmed. Leticia smiled back despite herself.

"Just wanted to check in on you," he drawled. "How are you both?"

"Good, sir," she said shyly.

"Any day alive is a good day, I say," Evanne announced. Mr. Foles nodded hesitantly. "See you at lunch, Leticia. Have a super day, Mr. Foles!"

"You too, Evanne. Now, Leticia, I saw Melba talking to you. I hope she wasn't too hard on you?"

Leticia shook her head. "No, sir, it's okay. I'm here to learn."

"You have a good attitude, Leticia," he said. "You're a real team player. I was impressed with how you comported yourself, yesterday." He paused, and then added, "You can always come to me if you need to." He glanced after Melba. "Not everyone has such a great attitude, and if you ever need, well, need any support or encouragement ... or help, I'm here."

"Thank you, sir."

He nodded again affably and sauntered off. Leticia watched him duck into another cube a little bit down to say hello to its occupant.

* * *

The next week roared in like a lion: a cold Monday morning buffeted by vast winds, heavy rains, and almost nonstop thunder. The Manhattan skyscrapers rose, dreary and bitter, into a cold and angry sky. To add insult to injury, the wind ripped Leticia's umbrella from her hands and tossed it away, and then whistled past her and nearly toppled the petite woman.

She stumbled into the building and over to her desk where she collapsed, dripping, into her chair. She could still hear the thunder outside.

"Girl!" cried Evanne. "I thought that was you; I saw your image dart past my desk. Ooh! You are dripping wet."

Leticia smiled soddenly for her friend. Today, Evanne was wearing a spiky, bleached blonde wig. Every day she got more outlandish.

"Come on, girl, let's dry off."

The two headed to the ladies' room. "Evanne, my dreads are totally soaked," Leticia said miserably, running her fingers across her hair. Both women pulled paper towels from the dispenser and started sopping Leticia's hair.

"Well, at least you won't have to wash your hair tonight," Evanne commented.

Leticia giggled, and Evanne started laughing with great guffaws, and soon, both of them were clutching at each other and gasping for breath. After they recovered, the two friends looked up into the mirror, grinning at each other.

Evanne said, "With your smooth ebony skin and my mixed-breed-nobody-knows-what-you-are skin, we can really fool the public. But honey, I am registered as black, and I'll keep it that way." She continued to help Leticia squeeze water from her hair, all the while pulling grapes from her pocket and popping them into her mouth. "Leticia, how old are you?"

"I am twenty-three," Leticia said as she dried her damp hair roots. "I'm a Christmas baby."

"Well, dear, I will be thirty-seven way down in September, but I tell everyone that I am only twenty-nine." The hazel-eyed, svelte, and toned Evanne chuckled.

As Leticia look at her friend in the mirror, she thought the blonde wig at least brought out the lightness in Evanne's bright eyes. Actually, it didn't really matter what her friend wore on her head or on her body; they always looked nice on her.

This made Leticia chuckle, and soon, they were both laughing all over again as they continued to compare their youthful features in the mirror. And while Evanne continued to eat her grapes. For the first time, Leticia really recognized that Evanne's charming personality was enhanced by her curvy Coca-Cola bottle figure. She whispered, "For thirty-seven, you have a hell of a body, especially your waistline! You look great!"

"Thank you, madam," Evanne said, preening. "But you would not believe what I have to do every day to get this way."

Leticia said shyly, "Well, I have to admit that I notice whenever you walk in the office, all the men, they just can't keep their eyes in their heads. But I see that no one dares to make any moves on you."

Evanne fired back, "Of course not! I work here; I do not sleep here!

Plus, my man and I have been together for umpteen years. I want nothing more from Lexhouse Advertising than a paycheck. Besides, girl, don't you notice some of the second looks you get?"

Leticia smiled a little. She whispered, "There was a guy last night."

Evanne turned to her in amazement. She grabbed Leticia by both arms. "Girl! Tell!"

Leticia laughed. "Well, it was this guy in a wheelchair."

"A wheelchair!"

Leticia nodded. "On my way home from the office. I was walking to the subway station, and he rode his wheelchair right in my way. He was this old guy, barely had any hair on his head, face looked like a dried fig. He stopped right in front of me and said, 'You are the most beautiful girl I've ever seen!'"

Evanne's eyes grew wide. "Go on! What then?"

"He asked if he could go out with me."

"And? What did you say!"

"I said I'd think about it. He asked for my number, and then I said I'd get his, and if I felt like it, I'd call."

"'Don't call me; I'll call you.'" Evanne laughed again with gusto; she wrapped her arms around herself and bent over with mirth. "You are too much, girl!"

Just then, a screaming sound echoed in the hallway. "Let-eeeee-sha! Let-eeeee-sha! Where are you?"

Evanne rolled her eyes. The screaming started again, and Evanne and Leticia ducked their heads out of the restroom door. They saw employees standing up in their cubicles and Melba tramping down the hall.

Evanne grabbed Leticia's arm and said, "Remember what I told you to expect."

Melba spotted them and came roaring up. With no greeting, she ordered, "Follow me." She pushed past them into the restroom. "Look at my skirt. I was fighting with the damn umbrella in the wind, and one of the spokes took out the hem on my skirt." Melba followed this with several colorful curses.

"I can't do anything about that," Leticia said.

Apparently, Melba did not hear or did not care. "There is a fabric store three blocks over; get some money from petty cash and get me some fabric tape."

"Melba, you cannot expect Leticia to go back out—in this weather!—to get you tape for your skirt," Evanne interjected.

"I was talking to Leticia, not you!"

"Well, I am telling you," replied Evanne, equally indignant. "I have some safety pins in my area. I will help you fix it; stay right here."

Leticia could barely look at Melba in the mirror. Melba wasn't very skilled at applying makeup ordinarily, frequently applying too much or too little, and opting for unflattering shades of color. Today was twice as bad: the storm had really messed up her makeup and tangled her hair. With raccoon eyes and crooked ruby lips, Melba twisted and turned in the mirror as she inspected the damage done to her skirt hem.

Leticia thought about what Evanne had told her, that Melba had gone to HR to get Leticia reassigned as her own personal secretary. She also thought about Melba's suspicious expense report, which she had delivered to accounting at the end of the day on Friday. She wondered what they'd make of it.

Melba was breathing like a moose in heat, but she didn't speak.

Evanne returned with a bowl of pineapple chunks and the safety pins. She used a safety pin to reattach the hem to the skirt as she chomped on her pineapple. "See," she said, "good as new. No one will even know your skirt's been damaged."

Melba just grunted and started out of the bathroom. Evanne rolled her eyes and made a face behind Melba's back. Leticia had to start coughing to cover her laughter.

The ladies walked down the hallway behind Madam Tiger, as they sometimes called Melba behind her back. Evanne reminded Leticia that they had an agreement for lunch: "Don't forget we're going to trade recipes at lunch today."

"I know; I'll see you then," said Leticia as each lady stepped into her respective cubicle.

At lunch, the two made their way to the break room. While Leticia nibbled on her eggplant and Swiss cheese sandwich, Evanne seemed to be in a race to eat her bag of ten plums and prunes. They both spent the entire thirty minutes laughing at the morning incident with Melba's dress. It ended with Evanne mouthing, "Let-eeee-sha, Let-eeee-sha!"

Fortunately, the rest of the afternoon passed without incident until it was just about time to leave. Leticia was organizing her desk and supplies for the next day when Melba passed by her cubicle. "Tomorrow, I'm going to need you very early, so be here by seven a.m.," Melba said and moved on.

Oh, Lord, thought Leticia. *This can't be good.*

CHAPTER 3

Monday's rains had fled and seemed to take all the moisture out of the air with them. Tuesday came cold but very dry: two conditions to which Leticia, with her tropical Jamaican upbringing, had still not accustomed herself. Having only been in the country for four months, her entire New York experience had been dominated by a wet fall and frigid winter.

The steely buildings crowded over her wherever she went. She was used to a canopy of wide open blue and warm, salty winds. New York was more like a valley of concrete and metal, and its winter was endless gray and drizzle.

She couldn't wait for these hot, humid summers everyone kept telling her to expect. She wasn't sure she entirely believed the stories.

"This place can never get warm," Leticia mumbled to herself as she removed and hung up her coat, an additional sweater, scarf, hat, and gloves. She also placed her sneakers and socks on a homemade rack in the corner of her cubicle, and replaced them with quarter-inch pumps.

She looked around. She had arrived early as Melba requested, and indeed, Melba was already here but deep in conversation with another account rep.

Leticia headed toward the break room, hoping that a cup of coffee would finally warm up the chill that never seemed to leave her bones. On the way, she overheard Melba's voice: "My dry cleaners are the pits; they are the worst. I cannot get them to stay open till my husband or I can get our clothes after work." Then Leticia was too far away to make out Melba's words clearly, but she thought she heard, "Get them for me."

After she returned with her coffee, she got to work and tried not to dwell on the fact that Melba had asked her to come in early, disrupting

Leticia's morning routine, but then hadn't bothered to approach her with any special tasks.

So the industrious young woman simply got to work on her regular assignments. Well, if they could be called regular. She was researching and copyediting reports for Melba's BALI account. Not Leticia's job, per her job description. But she was here to learn, and it was good information to know.

Evanne came by before too long, eating kiwi and star fruits out of a Ziploc plastic container. "Hello, sunshine! The wicked witch of the office come by yet?"

"I saw her, but she didn't come by," Leticia said. Some of her irritation seeped into her voice. "I heard her talking about dry cleaning."

"Oh, and here she comes now," Evanne whispered. She was looking down the hall. Leticia craned her head and saw Melba stalking toward them, a pillowcase stuffed with clothing swinging from her hands.

"Oh, Lord," Leticia muttered. "I should have known I'd be included in the subject."

Evanne seemed torn between chuckling and spitting. "Tell me everything later," she whispered and scampered to her own cubicle.

Melba stopped at the entrance to Leticia's cube.

Melba whispered, "A new account came in, and they gave it away to ding-dong Paul."

All Leticia could think to reply was, "Well, Melba, maybe they will realize that you are good and give you other accounts."

Melba didn't seem to hear. Her eyes never even blinked as she paced back and forth in front of Leticia's desk. "I will never get a decent promotion! My boss 'James Ass' just steals my ideas. He won't give me an account that could make me shine."

That didn't sound like Mr. Foles to Leticia, but the girl didn't say anything.

Melba continued, "I am so unhappy and frustrated here at Lexhouse Advertising. But, if I left, I'd be starting at the bottom of some other firm." She gritted her teeth. Leticia remained silent; she'd heard this speech, or some variation of it, before. Melba always ignored her anyway.

Melba took a tissue from Leticia's tissue box and blew her nose as if she had been crying. Leticia looked closely at her boss. Had Melba put on her makeup in the dark? She almost looked like a mispainted clown.

Melba threw the used tissue toward Leticia's trash can. She missed; it landed on the floor next to the trash.

"Pick that up, will you?" Melba instructed absently. "See, I can talk to you, Leticia. Because I know you're not going to repeat these things. It's a good thing they have you report directly to me. Don't forget that research I need from the BALI account. I want it on my desk by lunch. Oh, and I need you to stop by the dry cleaner for me. Here's the load." She thrust the bulging pillowcase at Leticia. "The cleaners are next to the deli around the corner."

Leticia didn't take the pillowcase, so Melba just dropped it. Orders issued and clothing deposited, Melba turned to leave.

"You want me to take your dirty laundry to the dry cleaners during my work time?" Leticia asked incredulously.

"Yes," snapped Melba impatiently. "You work for me. It won't take you more than a few minutes." Then she dropped her shoulders, shook her shoulder-length curly blonde hair, and strutted out of Leticia's workspace.

Leticia got up, pulled a new tissue from her box, and used it to pick up the soiled one. She placed them both in the trash can. She straightened and then looked over the short cubicle walls, watching as Melba darted down the corridor. She said hello to the executive account reps but nothing to any of the clerks. Mr. Foles and his protégé Paul always said hello to everyone.

For just a moment, Leticia wondered if Melba's lackluster looks could be the real reason she was being passed over. At thirty-five or so, she already looked fifty. On her two-and-one-half-inch heels, once again she struck Leticia as a stick with a blonde wig. But she dismissed the thought: that wouldn't be in character for Mr. Foles, and Melba brought everything on herself.

"That bony-ass woman would not last in a good windstorm," Leticia muttered, and then sat back down at her desk to work.

The bag of laundry didn't move all day, until Leticia got up for lunch and kicked it to the side.

She couldn't wait to tell Evanne. Somehow Evanne always helped the irritating become funny, and Leticia started laughing as she recounted the story. "Evanne, I can't believe this woman! I was so shocked I could barely speak."

But Evanne retorted, "No, that is not funny. Funny is if that super conservative bottled blonde Republican chick on *The View* had her baby and its first word was 'Obama.' That is humor. This is slavery with a measly paycheck."

Leticia chuckled and took another bite of lettuce-wrapped canned corned beef. "Like you said, watch her, and I am."

Evanne nodded solemnly. "By the way, what's up with that?" She nodded down at Leticia's lunch.

Leticia followed her gaze and looked up again, confused. "What?"

"You always bring something canned and usually eat it right out of the can. What's up with that?"

Leticia shrugged. "What else would I do?"

"Get some microwaveable lunches."

"Oh, that. I can't. I don't have any place to store them at home. My room barely fits me and a bed."

Evanne sighed. "Yeah. That's New York for you. You pay an arm and leg for a room here, mostly because the rooms are too small to fit both your arms and both your legs. That's why I live in Brooklyn." With that, she finished her kiwi, star fruit, and several nectarines.

Back at her desk, Leticia found the pillowcase no longer rested where she had kicked it aside. It was sitting in her chair. Leticia turned up her lips and felt the good humor from lunch leech away, replaced by more anger. What the hell was Melba's problem? Now she had to infect Leticia's chair with her funky dirty laundry.

Leticia called Evanne over to show her. Pete and Leslie, who worked in cubes nearby, also gathered to witness the laundry in Leticia's chair. They all stared at it.

"You should go to HR," Evanne advised. "She's a maniac and a bipolar bitch."

Leticia hesitated. "I'm new to this company," she pointed out. "This is my first job."

"Girl, newcomers and first-timers have the same rights as everyone else."

"I don't want to take the chance that this will be on my record, even if HR does something about it."

"I think you're right," Leslie said in a little, wispy voice. She looked very serious behind her rimless glasses. "HR isn't really here for the employees; they're here for the managers."

So Leticia left work fifteen minutes early, dropped off the pillowcase of laundry as instructed, and went home both sad and angry.

* * *

"Where is my pillowcase? Don't tell me you gave that to be cleaned, too!" raged Melba the next morning, first thing. "Where is the receipt?"

"They're both in my gym bag," Leticia said weakly, like a scared and wounded kitten.

"Gross! Isn't that where you keep your dirty sneakers? In that case, wash it before you return it."

"Yes, ma'am," was all Leticia managed.

Then she turned back to do the BALI ad account work that was rightfully Melba's. Her own filing duties, her primary job, were starting to stack up on one side of her desk. Once again, she wished she at least had windows to look out over New York City.

"Hump Wednesday," Evanne announced, effervescent in her cheer, a little later when she came by to say hello. She was eating a banana whose pale yellow color matched Evanne's wig du jour: long blonde tresses that fell past Evanne's shoulders. "Two more days to the weekend." She then looked closely at Leticia's face. "Oh, Lord. Don't tell me Melba has been at it again."

Leticia nodded. Her face felt hot, and she was close to crying. The frustration and irritation were nearly overwhelming.

"Well, if you can last for two more days, I promise when James gets back, it will all be okay."

Leticia felt some involuntary tears splash onto her cheek. Her throat and chest felt tight, and she felt doubly angry that Melba was even affecting her this much. Evanne came around to the side of the desk and patted her friend on the back while she continued to eat her banana.

Afterward, Evanne excused herself to the restroom. On the way, she saw Melba chewing out Berlina, but Paul's assistant Berlina had her back to Melba and was busily working and swaying to music from her CD player. She just totally ignored Melba, who turned and headed for Leticia's cubicle.

"Leticia, this is for the dry cleaning." Melba slapped thirty-five dollars on the desk. Leticia looked up. Once again, it looked as if Melba had put her makeup on in the dark. A little smear of lipstick stuck up at an angle from the corner of Melba's mouth. It actually gave the woman a rather sinister-looking fake half-smile. Like an evil clown. "Did you hear me, Leticia?"

The young Jamaican lady mumbled, "The cleaners said the clothes wouldn't be ready till five p.m." She paused, and then asked, "When will Mr. James Foles be returning?"

Melba looked suspiciously at Leticia. Her lips parted, and then she narrowed her eyes at Leticia. "James Ass will be back on Monday," she said. She seemed about to say something else but instead just stalked off. Fortunately—perhaps thanks to the implication that Leticia was going to talk to Mr. Foles—Melba did not bother Leticia for the rest of the day.

* * *

The following morning, Leticia came in with Melba's laundry. She laid it carefully across Melba's desk and laid the receipt on top with the total circled, so that Melba would see she had shorted Leticia by three dollars.

Then she returned to her cubicle and removed her outer clothes, got herself some coffee, and went to work.

It didn't take long for Melba to show up. But rather than give Leticia the additional three dollars, or even thank her for running the errand, she launched into an overheated rant. "I want to surprise my husband Jerry with a cake, but I have a conference call. The cake is ready at the LUC bakery two doors down, but Jerry is on the east side, so I need you to take a taxi and drop it off at his office, okay? Here is fifty dollars; that should do it for the cake and the taxi."

Leticia just stared openmouthed at Melba. She couldn't believe this woman's presumption! And yet, it seemed in character. If all her behavior came down to putting Leticia in her place, Melba would naturally follow up one demeaning task with another, just to show that she could and that Leticia would do it.

"Here are the directions; just ask for Mr. Grossott; everyone there knows him. Get going on this!"

Leticia looked down at the scribbled directions Melba had placed on her desk. She said, "Melba, I have a deadline from Paul for a new account, and I have to finish it before his conference call—"

"What new account?" Melba interrupted. "How did he get this account? When James Ass is not here?"

"I don't know, Melba. All I know is yesterday Paul had a conference call with me and Mr. Foles, and Mr. Foles asked me to compile these forms and give them to Paul. It's going to take me all day."

Melba wheeled out of Leticia's area and went into Evanne's, who didn't even give Melba a chance to get started. "Hell, no! I am nobody's errand gal. You need a cake to go to your husband, then you take it to your husband. I'll go to HR so fast you'll get whiplash!" Evanne shouted loudly enough that several workers in the office stood up to get a better view. Some people still had phones attached to their ears. The place became deadly silent; you could hear a pin drop.

Evanne's spiky-haired Patti Labelle wig seemed to emphasize her electrified anger.

Melba was beet red, nearly the color of her lipstick. "You'll regret this," she hissed angrily at Evanne and stalked off. Evanne met Leticia's gaze and rolled her eyes. She apparently didn't take Melba seriously, but Leticia thought Melba was perfectly capable of following through on her threat.

But she ended up too busy to dwell on it. She spent the entire day working with Paul, who was kind and nice and gentlemanly and had dreamy blue eyes. Leticia caught herself staring at him several times. Henry, who was also assisting Paul, noticed. Every time he caught her staring, he'd make some smart-ass comment like "Looks like Leticia's got other things on her mind than work."

Leticia would busy herself with the papers in front of her. "Just busy," she'd mumble. Evanne had previously described Henry to Leticia as "socially awkward."

Henry would laugh, an oddly sharp and not altogether pleasing sound. But Leticia actually felt sorry for him; he had a mole on the side of his nose. She had to force herself to look into his eyes when they talked, because otherwise she'd stare at the mole, but Henry seemed to have gotten the wrong idea. Every time he reached over to grab some papers, or to pass some to her, his hand would brush over hers. She knew he was doing it on purpose. She just wished Paul would do the same. Once, Henry winked at her, and she had to resist the urge to roll her eyes.

If Paul noticed anything, he did not let on. Before lunch, he said, "Leticia, I am so grateful for your help, and what a great worker you are!"

"That's true! Great worker!" interjected Henry. He smiled at Leticia, but his smile was a little too creepy-intense for Leticia's taste. She smiled shyly back at the two men.

"When James gets back, I have some things to talk to him about," Paul continued. "By the way, where are you from? If you don't mind me asking."

"Jamaica," replied Leticia with a bright smile.

"I like your accent. Very melodious."

"Thank you," she said, almost a whisper. Then it was Paul's turn to blush and turn back to his work. Henry looked back and forth, chewing on his lower lip.

That day, Evanne and Leticia shared a good lunch as Leticia related in detail all the events from the morning. Evanne had what appeared to be a pound of apricots, and Leticia nibbled on canned Vienna sausages.

Evanne said with outright curiosity, "I understand why you don't bring microwave food, but I notice you eat a lot of canned foods instead of fresh or homemade. Why is that?"

Leticia laughed. "The rooming house where I live, the owner, she won't let anyone cook in her kitchen. Because of a situation that occurred from over a year ago, the stove in her kitchen only has three usable burners. One of the tenants was cooking, and his food burned, and the pot burned, and till this day, the pot is still stuck on the stove. It melted into the burner!"

"So what do you do for hot food?" Evanne asked, puzzled.

"Well, I have a small electric teapot and mini-microwave hidden in my closet. Don't care how you search; you won't find it!"

They both burst into laughter on their way back to their cubicles. The afternoon passed quickly and enjoyably. Was it Leticia's imagination that Paul kept sending furtive glances in her direction?

CHAPTER 4

Finally, Friday came. Leticia arrived to find Melba rummaging through her desk. "Melba!" she said. What she meant: *Melba, what the hell are you doing rummaging through* my *area and* my *work and* my *things?*

Melba jumped up. For a moment, she looked back at Leticia guiltily, like a little girl caught doing something naughty. But then her usual haughty expression stole over her leathery features. "Where is the information for the work for Paul?"

"Paul has it," Leticia answered meekly.

"Paul has an assistant. Why did James Ass give this task to you and not her?" she asked, as if it were Leticia's fault. Leticia could only shrug. "Do you still have the instructions for the cake?"

"Yes," Leticia replied very meekly.

Melba thrust fifty dollars at her. "Then you need to leave now before traffic gets worse. And don't forget that BALI account is due today. Oh, when you get back, I want to send some gifts to the BALI executives. Take care of the paperwork. Then I need the research for the new presentation by the end of the day."

"The end of the day!" Leticia was so shocked by the new deadline the words just slipped out.

Melba didn't smile, but she looked grimly self-satisfied. "Yes, it should take you the whole day, don't you think?"

"And then some." Again, the words just slipped out.

"Well, that's fine. If you want to get anywhere, you have to do the time." Leticia took that to mean Melba was approving overtime. That helped. "Anyway, you better get going, hadn't you?"

Leticia didn't reach out to take the money, so Melba slammed it onto Leticia's desk and walked off. Leticia debated for a moment what to do.

She decided she needed to keep her priorities straight. Work comes first. Even when half her work was actually Melba's work.

Evanne and Leticia shared their usual lunch, Evanne with an assortment of pears, Leticia with a canned potted meat sandwich. Leticia described the morning's confrontation.

Evanne leaned toward her friend with a glossy stare. "Leticia, just wait till Monday, when James returns. That's all I'm going to say. Let's just enjoy Friday."

The two ladies lifted their water bottles and toasted, "To Friday."

Leticia decided to take care of the cake immediately after lunch. She thought about putting it off to the end of the day, but she had a morbid curiosity to see what kind of man would be married to such a mean individual as Melba. If she waited till later, he might have left for the day. It galled her to take work time, though, because she knew she'd just have to stay late to finish the work Melba had assigned her.

She wondered again what her parents would make of all this. Her father's advice had been to "lie low." He just wanted her to learn everything she could about business and what he called "the New York way." Then, he had told her, she'd be able to use the best of both worlds, the best attributes of her Jamaican heritage, and the best parts of American and New York business culture.

But her mom was a little more strident. She always told Leticia to be the best at whatever she was, wherever she was. Never let anyone show her up. And wasn't that exactly what she was letting Melba do? But how should Leticia respond? It was a conundrum.

She stopped first to pick up the cake. "She made me re-ice cake," Mr. Luc, the proprietor of the bakery, complained to her through a thick Asian accent. "Even though she day late. She late! That woman, I want no more business from her. She make crazy. No more cake for her."

His assistant, perhaps a daughter or granddaughter, translated for Leticia, "We don't mind if a customer can't pick up the cake till the next day; it happens, but if it happens again, we'll have to charge for re-icing the cake."

"No," Mr. Luc insisted. "No more cake for her."

Leticia smiled sympathetically. Apparently, it wasn't just coworkers that Melba tried to bully. She paid for the cake with the money Melba gave her, but that left only twenty dollars. She didn't think she'd be able to get to the address from Melba's directions for only twenty dollars. Indeed, she ended up paying an extra ten dollars out of pocket for the cab fare.

When she arrived at Mr. Grossott's office, the receptionist called the man to pick up his package.

The receptionist sat at a semicircular desk in front of a clear glass wall, behind which Leticia could see all the office cubes. The business name, Georgeman and Associates Accounting Services, was etched into the glass.

From where Leticia stood, she could see the man who got up and headed for the front. He had to heave himself forward; he must have weighed three hundred pounds with tufts of thinning blonde hair on his pate. The short walk from his desk to the reception area left him huffing and puffing like an out-of-breath dog. His stomach hung over his pants.

He eyed Leticia up and down. "So, you're that new domestic Melba said she was hiring?"

Leticia's eyebrows shot up. *What?* What the hell was Melba telling people about her? "No, sir," she said demurely. "I work with Melba at Lexhouse Advertising."

"Oh. Well, she told me she had a new personal worker from one of those places that don't speak proper English."

Leticia bit back her anger. "I'm from Jamaica, sir."

"Yeah, that's what I thought." His eyes roved over her body again. "You know, Melba was wrong about you. You're not trashy at all. You just look exotic." He licked his lips. "Are you sure you don't want to be our new domestic? We'll pay cash. Immigration would never have to know. And you'd have plenty of opportunities for bonuses." He leered at her as he said this.

Leticia managed to keep the disgust off her face. "No, thank you," she said and turned and walked away. She could feel his eyes on her all the way to the door. It figured that Melba would marry a man like him. They were a perfect pair.

She fumed all the way back to the office, but she dared not confront Melba. She debated whether she should tell her mother all this. She was here specifically to learn how to deal with people, especially those like

Melba. She couldn't go running to her mama every time someone was rude to her.

But the temptation was great, as she knew her mother would take decisive action on her behalf. Her mother was a powerful woman. Leticia probably would say something, in the end, but she would try to deal with Melba on her own first. Still, part of her remained morbidly curious about what her mother would do to Melba if she knew how her baby was being treated.

She had barely settled back into her desk at the office when her phone rang.

"Leticia Patrick?" a curious male voice said.

"Yes," she answered. "Here."

"This is Mark in accounting. I was just looking at the expense vouchers you submitted for Melba Grossott."

Here we go, Leticia thought to herself. "Yes?"

"There are some irregularities."

Leticia's heart started thundering. Even after her false accusations had been disproved, was Melba cheating on her expense report going to fall on Leticia and get her fired?

CHAPTER 5

MARK STARTED ASKING HER QUESTIONS about specific charges and receipts. After three or four "I don't know" replies, Leticia interrupted, "Melba asked me to prepare the report, but they're her expenses. She'd be the best person to ask."

A moment of silence. "Thank you," he said and hung up. He sounded irritated, which annoyed Leticia. It wasn't her fault that it was so difficult to work with Melba.

But then a bright thought occurred to Leticia: if Melba had faked the expense reports, as Leticia suspected, she had just been caught. A slow smile crept over Leticia's face. She just hoped she'd be there when Melba got her due.

* * *

Leticia spent the whole weekend in anticipation of Monday's impending drama. Accounting was asking questions about the strange expense reports Melba had asked Leticia to prepare. Melba had behaved even more disrespectfully than usual all week, or at least when Mr. Foles was in the office, Melba wasn't so obvious about taking advantage of the young assistant.

But now, Melba had overreached, and she would soon get her own.

It was also eye-opening to realize that other people did not like or fear Melba either. Evanne never let anyone cow her, and even Paul and Mr. Luc didn't put up with her bullying ways. Plus, Paul was going to talk to Mr. Foles about her! She felt excited about that. Paul was so much nicer than Melba, so smart, so kind, so handsome. Maybe Paul would request that Leticia work more closely with him.

She could not wait for Monday.

The week woke with a wet kiss from winter. A chilly rainstorm drenched the city, just like the previous week. But this downpour couldn't dampen Leticia's spirits. She dressed as warm and cozy as a Jamaican Eskimo.

"Good morning, Leticia," Melba greeted her almost immediately. "How was your weekend?"

Leticia could only stare back. She couldn't believe Melba had just greeted her as if they were old friends. Suddenly, she was filled with suspicion.

Her eyes focused on the bully's pinstriped skirt suit. Melba merely smiled at her only charge and walked confidently down the row of clerical cubes, greeting everyone. Some people reacted like Leticia, with disbelieving silence; others said good morning back, but it was obvious they just did so automatically, and then started when they realized who had greeted them.

"Good morning, Leticia." This time it was Paul, with a smile. He continued, with a mischievous grin. "James and I had breakfast this morning. You were one of the topics. He'll be meeting with you privately today, so keep up those warm trade wind spirits." He reached out and patted her on the shoulder, and then sauntered down the clerical cube aisle and shouted to everyone, "Happy Monday morning!"

In virtual unison, everyone answered, "Good morning, Paul!"

Evanne entered the office, singing. Leticia was apparently not the only one to have a good weekend. She ran her fingers through a new raven black bun-in-the-back wig.

"How was your weekend?" Leticia greeted her friend.

"Glorious! Church was nice, we went to the movies, and my sweetie and I had sex. Matter of fact, great sex!" Evanne practically sang to her coworker.

Leticia laughed and blushed at the same time. Evanne was frank about everything.

"Burn anything at the rooming house?" Evanne joked.

"No, no, I stay away from Miss Martha's kitchen. I only use the fridge; that's all she allows." Then she added slyly, "I did meet a nice young gentleman."

Evanne's eyebrows shot up. "A new one? Do tell."

Leticia nodded. "He came to see Miss Martha about a room. He was tall and skinny, and he wore glasses, and he had the palest white skin I've ever seen. He looked like someone had painted him white."

"Mm-hmm," Evanne hummed. "Well, what then?"

"Oh, I didn't tell you about his teeth. He had this huge overbite and these great big buck teeth."

Evanne started laughing. "You're pulling my leg!"

"No! Oh, no. His name was Bill. He was looking for a room, and when he saw me, he just kept staring. It made me feel very uncomfortable. But then Miss Martha introduced us, and Bill said he looked forward to getting to know me. Then he started laughing. He sounded like a donkey."

Leticia made a couple of loud braying laughing noises, and Evanne broke down into full on guffaws.

"Leticia, you meet the strangest men."

"You're telling me!"

"Well, maybe one of these days you'll meet a fella who will light your spark!"

"Evanne!" But Leticia kept laughing.

"Anyway, since I had such great sex, I thought I would bring you something. A banana nut muffin! Bananas and nuts! I thought that was appropriate."

Still laughing, Leticia thanked her friend and then proceeded to enjoy the muffin with her coffee.

But as the day wore on, things started to sour, and Leticia got a bad feeling in the pit of her stomach. Mr. Foles had greeted everyone, Leticia included, when he breezed through the office, and Leticia thought his greeting to her seemed especially bright and cheery.

Then she saw Melba walk into Mr. Foles's office carrying several file folders. A couple of people were already in Mr. Foles's office. Leticia recognized one, a pretty lady from accounting. The Jamaican admired the woman's long red hair, but she couldn't remember the lady's name. Leticia didn't recognize the other at all.

Leticia turned back to her work with a satisfied smile. So it was about to happen. Good!

She kept one eye on her work, but every so often, she'd lift her head to look over her cube wall at Mr. Foles's door.

After about half an hour had passed, she looked up to find the whole group standing outside the office door. Mr. Foles looked somber, but Melba was laughing. Leticia frowned, confused. Why would Melba be laughing? The accountants were smiling, too.

No, no, no. Melba was supposed to be getting in trouble. She was supposed to be cooking in her own juices. She was supposed to be reaping what she'd sown.

Instead, she was smiling and laughing as though she were having the best time ever.

Then Mr. Foles saw Leticia looking at them. His somber expression darkened into a frown, and he turned away and went back into his office. The accountants followed him and shut the door.

That's the moment when Leticia's heart started beating harder.

Melba looked over and saw Leticia looking. She waved, her long bright red nails gleaming under the fluorescent lights. Melba smiled, but even from a distance, Leticia could see something in Melba's eyes. Her boss was a predator, and she had just cornered Leticia.

The young Jamaican sank back into her chair. She had a very bad feeling about this turn of events.

She was quiet through lunch. Evanne asked her what was wrong, but Leticia avoided the question. With every passing moment, she was dreading the impending meeting with Mr. Foles even more.

Evanne chattered on, her good mood unbroken. She had wanted to eat on the plaza, but they stayed in the lunchroom. Indeed, the weather had turned fierce again. How Leticia longed for the warm and tender caress of the Jamaican sun, air tangy with salt, and clear azure blue all above, unobscured by human-made monstrosities rising into the sky.

Leticia sipped on her cold zucchini and tomato soup, while Evanne peeled and sliced her avocado.

While they were still eating, Mr. Foles's private secretary, Frances, came to Leticia. The elderly woman, gray hair tied back in a ponytail, whispered that Mr. Foles would like to see her right after lunch.

Leticia thanked Frances for the message with an innocent smile, as though she had no idea what was going on.

The two women continued their lunch. Evanne asked, "Is something up?"

"Up? No," said Leticia, "not that I know of."

"Mm-hmm." But Evanne let it drop. She started singing some Barry White song.

On the way back from lunch, Leticia said, "I'm going to put my lunch stuff away and refresh my makeup before my meeting."

"Okay. Good luck, and give me all the juicy details afterward!"

"Okay, I will," Leticia promised.

Evanne stopped in the ladies' room, while Leticia zoomed to her cubicle. She picked up the phone, dialed, and then whispered urgently, "Give me about twenty minutes, and then call the main number and please remember what to say. All right? Good."

She headed for Mr. Foles's office and greeted him with her warmest smile. "We missed you last week, sir," she said. "I have always heard to be missed is a good thing; it means you are useful."

Mr. Foles said, "Thank you, Leticia. I've heard the same thing." He wasn't smiling.

He closed the door, and they sat at a small table in the corner of his office. His desk was cluttered with papers and files, and a couple of bookshelves along the wall overflowed with books and three-ring binders. Outside his corner window, the sky still looked dark and damp.

"Leticia," Mr. Foles started, and then hesitated. He looked down at the table and chewed on his lip for just a second, apparently trying to find the right words.

"Yes, sir?"

"Leticia, I've had two people talk to me about you today, and I admit to being confused and disgruntled by what I've heard."

Leticia's smile disappeared, replaced by a look of confusion and polite attention. "Sir?"

CHAPTER 6

"First, Paul came to me first thing this morning. He said you had a horrendous week with Melba. Let's start there. Tell me about it." Finally, he offered her a smile, encouraging, almost fatherly. His brown eyes seemed warm and deep behind a weatherworn face. His face was red from too much sun on his vacation, though.

She recounted a CliffsNotes version of the events of the previous week. "Hmmm, hmmm," was all he said during her explanation, tapping his pen on the table.

After Leticia stopped talking, they sat in silence for a moment. "Well," Mr. Foles said. "Paul is very fond of you, and appreciative of your work. He's asked that you be moved to his group."

Leticia smiled shyly. "That's very nice of him."

"Hmm. Unfortunately, there's another problem."

"Sir?"

"Accounting noticed some discrepancies on an expense report you prepared for Melba."

Leticia nodded.

"You know what I'm talking about?"

"Yes, sir. Melba asked me to prepare them. I didn't understand all the numbers, but when I asked her about them, she told me they were correct and just to enter the numbers she gave me. Evanne was there. She heard what Melba told me. Evanne heard everything."

"Oh, there was a third party present? Excellent." Mr. Foles scribbled a note. "At any rate, Melba told us those weren't the numbers she submitted. She was able to provide receipts and notes that matched. She seemed shocked at what had been submitted."

Leticia frowned. She felt a flash of anger so intense it almost surged out her mouth in the form of a string of expletives. Instead, she just said, "I don't know what to tell you, sir."

"You don't like working for Melba, do you?"

"I'm learning a lot from her, sir."

"But you don't like her."

Leticia frowned again, this time out of confusion. "It's not that, sir. I'm learning a lot from her, which is what I'm here to do. That's what I want to do. If she helps me with that, that's all that matters. Anywhere you work, there is always someone who will not treat you with respect, despite how much respect you show that person."

"But if she were to get you in trouble, you'd have to be moved to someone else's group, no questions asked. And Melba might get in trouble. Since Melba hasn't treated you with respect, I wouldn't blame you if that was appealing to you."

"No, sir. That would be beneath me."

Mr. Foles pursed his lips and studied the young assistant. Apparently, it wasn't the answer he'd been expecting. He was just about to speak again when Frances burst into the office. "Leticia! There is an emergency call for you." She looked at Mr. Foles and nodded, just slightly, as if to say, *It's legit*. She continued, "The person said they've been calling your direct line but obviously haven't been getting an answer."

"Who is it?" Leticia asked, a quaver of nervousness in her voice. Although she knew perfectly well. The supposedly poor immigrant was about to give the best acting performance of her lifetime.

"Your landlady," Frances said. "A Miss Martha. She said there's an emergency with your mom."

"Leticia, you can take the call in here," Mr. Foles interjected. "Frances, send the call to my phone."

Frances dashed out, and Mr. Foles's phone line instantly lit up.

Leticia picked up the phone, shaking like a leaf in a light breeze. "Hello?" Her mouth went slack, and she gripped her stomach and bent over. She started bawling, tears just rolling down her face. She shouted, "Lord Jesus Christ! Is Mama dead?"

Mr. Foles had stepped outside with Frances but hadn't shut the door. He turned around and looked at Leticia, whose eyes were wild, tears splashing down her cheeks, clutching at her stomach.

"Lord, sweet Lord, when did it happen? Oh, God! Which hospital they have her? Mercy! Oh Lord!" Leticia wailed.

The phone tumbled from Leticia's hands. Leticia herself followed an instant later, crashing to the floor with a loud thump.

"Call 911," Mr. Foles instructed.

"She's moving," said Paul, who had run up to the office to see what the commotion was all about.

Frances charged in with a cup of ice and water. She stooped down as Leticia sat up and said, "Here, Leticia, drink this."

Paul helped Leticia to a chair.

"God, me feel better," Leticia mumbled, emphasizing her Jamaican twang.

"What happened, Leticia?" Mr. Foles asked.

Breathing heavily and still crying a little, Leticia explained, "Sir, according to Miss Martha, a minibus in Kingston hit Mama on her way to the market. You don't know how people drive there! Now she is in the hospital in critical condition. They don't know if she's going to make it." She choked out a fresh round of sobs.

Frances patted Leticia's back comfortingly, and Paul held her hand, while Mr. Foles stood awkwardly by. Paul massaged her hand with his fingers, stroking in a circular pattern. It felt very nice. More than nice, actually. She squeezed his fingers ever so slightly, and he reciprocated, watching her in sympathy and kindness. Then he noticed the crowd of onlookers that had gathered at his door. He shooed them off and closed the door.

Leticia calmed enough to say, "My family is very poor. My parents have four children, and we live in the countryside. I am the oldest, and I got to come to America to work. So I can send money back to support my family."

"That's good of you," Paul said.

"It's just such a hard life. My father takes the family donkey and does farming in the bushes. All the crops he reaps, Mama take them to the market in the city on Fridays. She sleeps in the market on Friday nights, and on Saturday she sells again. She comes home for church on Sundays, but she has to go back on Mondays because anything that doesn't sell on the weekend, you sell again cheaper on Monday. That's why it's so crowded on Mondays. She doesn't even have a stall; she just spread some crocus bags and put the food on it for people to see. And if it rains, she has to cover it and herself with a tarp hitched with some sticks."

Leticia took a deep breath, then added, "Oh, Mama!"

"I'm sure she's going to be okay," Paul said, but he didn't sound so sure.

Mr. Foles was shaking his head. "What a life," he muttered.

"Can you go home to Jamaica?" Frances asked.

"I don't know!" She looked up at Frances with horror, as if that question hadn't even occurred to her yet, and then another flood of tears burst forth. She just kept repeating, "Oh my God! Oh my God! What am I going to do?"

Paul hugged the crying file clerk. She could smell his cologne. It smelled tangy and sweet at the same time. She liked it. "We are going to take up a collection for you," he said. He stood up. "I'll get it started right now." And with that, he left her in Frances's care and stepped out of the office.

"You poor thing," Frances said.

After a moment of apparent indecision, Mr. Foles took out his personal credit card and called American Airlines. Leticia was so shocked that she didn't even hear when he asked her what airport in Jamaica she needed.

"Kingston," she finally answered, in a whisper. Mr. Foles could tell she was in a daze.

"The last name is Patrick, yes, exactly, Leticia Patrick."

At that moment, Melba burst into the office. She took in the scene, and then strode up and knelt by Leticia. "Don't worry, Leticia," she said. "You are a great employee, and everyone will do what we can." She graciously handed the weeping assistant a crisp hundred-dollar bill. She held it up to make sure it was visible to everyone. "Here's one hundred dollars for you."

Leticia, despite her tears, noticed how Melba's gaze darted toward Mr. Foles when she announced the amount of her contribution. But all she said was, "Thank you, Melba. I will give both you and Mr. Foles your money back."

Melba nodded, but Mr. Foles said, "No, don't worry about it, Leticia. Go look after your mother."

"That's right, Leticia," Melba said instantly, although she didn't seem thrilled about it. "Right now, all you need to worry about is your mother."

"Thank you," Leticia whispered.

"You have an electronic ticket," Mr. Foles said. "I'm printing it now. You leave tomorrow morning at six a.m., and you'll return the following Sunday. If you need more time, call me."

"Thank you, sir. God bless you and your family. We don't have a phone, but I can go to the post office and call."

"You can call me collect if you need to stay longer. Go home now and look after your mother."

"Thank you, sir."

"Leticia, family comes first. We're sending you home for the next week because it's the right thing to do. But what we were discussing before, it's a serious issue. I'm going to give you the benefit of the doubt and assume it was just an error." But Mr. Foles was actually looking at Melba as he said this, and Melba nodded vigorously. "I'll also speak with Evanne about it." A look of shock and uncertainty passed over Melba's face, but she schooled her features quickly. Mr. Foles looked at Leticia and said, "Just watch closely for any more errors, okay?"

"Yes, sir," Leticia said meekly, as if he was talking to her and not looking at Melba. But what the hell was she supposed to do if Melba was bound and determined to lie and cheat? Or was he talking in code about watching out for Melba's antics? Her gaze slid toward her boss. Melba nodded again, expression perfectly balanced between stern and sympathetic. But beneath the paint and deception, she could see Melba's hypocrisy clearly. She looked at Melba for a long moment, long enough that an edge of discomfort and uncertainty crept into Melba's countenance.

Leticia became aware of something new in herself, as well. Before, she had been too uncertain to take any kind of concerted action against Melba. That time had passed. Her father's advice to "lie low" only made sense if Leticia were able to just come to work and do her thing. But she couldn't; Melba had declared war on her.

Leticia turned back to Mr. Foles and found he was also glancing at Melba. When he looked back at Leticia, a warm and sad smile flitted across his lips, and then disappeared again. Interesting. Her eyes darted between her two bosses a couple of times. Melba wasn't the only one playing a dangerous game here. Somehow, Leticia was in the middle of it.

But not for long. Soon enough, she would find a way to be in control of it. She could almost hear her mother's voice in her head. "You're the only person stopping you from being in control of any situation. Most people, they're sheep. How do you think such crazies get elected to lead nations? People will follow anyone who speaks and acts with enough force and confidence."

And yet, Mr. Foles was clearly a born leader, and powerfully entrenched at Lexhouse. To meet Melba's declaration of war, Leticia would have to be careful not to inadvertently challenge Mr. Foles's authority, too.

"I understand, sir," she said in what she hoped was a sufficiently contrite voice. With some more sniffles for effect, Leticia whispered another grateful "thank you."

Melba walked Leticia back to her cube. "Go home and get yourself together," Melba said in a gentle, saccharine voice. "If there's anything you need, just let me know." Melba didn't wait for an answer; she just walked away with her usual uplifted nose. Leticia watched her leave. The hypocrite had been perfectly willing to throw Leticia under the bus for her own lies.

Evanne walked up and wrapped Leticia in a huge bear hug. "Oh, Leticia sweetie, I'm so sorry. It's all going to be okay. We're all going to pray for you and your mama."

"Th-thank you," Leticia gasped through the breathless embrace.

"What time is your flight?" Evanne asked, releasing her friend.

"Six a.m., so I have to be there by four a.m.," Leticia replied.

"How do you plan to get to the airport?"

"A taxi, I guess. The only person at the rooming house that has a car, well, he works nights. I know that he will be able to pick me up, but he won't be able to take me."

"Okay, then I will pick you up at three a.m."

Leticia blew her nose loudly into a tissue. "Won't that be hard for you?"

"Look, you go home now, pack your things, and I'll pick you up at eight o'clock tonight. You can spend the night at my place, and I'll take you in the morning. Then I'll come into work and leave early tomorrow. That will work."

Quickly, as if she just remembered, Leticia said, "Please, Evanne, before I forget. Miss Martha doesn't like people coming to her house, so I will be waiting at the doorway; just blow your horn and I'll come out."

"Okay, sweetie, it's a plan."

By the time Leticia left the office, she had a paid ticket to Jamaica, a ride to the airport, and $272 in collection money. Paul had even squeezed her hand when he gave it to her.

At the elevator, she looked back over the office. She'd only been here for a few months, she already had a week of paid vacation, and when she got back, she would take care of Melba for sure.

CHAPTER 7

Leticia's Aunt Martha stood in the doorway and watched Leticia pack. "You have a paid plane ticket, cash, and a friend to take you to the airport," Aunt Martha marveled, laughing.

"They are very kind to me." Leticia's eyes twinkled. "Imagine one whole week in Jamaica! Never did I think I'd be here for four months and already have a week of paid vacation. I can't wait!" She paused, and then shook her head. "Auntie, you should have seen the look on their faces. All those sympathetic hugs and stares. The comforting and supportive words. They all believed that I am from the countryside, and my family in Jamaica is poor. They bought my story hook, line, and sinker, and they don't need to know any different."

Aunt Martha laughed again.

"Well, after I made the call this morning, I was expecting you to come straight home. I did not expect them to send you to Jamaica." Martha spoke with eloquence, her accent a mixture of her native Jamaica and Britain, where she had been educated.

"Me neither!"

"You have them wrapped around your little finger, as they say."

Leticia chuckled. "No, it's Melba who makes everything like this. I should thank her. I just wanted to go and work and learn. But she had to make everything difficult. But I know how to play her game."

"Apparently. Now, you have to take one of my suitcases because I want to send a dress for Sonia, a pair of shoes for Madge, and some briefs and shirts for Cecil. I wonder what I should send for my sister?"

"Well, Auntie, you know how Mama loves perfume."

"Good. I will send her a bottle of Anais Anais. I'll go shopping right now before you leave. By the way, I made some jerk chicken, rice and peas, corn, and some fresh ginger beer, so you can eat your dinner whenever you're ready."

"Auntie! Don't buy a whole bunch of things, because I can only carry a medium-sized suitcase. Evanne would want to know why I have such a big suitcase for a short trip."

"True, true. Leave no suspicions. I'll be back by six o'clock so you can get fully ready."

"Also, Auntie, when she comes to get me, she is going to blow her horn. I told her she can't come to the door because my landlady doesn't like visitors in her rooming house," Leticia said.

Aunt Martha burst out laughing again. "Child! You and your stories. I forgot that this is a 'rooming house.' Why did you start telling your coworkers that you live in a rooming house?"

Leticia chuckled as she responded to her only aunt. "You see, Auntie, from the day I started working at Lexhouse and everyone learned that I am from Jamaica, it became obvious they assumed that Jamaica is third world, and I am impoverished and destitute. One day, one of the staff told me that most third-world foreigners live in a rooming house when they come to New York. And if that is what it took to get their confidence and friendship, so be it. Therefore, Auntie, your home became a rooming house, and I am one of your poor third-world tenants."

"Again, my only niece, you and your stories."

"It's what you have to do," Leticia said.

Aunt Martha laughed. "That's our family motto, isn't it? Do whatever it takes."

Leticia nodded, completely serious. "Yes, precisely. That's what Mother always says. 'Do whatever it takes to succeed.' If that means playing on other people's prejudices, then so be it. If they're fools enough to make those assumptions about me, then it's their fault, not mine."

"Sister—your mother—was always very ambitious," Aunt Martha mused.

"We all are."

"Mm." Aunt Martha stroked her chin thoughtfully. "That we are. And we're survivors. We don't let the Melbas keep us down."

Leticia folded another shirt and placed it in her suitcase. "No, we don't. We always do the smart thing."

"That we do. So don't forget to pack 'the thing'! Put it in a Ziploc. I promised your mother I'd remind you. She's been hounding me about it."

Leticia nodded solemnly. "I will remember. Yes, Auntie."

Aunt Martha gave Leticia a peck on the cheek and then ducked out of the room to start her shopping. Leticia finished packing and then enjoyed a fantastic dinner, as she usually did each night, courtesy of her aunt.

By 7:45 p.m., Leticia was packed with gifts and letters to deliver. She had already said goodbye to her two cousins, and she kissed Uncle George farewell. She waited for Evanne's honking horn with Aunt Martha at the door. The honk came at precisely 8:00 p.m.

Leticia was ready. She sprinkled some ground black pepper into her palm and then sniffed it. Her nose and eyes started burning immediately from the spice, and she let out a little gasp. She felt her eyes water.

Aunt Martha just laughed. The two women hugged, and Leticia and her red-rimmed, teary eyes stepped outside.

Evanne stepped out of the car and greeted Leticia and Miss Martha, whom Leticia introduced simply as "Martha." Martha didn't say much, just smiled and nodded at Evanne's pleasantries. Leticia remained somber and taciturn.

Evanne helped Leticia load the suitcase in the trunk. For only being medium sized, the weighty parcel was crammed full.

Leticia's friend chattered on during the drive, mostly gossip and meaningless anecdotes, punctuated every so often by something like "But don't you worry about us; you just take care of yourself and your mama while you're gone. Lord knows, our prayers are with you and your family."

Leticia would respond with a strained, whispered, "Thank you."

The valley of skyscrapers gave way to brownstones, as urban melted into suburban. Finally, they arrived at Evanne's house. Leticia's friend opened the trunk, but Leticia stopped her. "You don't have to take the suitcase out of the car. I brought my necessities for the morning, and I'll just be wearing these clothes that I have on."

"Oh, you're so thoughtful," Evanne said. "Poor girl." She shut the trunk with a loud bang and led Leticia inside. "Just come on in. You can sleep in this room. Make yourself comfortable!"

Leticia stared in amazement at one side of the room, which was filled with store-like shelves, every one holding wig after wig after wig sitting on stands. There must have been dozens. All colors, shapes, and sizes. The majority of them were shaded brunette or red, but a few stood out with wilder or starker colors. Only a single wig stand was empty, doubtless for the one now gracing Evanne's head.

"I call this my happy room," Evanne said.

"Your happy room?" Leticia echoed.

"Mm-hm," said Evanne. "Because all this makes me happy. They make me feel as though I'm alive and okay."

In front of and around the shelves stood at least two dozen mannequins dressed with ladies undergarments: girdles, corsets, bustiers, various slimming body wear, and some garments that Leticia didn't even recognize.

A twin-sized bed was tucked almost discreetly in a corner of the room.

"Have you eaten?" Evanne asked, startling Leticia out of her reverie.

"Oh! Yes, thank you, Evanne. I had a can of soup." She looked back at Evanne with red eyes. She'd been rubbing at them most of the day to keep them that way.

Evanne nodded and whipped off her wig to reveal matted hair, maybe a couple of inches long, with small patches of her scalp showing. She placed the wig on the empty wig stand. To Leticia's surprise, Evanne continued to disrobe. Before she knew it, Evanne was standing in just her bra and panties.

She looked nothing like she did when dressed for the day. Instead of trim, she was shaped like the number 16, with a belly that hung practically just above her knees and no buttocks. Her butt was flatter than Melba's, which was saying something. And when Evanne whipped off her bra, apparently unconcerned with Leticia watching her, her breasts pointed straight to her stomach. In fact, her nipples nearly touched her belly, and she was standing!

Leticia was awed. How Evanne managed to transform her physical appearance so dramatically just using her clothing and wigs, that was a feat! Leticia could hardly recognize this new person standing in front of her.

She was so used to workplace Evanne: immaculately dressed, tight pants or skirt around a seemingly tiny waist, with dramatic and striking hair. Now she found someone who was shapeless, almost blobby, with short and patchy hair.

She was reminded of something her mother said every so often: "Leticia, almost no one is who you think they are. You don't know anyone as well as you think you do."

Once or twice she had asked in return, "How do you get to know someone then?"

"You have to really look," her mother replied. "But almost no one does that. Because other people always end up being mirrors, and no one likes looking at themselves."

It made her wonder: was this even the real Evanne? Because Evanne surely knew Leticia was looking.

Leticia wanted to start laughing. Not at Evanne exactly, although her friend's physical transformation was astounding. But at the proof of her mother's wisdom undressing in front of her. No one really knows anyone in this world, least of all in a city like New York, where everyone was stacked against each other like the sardines in one of Leticia's canned lunches, yet never saw each other—on purpose! Just as her mother said. "Almost no one ever really looks."

To keep from laughing, Leticia started wailing. Tears leaked out of her eyes like a dripping faucet. Evanne paused mid-movement, startled, and then rushed to hug her friend.

Being embraced by her naked friend made Leticia want to laugh even harder; instead, she poured all that energy into her sobs.

"Oh, there, there, sweetie," Evanne cooed. "Are you sure that you're not hungry? Just come with me to the kitchen," she insisted. "Eating something will make you feel better."

Evanne, still half-naked, led Leticia to the kitchen. Leticia expected to see cornucopias of fruit filling Evanne's kitchen. But no, she was in for another shock. Large bags of potato chips, corn chips, every type of chip imaginable lined every single shelf of the pantry.

"Go ahead, honey; take a bag; it will make you feel better."

Leticia sniffled and hesitantly grabbed a bag of Ruffles. Evanne grabbed two bags for herself, and they proceeded into the living room to watch some television. On top of the TV were several framed pictures. One featured a beaming Evanne and a very large guy, tall and portly, a little like Mr. Grossott. They were holding hands, and Leticia wondered if that was Evanne's man.

After eating a quarter of her chips, Leticia noticed that Evanne had finished both her bags. *Wow*, Leticia thought. She didn't know what to think about these revelations about Evanne. Part of her was impressed. Her mother had taught Leticia that she could control how people saw her, and Evanne had obviously mastered that lesson as well! She had certainly fooled Leticia. But that irritated the young Jamaican, too.

She excused herself for bed.

"Okay, honey," Evanne said. "I've set the alarm for two thirty a.m."

As Leticia nestled down into her surprisingly comfortable bed, she heard a muffled "Hello, sweetheart!" through the door.

Another party, voice deep and male, replied, "Good evening, my precious honey cake."

The two giggled. Leticia could hear the couple kissing even from inside her room. She visualized the picture from atop the TV.

Silence followed, and Leticia drowsed into sleep. Two thirty came more suddenly than was welcome. Evanne woke Leticia with a fresh cup of instant coffee.

"Thank you," Leticia mumbled blearily.

"You are welcome. I've already had my shower, so the bathroom is all yours."

Leticia took her shower, drank her coffee, and proceeded to dress. She was just finishing when Evanne knocked on the bedroom door. "Here, you are going to need these." She handed Leticia a pair of rawhide leather gloves. "These will keep your hands safe." Safe? "I don't want to wake Tony, so you are my helper today."

Evanne put on, or at least attempted to put on, a girdle with an open fly crotch. Ultimately, the two ladies had to pull the monstrosity over Evanne's knees. They stopped for breath several times in the process, as Evanne pulled from the front and Leticia from the back. It took them a full ten minutes to get the girdle to reach Evanne's waist. Instantly, Evanne lost the lower part of the number 6 from her figure. Leticia marveled.

Then Evanne went to the closet and retrieved a piece that looked like an eighteenth-century torture device. It had strings that tightened from the back like lacing sneakers.

Leticia's job was to pull the laces and tighten them as hard as she could. At the end, Evanne's Coca-Cola figure re-emerged, with an ass. Leticia was so tired she just breathed hard. Her friend worked hard at her physical transformation.

"Honey, that is why I live with a big man! So he can help me with this. He's been with me through thick and thin."

Leticia nodded as if it all made perfect sense to her.

"I have cancer, you see."

"Oh! I—oh!"

"Well, had. It's in remission." She ran her hands over her scalp. "That's why all this makes me happy." *Makes me feel alive and okay*, she had said the night before.

Leticia's mouth made a little O. She didn't know what to say, and while she struggled, Evanne went blithely on. "That's why I eat all that fruit. Antioxidants or whatever. But it's also why I always have a pastry after good sex." She laughed. "I enjoy the good things in life, you know, because life's too short."

Leticia smiled and nodded.

"It was rough," Evanne said conversationally as she adjusted her undergarments. She didn't seem on the edge of tears or anything, as Leticia would have expected. But then, Evanne was made of stern stuff. "I wouldn't wish it on my worst enemy. You have no idea how bad it is when the cure is worse than the disease. Every day becomes an adventure in suffering." Evanne paused and stared off into space for a long moment. Leticia instinctively reached for her friend's hand. Evanne accepted the handclasp wordlessly; she squeezed Leticia's hand.

"If it weren't for Tony ..." At this statement, Evanne's eyes watered, and she swiped quickly at them with her other hand. She looked at Leticia, right in the eyes. "It changes you forever. Cancer. Sometimes I feel as if it's a guaranteed death sentence if you get cancer, because you do die, even if you live. The poison they treat you with, it kills parts of your body, no matter what. And the person you were before, you're never that person again. That person does die."

Leticia couldn't look away from Evanne's gaze. The sorrow she felt for her friend was formless and turbulent, battering at her heart. She couldn't put words to it, or understand what to do with it. She felt awkward and ineffectual; she didn't know how to express her feelings, and she didn't know what she could do for Evanne.

Failing to find anything to say, she reached out and gave Evanne a hug. At first, Evanne stiffened. Whether she was just surprised or didn't welcome the hug, Leticia couldn't say; but after a few seconds, Evanne relaxed and Leticia felt the older woman's hands on her back. The hug lasted no more than a few seconds, and when they broke apart, neither said anything about it. But for those few seconds, real warmth and compassion moved between the two.

Both ladies completed dressing in silence and then took off for the airport. They made their farewells tearfully, kissed each other on the cheek. "Please go take care of your mother and pray. I will be praying for her, too."

"Thank you, Evanne," Leticia whispered. She admired once again how completely Evanne had transformed herself—even more completely than Leticia had recognized. She wondered suddenly how long Evanne had been in remission. She'd never even had the faintest clue that Evanne was sick. To her knowledge, Evanne hadn't ever been out of work sick, and the wigs were just some personal eccentricity.

But in a perverse way, Leticia was inspired. If Evanne could transform illness into a vision of health and vivacity, Leticia could transform herself, too, into whatever she needed to be to counter Melba's awful influence. She would put her time in Jamaica to good use—certainly her mother would know exactly what to do—and when she got back, Melba wouldn't know what hit her!

PART TWO—MAMA DASSA

CHAPTER 8

AFTER A LONG DELAY DUE to inclement weather in New York, Leticia finally landed in Kingston Airport in Jamaica. Leticia had thought that she would be home for lunch; instead, the delay pushed her arrival to later afternoon. As she stepped out of the customs area, her excitement at being back home eclipsed her fatigue from the very short night. After the endless chill and gray of a New York winter, the warmth and bustle of the Kingston airport delighted her. A mass of humanity throbbed in every possible direction as endless streams of people shuffled past each other. The airport was filled with the loud buzz of many simultaneous conversations.

She weaved her way through the throngs. Some children bumped into her, but they moved along without a word or second glance. To her left, a mother wrapped in a sumptuously colored African dashiki was reprimanding her teenage son, who ignored her glumly. To her right, a reunited family were laughing and embracing, passing people around to hug as though they were living teddy bears.

A grin broke out on Leticia's face as she sucked in great draughts of the warm, tangy Jamaican air. Home!

She spotted her brother Neville waiting patiently for her. He broke into a grin at the sight of her, and they rushed into each other's arms, laughing.

"Little girl, I missed you!" Neville said as he took his younger sister's suitcase. They headed toward the car park, as parking lots were called here. He stopped at a brand new Toyota Camry, gleaming blue with dark tinted windows.

"I've been gone just four months, and you have a new car already?" squealed Leticia.

"Oh, no, not me. This is Mama's new car. Daddy surprised her with it last month. She only let me drive it so I could have it washed and detailed. But I was glad to. It's a smooth ride!" He beamed at his sister as they deposited her bag in the trunk and settled into the plush, overheated interior. It still held the fragrance of a new car. It certainly put Leticia's bus and subway rides to shame. Alas. That wouldn't last forever.

"Where is Mama?" Leticia asked. She was delighted to see Neville, and only slightly surprised not to see Mama or Daddy. She knew they were quite busy. Still, she tried not to feel hurt that they hadn't been waiting along with Neville.

Neville just laughed again. "You know Mama. She just wants to look good for her only daughter. Or, as Mama calls you, her 'baby girl.' Wait till Mama and Daddy see the dreadlocks!"

As the siblings passed through the busy marketplace of the inner city, Leticia realized that she had never fully appreciated the quiet and tranquil environment of her family's suburban home. She gazed at the manicured lawns and overflowing flower beds kept safe behind decorative iron fences and gates. A rainbow of crepe myrtles—royal violets and fiery reds, golden oranges and pristine whites—danced in the breeze.

As they entered their own securely gated community, she smiled at the gardeners and workers tending to the well-heeled estates. They continued to ascend into the hills around Kingston, and she looked down on the busy city below. She had always thought Kingston was a busy, bustling city, but it didn't hold a candle to New York's towering steel and glass buildings. The fast faces of the many people passing each other without a word of hello. The sea of yellow taxis swarming around downtown New York.

They continued past the elementary school that she and her brother had attended many years ago. Chauffeured luxury vehicles were delivering children from school to their respective homes.

She was delighted to be back.

At home, the Patrick family's housekeeper greeted Leticia enthusiastically.

"Peggy!" Leticia cried, embracing the stick-thin older woman.

"Hey, gyal, yuh luk good eh! Merka, she 'gree wit' yuh!" It took Leticia just a moment to work through Peggy's words. Usually Peggy spoke proper English, but her excitement had clearly gotten the better of her tongue. *Hey, girl, you're looking good! America must agree with you.*

They continued to hug, and Leticia whispered in Peggy's ear, "I missed everyone, but especially you, Peggy!"

"Course yuh did, pickney!"

With a final squeeze and a laugh, they separated.

"Did you fix my favorite dish?" asked Leticia hopefully.

"Course!" Peggy looked put out that Leticia even suspected she might not.

She returned to the kitchen just as Leticia's mother pulled into the driveway with Neville's car: "A brand new Accord!" Leticia marveled. "Did everyone get a new car while I was gone?"

"No, no, Letty. Daddy still has the same SUV that you left with him." Neville grabbed his sister's suitcase and dashed into the house. He shouted over his shoulder, "I'm putting it in your room."

"Thanks, big brother!"

Mira Patrick was so excited and delighted to see her only daughter. She practically leapt out of the car, tangling herself with the seatbelt in the process. Finally, she freed herself and grabbed Leticia, who had already sprinted to the car to hug her mother.

"Oh, Mama! I missed everyone, especially you!"

"My youngest baby is home!" cried Mrs. Patrick. She wiped at the tears running down her face.

"So, Mama, what do you think about my dreadlocks?"

Mrs. Patrick shrugged. "Darling, if you like it, I love it. Your dad just called on my cell phone and said he should be here in about an hour."

Still holding on to each other, the two women walked in the house, where they could smell the aroma of Leticia's favorite dish.

Leticia dropped her handbag on the white leather sofa, and they headed straight for the kitchen.

Peggy had, in fact, outdone herself. In addition to the wonderfully aromatic stewed peas and rice, she had also prepared fried plantains, roasted breadfruit, and sweet potato pone pudding for dessert. There was coconut cake and enough fresh fruits to make Evanne's mouth water. In fact, Evanne probably wouldn't know what to make of the fruits like sweetsop, soursop, ginnep, and star apples.

Leticia was in food heaven.

"Oh, Peggy!" Leticia cried in delight. "I am so hungry. I missed lunch, and I have been saving my appetite just for this."

"Letty, let's hurry and eat this before your dad returns, because you know your father will only eat stew peas made with salted beef."

Leticia chuckled. "I remember. Papa refuse to eat pork."

At that moment, Peggy pulled two ham hocks from the steaming pot of stewed peas and placed them each on a plate. The mother and daughter ate them so fast, neither uttered a word. The meat was luscious and tender and melted in her mouth, the flavor exploding. Not even Aunt Martha's wonderful cooking could match Leticia's favorite childhood meal.

Leticia giggled through her mouthfuls. "I can't believe Daddy has never caught on."

Her mother laughed softly. "People don't catch on when they don't want to."

Leticia nodded and chewed. Maybe that's why Melba got away with so much.

Mrs. Patrick added, "Deep down, he knows what makes it so delicious. But he loves the flavor of Peggy's stew peas so much, he doesn't want to know that he knows!"

After gobbling all the meat, Peggy took the plates with the bones. She wrapped them in some paper towels and dropped them in the trash. Not a moment too soon, for Mr. Patrick burst through the door, dashed right over to Leticia, and literally picked his daughter up.

She burst out laughing and cried, "Daddy!"

He must have held her for nearly five minutes. He was tall and strong, and he smelled spicy and sweet at the same time. His whiskers tickled and made Leticia laugh even more. Mrs. Patrick took in this happy reunion with a smile.

"So Daddy, what do you think of my dreadlocks?" Leticia asked finally.

"Baby child, if you like it, then I love it."

Peggy interrupted the joyous occasion to announce that dinner was ready. Mrs. Patrick called for Neville to join them, and everyone sat down around the table. "I wish Denver were here," Leticia's mother mused. "I would love to have all three of my beautiful children here to enjoy this supper."

"Honey," Mr. Patrick said gently, "Denver is a grown man now and busy with all the good things happening for him. We just have to be happy for him."

That sparked Leticia's interest. "What's happening with Denver?" she inquired.

A marvelous smile spread over Mrs. Patrick's smile. She leaned toward Leticia, almost conspiratorially, and reached out to place a hand on Leticia's arm. "He landed a prestigious position as an electrical engineer at BMW. In Germany!"

"Oh, that's wonderful news!" Leticia exclaimed. "That's just what he wanted to do."

Her mother and father nodded. "And he's able to take his wife and son with him," Mr. Patrick added. "He is a happy man. Letty, make sure your mother shows you the latest pictures that Denver has sent us."

"Oh, I already have them! Denver e-mailed them to me, too. I just didn't realize he'd gotten the position. I'm so happy for him. I wish I could give him a big hug."

With that, Peggy entered with the beginning of her feast. Mr. Patrick led them in a solemn prayer that dwelled on thanks to God and Jesus for bringing Leticia home to them.

Every special meal in the Patricks' home had to start with the peppery and fragrant spicy goat soup. Then they dined on jerked smoked brisket, followed by the best rice and peas with Peggy's own freshly grated coconut milk.

After Leticia announced that she couldn't eat another bite without exploding, she pushed away from the table and said, "I am going to get some rest. I have been up since early, early this morning, and I am so very tired now."

"Of course, sweetheart," said Mrs. Patrick. "Get some rest. Your dad has some very important meetings tomorrow, and Neville is attending a seminar. So you and I will have all day to talk."

Leticia kissed both her parents on the cheek and went directly upstairs to her room. In no time, the gentle breeze stirring through her open window lulled her into a fast sleep.

A knock on her bedroom door woke Leticia. "Come in," she said groggily.

Mr. Patrick poked his head into the room and smiled at his daughter.

His warm brown eyes twinkled at her. "Letty, I will be gone all day tomorrow, but after that, I'll take off so we can spend time together."

"But, Daddy, you own the company. You have four branches. Is there not someone else who can do these things for you?"

"Oh, baby child, I'd love to spend every minute with you. But that is just the reason why I have to be there. Some people are flying in from Canada for a major order, and I personally want to seal the deal. That way, I don't have to pay any implementation commission.

"I didn't get to be the largest importer of foreign top-shelf liquor into Jamaica by letting others handle the important deals," he reminded her.

Leticia nodded with comprehension. "Okay, Daddy, I understand."

Her father supplied the high-class tourist resorts and hotels with all their liquor needs, and he was constantly dealing with foreign distributors who wanted their products to reach the natives and tourists of Jamaica. "We cannot live off our rum alone," Mr. Patrick often said. And foreign liquors had to be imported by someone.

She paused, and then added, "Daddy, I missed everyone, but especially you." Mr. Patrick gave her a proud smile and shut the door.

Leticia went back to sleep. She woke, after a long dreamless slumber, to the sound of her mother singing.

"Good morning, pretty!" Mrs. Patrick said when she noticed Leticia was awake. She pushed a window open and let the bright Caribbean sun splash into the room. Bright green ivy curled around the edges of the window. "Did you sleep well?"

"Oh, it was a perfect sleep. I am well rested," replied Leticia as she headed for her private bathroom, her mother in tow.

While Leticia used the bathroom, Mrs. Patrick perched on the edge of the bathtub and said, "Your breakfast is ready. After you finish, we have a lot to talk about, because I want you to tell me everything. Do not miss anything, you understand?"

"Oh, yes, Mama, I can't wait to tell you all about it."

Mrs. Patrick kissed her daughter's forehead and left for downstairs. Leticia called out after her, "Oh, Mama, I almost forgot! The things on the chair in my room were sent by Aunt Martha. She sent the perfume for you, Mama."

Mrs. Patrick picked up the parcels and opened the perfume. "Wonderful!" she said. "Anais Anais, that's my style."

Leticia's mother ducked her head back into the bathroom just as a naked Leticia stepped into the steamy shower. "I'll give these things to everyone. You won't have time to see everyone, so I'll take care of it. You are here for one reason and one reason only."

Leticia froze. She'd told her mother a little about her work situation. But then, her mother had an uncanny way of always knowing exactly what was going on with all her children. It used to scare her. When she was a little girl, Mama always knew not only that she'd done something naughty, but usually what it had been! As she had grown, though, she'd learned to take comfort from it. Mrs. Patrick was fiercely protective of her brood, and whenever she got involved, their problems seem to take care of themselves.

"In fact," continued Mrs. Patrick, "you have an appointment tomorrow at eleven a.m. with Mama Dassa."

Leticia nearly dropped the soap.

"Mama Dassa?" she squeaked. She knew the name by reputation only, and she was astounded to hear her mother mention it.

"Yes. It's going to be a long drive, so we have to head out early."

"Mama Dassa?" Leticia asked again.

"Yes!" A note of irritation crept into Mrs. Patrick's voice, like iron filings mixing with sugar. Leticia clamped her mouth shut. After a moment, Mira's voice returned to normal, and she said, "Okay, baby girl?"

"Okay, Mama. Can we talk in my room so no one can interrupt?" shouted Leticia over the pouring shower.

"Of course, darling."

Leticia stepped out of the shower and shivered, but the plush towel felt wonderful over her skin. She fixed her hair and went downstairs to eat. Peggy smiled to see the young lady and dished out some traditional Jamaican fare like ackee and saltfish stew, fried cod fish fritters, fried fish, smashed green plantains, fried dumplings, and home-grown peppermint tea.

Once again, Leticia cleaned her plate and afterward joined her mother on the verandah. They sat in companionable silence for a while.

Leticia noticed that the ornate six-foot iron fence surrounding their manicured lawn had the letter P on its crest. She was amazed to realize she had never noticed that before. Perhaps it took leaving the country and coming back to notice the details she had always taken for granted.

Many-colored hibiscus flowers draped themselves over most of the rest of the fence, lending some additional privacy to their yard. Their garden was full of bright flowers of every conceivable hue. Leticia's favorites remained the miniature roses, orange and peach-like, that crept close to the verandah.

Meanwhile, they enjoyed some cool, freshly squeezed lemonade as the towering heat beat down on the home. But with the shade, the soft breeze, and the icy lemonade, the two women felt perfectly comfortable.

Leticia found herself telling her mother about her friend Evanne and the cancer, the wigs and body contour extravaganza, and Evanne's obsession with fruit and chips.

Mrs. Patrick laughed to hear about the wigs and dressing room, and nodded soberly about the cancer. "Your friend sounds like she'd make a good spy," she commented.

Leticia chuckled. She had wondered how her mom would respond to the revelation. Some kind of pithy wisdom about crafting the image you project to the world? Or a bit of humor?

They were both laughing so hard that Fala heard. The golden retriever came running from the back and lunged for Leticia's lap.

"Oh! Get off me!" Leticia yelled.

"Letty, he missed you, too." Mrs. Patrick smiled. Her tone was gently chiding.

Leticia held the dog by the face and said matter-of-factly, "I missed everyone, except you."

After that, they returned to Leticia's room, where Leticia locked her door and told her mother everything about Melba, the office politics, her last meeting with Mr. Foles, everything she could think to add.

Mrs. Patrick did not interrupt to make a single comment or ask a single question. But as Leticia delved deeper and deeper into her explanation, Mrs. Patrick's face grew rigid and dark, like storm clouds poised just before a thunderous downpour. By the end, she was fuming mad and pacing around the room.

Leticia sat silently on the bed. She was just glad she wasn't the object of her mother's ire.

"Mistreat my child!" Mrs. Patrick snapped to no one in particular. She turned to her daughter. "Leticia, you must tell Mama Dassa everything. All the details: do not leave anything out, even the most minute detail."

Almost timidly, Leticia said, "I will, Mama. I was writing notes about certain things during my flight."

Mrs. Patrick's countenance relaxed, and she smiled again. It seemed as though the sun came out again from behind a cloud, and its hot and forceful light shoved into the room once again. The verdant growth outside the window rustled in the wind.

Leticia regarded her mother with no small wonder, and it wasn't the first time. Her mother had the strongest, most powerful personality of anyone she'd ever met. If Mrs. Patrick ever met Melba face to face, Leticia was sure Melba would melt like a wax dummy, rivulets of makeup and old white wrinkles running down her face.

"As soon as your father leaves for work in the morning, we'll leave to see Mama Dassa. It is a bit of journey."

"Mama?" Leticia asked.

"Yes, baby child?"

"Mama Dassa. Isn't she … well, isn't she one of those … mystery women?" She used a euphemistic phrase.

Mrs. Patrick responded with an enigmatic smile and an equally puzzling answer: "She's a wise old woman who knows how to make the wind blow her way."

"What will she be like?" Leticia asked. "This Mama Dassa."

Mrs. Patrick shrugged. "She's different for everyone. She'll be whatever you need her to be."

"Have you …?" Leticia started but found she couldn't finish the question.

But Mrs. Patrick just chuckled under her breath. "How do you think I married your father? It's been a long family tradition to see this Mama Dassa and her ancestors. Our class of people don't normally associate with these mystery women, but most of them are just shams. We recognize real power when we see it, and Mama Dassa has real power in her line. My mother—your grandmother—went to see Mama Dassa's mother in her day."

"Really?"

"Oh, yes. Long ago. Our family wasn't always where we are now."

"And because of Mama Dassa you met Daddy?"

"Oh, no, I had already met him! We were courting, in fact. But I was ready to get married, and he was not. It's not that he had a wandering eye or any of that nonsense. It was just that your father couldn't see that final step as opening the door to a new and better future together, not until he actually stepped through it. He just saw it closing the door on the past, on whatever picture he had of himself as some kind of playboy." Mrs. Patrick laughed. "But he was ready in his heart, if not in his head. He was devoted, even then. And he was so handsome, and I knew he would make a good husband and a good father. He would be loving, and he would make sure our family was always taken care of. He would be a good provider. And I was ready to get a move on!"

Leticia and her mother shared a laugh. "So you went to Mama Dassa to make Father marry you?" the young woman asked.

"Not 'make' him! What kind of woman do you think I am?" her mother chortled. "No, to *encourage* him! And *my* mother was just as impatient as I was. She was ready for you grandchildren to be born. So she sent me off to Mama Dassa. Our family have been going to see her family for generations. Oh, and what it took to work her mystery! Do you have any idea how long it took me to get some of your father's pubic hair to take to her!"

"Mother!"

Mrs. Patrick laughed gleefully, like a little girl. The laughter rocked her whole body. "In those days, young couples didn't do such things before being married; initially, your father and I were sort of dating. And I needed to push him along." She laughed again. "Martha and I were reduced to stalking him, sneaking into his bathroom, and looking for hairs fallen into the drain. We even resorted to having Martha distract his family's housekeeper while I rummaged through the dirty clothes hamper."

"Urgh!"

"Indeed. And at the beach, I would hug on him and try to grab some hairs. I thought I would be smooth and surreptitious, but it really isn't as easy to grab a handful of pubic hair without being obvious as you might think. Gladly, I only needed a few."

"Mother!"

"And I'd buy him gifts like boxers and make him try them on

immediately, and then look through them later for spare hairs. But eventually, I got what I needed."

"I don't think I need *all* the details," Leticia protested. Mrs. Patrick laughed again, but a sudden horrifying thought struck Leticia. "Is Mama Dassa going to make me—Melba—no!"

But Mrs. Patrick didn't laugh. She just looked thoughtful. "How could you? She's a thousand miles away. But that's the way the mystery works. You have to do, too. Mama Dassa can't just do it herself; you have to put into it, too."

"What does that mean?"

"It means you pay a price for what you want, and part of that price is active participation. It's not magic, not what Mama Dassa does. It's mystery."

"I wonder what I can expect?"

"The unexpected. Mama Dassa will keep you on your toes; that's for sure."

"Oh, Mother! Do you think she could help Evanne, too?"

"Perhaps, perhaps." Mrs. Patrick nodded sagely. "You can ask, certainly. But what if you have to choose? What if you can only do one, help your friend, or help yourself?"

"Oh! I—I don't know." The two women were silent a moment. Then Leticia added, "Well, Evanne did say the cancer was in remission."

"Whereas Melba is a very current problem. Well, my beloved daughter, all you can do is ask and see what Mama Dassa says."

Leticia found she could not wait until tomorrow.

CHAPTER 9

"WAKE UP, MY PRECIOUS SLEEPING beauty," said a singing Mira Patrick. "We have to be on our way." That's how her mother woke Leticia with eagerness and comfortable supporting love.

As Leticia washed and dressed, she had an uneasy feeling. She felt a little flutter every time she pictured herself meeting this formidable woman.

What did it portend? Having had a night to sleep on it, she found herself shocked that her mother and *her* mother before had used the services of a mystery woman like Mama Dassa. That just wasn't something their class of people did. It just didn't fit her understanding of her family's place in the world. They had money, connections, influence; they purchased their goals with those currencies. Not with the superstitious, unfathomable mysteries to which common people always turned.

But her mother had said their family could always recognize real power.

Leticia and her mother waited for Mr. Patrick to leave before making their move. As soon as he made it past the gates of their posh Glendale Estates home, Leticia and Mrs. Patrick set out.

Mama Dassa lived nearly 120 miles away from their home. In addition to the distance, the condition of the roads made the trip sometimes dangerous. And indeed, the traffic was horrific at many points along the journey. Most of the cars sped well over the thirty-five-kilometers-per-hour speed limit.

Hairpin curves, deep gullies, and steep hills made the road to Mama Dassa treacherous. At one point, a shallow river even spilled water onto the street. It was impossible to tell the direction of the water flow, or even exactly how deep the water had flooded.

None of this deterred Mrs. Patrick. She was absolutely determined for Leticia to see Mama Dassa.

Leticia kept mostly quiet on the drive. She mused about the old mystery woman. She'd heard of Mama Dassa, mostly innuendo and stories. Nothing too alarming. She knew Mama Dassa wasn't some kind of voodoo priestess. This wasn't Haiti, thank goodness. But all the stories painted Mama Dassa as otherworldly, a wise old woman who tapped into a wisdom that shouldn't normally be available to ordinary people. The more embellished stories portrayed her as a person with a wicked streak a mile long.

It also occurred to Leticia to wonder about the price of Mama Dassa's services. These things didn't come cheap. The Patrick family could afford nearly any financial amount, of course. Despite the impression she had given her New York coworkers so they would underestimate her, her family had plenty of money.

No, it was the non-financial price that caused her to wonder. She was young, but she knew well enough that these things always came with a price.

She glanced at her mother, but Mrs. Patrick was focused on the road as she tried to avoid the worst offenders: the minibuses. Always overcrowded and nearly bursting with passengers, the buses were too large for a too small road, and they always traveled too fast, always just on the verge of tipping over as they swerved around a sharp curve.

But Mrs. Patrick took a perverse pleasure in passing them. With every narrow miss, the minibus just inches from their car, Mrs. Patrick shook her head and chuckled. Leticia, meanwhile, had a tight-knuckled grip on the car door. And she was used to Jamaican traffic!

Her mother was made of sterner stuff than she was, apparently. But she already knew that.

After a while, her mother began chatting with her about daily life. Leticia just sat and absorbed it all. Mrs. Patrick described her numerous responsibilities at the family church.

"I don't know what those ladies would do without me," she said. "I wasn't able to organize the ladies' tea party last week, so Camilla handled it. That woman has no head for details! It was terrible. Of course, I told her how much I enjoyed it. Elisabeth wasn't so diplomatic, however."

"How much do you do at the church, Mama?"

"Well, more now that you and Denver are gone. I need something to occupy my time, you know! So I organize a couple of the ladies' groups, and I'm the church coordinator for evening events with our sister churches. And I lead every other women's bible study group. The good book offers a lot of valuable wisdom. You should remember that, young lady."

"Yes, Mama," Leticia said. The good book and mystery women both, apparently. It was a jarring juxtaposition. Yet her mother seemed so earnest about it all. But then, her mother had once told her, "Leticia, if you're going to fake something, you might as well fake it as though it were true."

But sometimes, that made it awfully hard to tell where truth ended and fake began.

After a couple of hours of driving, the ladies stopped at a gas station to stretch their legs and use the toilet. But with no time to waste—they wanted to be home in time to avoid any undesirable questions—they got moving again quickly. This time, Mrs. Patrick herself was speeding at fifty kilometers per hour.

They turned a corner and nearly crashed into a police road block. Two of the officers, both dapper and menacing in their uniforms, frowned and squinted at their car. They approached and came to stand, one on either side of the vehicle.

The one on the driver's side tapped the window.

Mrs. Patrick lowered it and smiled up at the officer. Well groomed, with fancy makeup, lipstick, false eyelashes, and manicured nails, she looked like exactly what she was: a high society lady out for a country drive. The light-skinned Mrs. Patrick said, "Good morning, gentlemen."

As soon as he had seen her, the officer's entire demeanor had changed. Originally irritated at a speeding car nearly bursting into their barricade, he became respectful and solicitous. "A good morning to you, too, Mrs. Patrick. Please go through."

Leticia's mother offered the officer another sunny smile. She continued past all the other vehicles whose drivers were being interrogated.

"It pays to have money and be married to the top importer of fine wines and spirits from all over the world," said a proud Leticia.

"Yes, honey, your daddy is well known and well respected by everyone. Almost every other week there is an article in the paper where your father's name is mentioned." Not to mention the high-level connections her father had in both business and government, and the effects of generous political contributions. It was a game both Mr. and Mrs. Patrick played very well. Leticia hoped she was learning to exercise the same level of skill.

After a bit more driving, Mrs. Patrick said with a broad grin, "We are here."

She stopped the car and heaved a big sigh of relief, and then reached into the backseat to grab their two bags.

Leticia looked around, confused. They were in a lonely, thickly forested part of the island. "I don't see anyone or anything, Mama."

Mrs. Patrick just handed Leticia a pair of shoes they had packed. "Put yours on. I just have to drive up this hill to the flat, so let's get ready now."

They took off their elegant footwear to replace them with well-worn old shoes with holes in the toes and heels. Then they donned their respective wigs. Leticia couldn't help but think of Evanne, and wondered which of Evanne's endless wigs the native New Yorker had chosen for today. She also thought of her other coworkers, all imagining Leticia to be huddled next to her mother's bedside in the hospital, and she snickered.

Mrs. Patrick just gave Leticia a brief glance with an uplifted eyebrow, but Leticia didn't say anything, and Mrs. Patrick didn't press.

Meanwhile, Leticia's mom wiped off most of her makeup, removed her lipstick, and put a torn scarf over her head, tied under her chin. Leticia followed suit. Then they removed their dresses to reveal tattered, wrinkled skirts and blouses. Leticia's was pale yellow with large sunflower print.

They each finished their ensemble with a pair of dark, oversized sunglasses that took up nearly half their faces.

"What if someone sees us, Mama?" inquired Leticia. People of her class did not visit women like Mama Dassa. It just wasn't done.

"Not like this," answered Mrs. Patrick. "No one would know us. Are you ready? Do you have everything?"

"Yes, Mama!" Leticia was smiling from ear to ear. She could feel her heart thumping with anxiousness, but she was excited, too. Mama Dassa lived in a world in which Leticia had never set foot. Perhaps literally.

Superstitions belonged to the poor, but if her mother—whom Leticia respected above just about anyone else—had brought her here, obviously this Mama Dassa had something real and tangible to offer.

The ladies rearranged themselves in the car once more. "Keep your seatbelt on tight," Leticia's mom said. "It's a steep hill to climb to get to the flats, and the road might not be paved."

"Mama," Leticia asked curiously, "how would you know about the road? Is it the same road from your days?"

Mrs. Patrick chuckled. For a moment, Leticia didn't think she was going to answer. Then her mother said, "How do you think your brother got his one-of-a-kind job in Germany?"

Leticia didn't know how to respond to this.

"I take care of my three children, no matter what it takes," replied Mrs. Patrick firmly. Leticia glanced at her mother askew. "And furthermore, your father's success is set in stone." At first, Leticia assumed her mother was just talking in idiom, but then Mrs. Patrick added, "One day, I'll show you the stone."

Perhaps it was the nervous energy nearly sparking around her, but this comment cracked Leticia up. She burst out laughing. She was bewildered and delighted, frightened and enthused, all at once.

At that moment, a small sign nailed onto a coconut tree came into view. It read, "The Flats."

"See, Letty, there is no road for the car, just a lane. We have to park and wait here for the ride to get to her house."

Immediately, they spied two men coming down the lane with two animals. The older of the men had about three teeth in his mouth, obvious because of his wide grin. He wore a sleeveless T-shirt, torn pants, and a pair of sneakers without any laces. The younger man, also smiling, had a cap on his head. He wore similar tattered clothes with many holes in them.

Leticia repressed a vague surge of discomfort.

"Morning, madam; morning, miss," said the elder man. Leticia was surprised at how well he spoke. "You have an eleven a.m. with Mama Dassa."

"Yes," replied Mrs. Patrick.

"All right," said the elder. He guided his mule over to Leticia. "This is my son, Kevin. He and I will lead you up. But where are my manners? I am Joseph, but everyone calls me JoJo."

Leticia stared at the man in open amazement. Everything about him defied expectation. His unkempt, toothless appearance said poor beggar, low class, uneducated. But he spoke with such dignity and clarity.

"Have you ever been on a mule before?" asked Kevin.

"No," said Leticia. Her mother said yes at the exact same instant. Leticia was about to ask, but then she remembered her mother had come here before.

"Well," said JoJo. "Kevin, help the mother on Horse, and I'll put the young lady on Donkey."

"I thought you said they were mules?" inquired Mrs. Patrick.

JoJo and Kevin both laughed. "They are mules," JoJo replied. "One is named Horse, and the other Donkey." Kevin was laughing very loud. "Be quiet, Kevin, so I can explain! My granddaughter was asking one day how come mules can't have baby mules. So I was trying to explain that when a horse and a donkey mate, they have a mule. It became very confusing, so by the end of the conversation, one was named Horse and the other Donkey."

This time, the ladies joined Kevin and JoJo in laughing. In fact, they were so amused by JoJo's stories they barely felt the rough, rocky passage as they climbed up the steep narrow lane.

The lush forest pressed against them. The thick canopy of leaves high above covered them from the sun, but the clustered trees and thigh-high grasses and wildflowers made the air thick. Leticia steadied herself against ivy-strewn tree trunks as they made their way up the steep hill. And yet, the air was pleasant, almost cool—not too hot, not too stuffy, not too humid. It surprised Leticia.

Soon enough, they arrived at Mama Dassa's house. They passed through a wooden archway, its white paint peeling from the strong sunshine. Leticia stopped cold at her first sight of Mama Dassa's house, and her eyes widened appreciatively.

Mama Dassa had done well for herself. The house bore signs of wear—roof shingles askew or missing, paint peeling, pieces of wood missing here and there among the balcony railing. But on the whole, the house stood sturdy and strong and welcomed its visitors. White wooden latticework decorated the railings and eaves of the house, and a wide veranda swept around the house on both the ground and upper floors. Though the house appeared to be made of wood, the entryway was paved with stones. Behind the house, foothills carpeted in green gently sloped upward into a low-lying cloud. Meanwhile, billowing trees framed the house on either side, swaying in the breeze, and the front door yawned open as if in greeting.

An old woman, chubby and bent over, stood in the doorway. She spoke with a British accent rather than a Jamaican one, and she seemed very dignified. Her dress was plain, albeit nicer than JoJo's and Kevin's clothing. At least it didn't have any holes in it.

Estrella, the old lady, offered them a cold purifying tea that Mama Dassa required all visitors to drink before entering the house. Leticia looked down into her glass, but it just looked like ordinary tea to her. She sipped at it. Tasted ordinary, too sweet for her taste, but nothing unusual about it.

"You are Mama Dassa's only client for this hour, dear," Estrella told Leticia. "Booked for one full hour."

Strangely, Estrella reminded Leticia of Frances, Mr. Foles's private secretary.

"Use it wisely, love," Mrs. Patrick said as Estrella took their glasses and led Leticia deeper into the house.

Leticia looked all around, trying to soak in all the details. The house was a surprise: it was neither the ramshackle hut one might expect of someone barely making a living, nor the worn but comfortable home the exterior suggested. Instead, it was the opulent estate of someone who apparently had the power to bring good fortune to herself as well as her clients.

Leticia look around in wonder. The gleaming floor beneath her feet was polished marble. The walls were painted a bright, pale blue that echoed the color of the skies. Unlike the archway in the yard, the paint looked so crisp and vivid it might have been recently painted.

Fresh flowers lined the entryway, placed in gorgeous ornate and multi-hued vases, gleaming as though they were made from mother of pearl. Original works of art, most depicting scenes around Jamaica, lined the walls, each with a small light shining on the picture. Leticia was stunned. She could have been standing in the middle of her parents' own estate; this kind of art and decoration filled their home as well. What kind of woman was Mama Dassa, that the exterior of her house should appear pleasant but humble, while the interior should reflect an entirely different class of woman altogether?

"Stay here, dear. I'll be back to take you into the ceremonial room in a moment."

Leticia nodded, and Estrella disappeared through a door. Leticia nervously rocked from foot to foot as her gaze traveled through the hall. Everywhere she looked, she discovered new finely crafted and unexpected details: a trompe l'oeil mural on the far end of the hallway, so intricately painted that it took several seconds of gazing to realize it was actually a painting; an artful arrangement of flowers and silver candlesticks tucked into a small alcove in the wall; even a maid in a sharp uniform crossing from one door to another farther down the hall. Leticia just marveled.

True to her word, Estrella returned only a minute later, and she led Leticia into another room.

It was dark except for glittering candles as Leticia stepped in. A cloud of incense smoke wafted past her. The room either had no windows, or any windows were very well covered. At least one hundred candles were scattered through the room. They warmed it and cast a flickering yellow-orange glow over everything. Shelves along the wall held dozens and dozens, perhaps hundreds, of bottles and strange balls made from some kind of straw material. A desk sat against the far wall.

"Have a seat, child," Estrella instructed. "Mama Dassa will see you in a moment." She lit five additional candles and set them in what seemed like strategic spots around the room.

Soon thereafter, a fat lady emerged from a door behind the desk. Leticia hadn't even realized it was a door.

The lady, surely Mama Dassa, paused as she surveyed Leticia. Her jowls shook a little, and her eyes were both bright and beady as they studied the young woman. Mama Dassa wore at least three layers of clothing. Her head was wrapped with the remnants of many cloth swatches, all different colors and patterns, with a feather stuck in the side of the headpiece. Her voluminous robes cascaded to the ground, and she must have been wearing at least a hundred small beads around her neck.

With a grace and stealth that defied her bulk, Mama Dassa walked slowly over to Leticia. She put her hand on Leticia's forehead. The hand was hot but perfectly dry. Mama Dassa then pulled a chair from next to the desk and sat.

"Look me straight in the eyes, child," she commanded. "Look at me as if you can see right through me."

The incense was making Leticia feel lightheaded, but she complied as best she could. Mama Dassa's voice was a rich timbre, very deep, gravelly, almost manly. Leticia wondered idly if a man was hiding himself amidst the thick cascades of cloth. The mystery woman spoke with a pronounced Jamaican accent, but her words were crisp and enunciated.

Mama Dassa started laughing, a deep and soulful belly laugh. Leticia smiled but didn't know how to respond. She was mildly alarmed that Mama Dassa might have read her mind. After a few seconds, the laughter passed and Mama Dassa observed, "You are hot. That is good. Now, tell me everything. I want to hear it all. Tell Mama Dassa all your worries and concerns."

Leticia nodded and started her story. She related everything that had happened from her first day on the job at Lexhouse Advertising. Melba, Evanne, Mr. Foles, Paul. Everyone featured. She did not miss a single syllable from her tale.

Mama Dassa listened attentively. From time to time, she rose up and down as if she was about to have some kind of fit. Occasionally, she mouthed something wordlessly; at other times, she would moan softly, "Ooooh." It was as though Mama Dassa was half present and half … elsewhere. Leticia just kept looking straight into her face and continued to offer up all the facts.

"Did you bring the thing?" asked Mama Dassa promptly when Leticia had finished.

"Yes!"

Mama Dassa reached into a desk drawer and pulled out a purple bottle of water. At the same time, Leticia opened her handbag and pulled out a Ziploc bag. She handed Mama Dassa Melba's pillowcase, which she had never returned to her boss.

Mama Dassa shook the pillowcase and tied it in a knot. Then she loosened the knot and startled sprinkling the water from the bottle all over the pillowcase. Next, she wrapped the case around both of Leticia's hands and smiled as she sprinkled both the girl's hands and the pillowcase together.

Finally, Mama Dassa lifted her steady gaze to meet Leticia's. Leticia fought an almost overwhelming impulse to look down, or up, or anywhere rather than meet the woman's powerful and commanding eyes. She felt dizzy, and she tried to blame it just on the incense. But something was swirling around the room, some energy, something sizzling silently, and it wasn't the cloud of incense.

If Mama Dassa sensed Leticia's sudden spike of fear, she said nothing. "Now, my child, go through that door and don't let this out of your hand. Keep twirling it in your hands, twisting every chance, and just walk among the flowers. I will call you in when the time is right."

Leticia stepped out the door Mama Dassa had indicated. At first, she had to shield her eyes from the sudden intense glare of the sunshine, but after a few moments of rapid blinking, she found herself in a little grotto on the backside of the house. It lay downhill, and Leticia followed the downward-sloping path.

She marveled at the cascade of flowers blooming all around her. Amazingly, none of the flowers were native to Jamaica. In fact, she didn't even recognize many of them, and she marveled at Mama Dassa's apparent ability to grow such an exotic variety of blooms. And not just grow, but truly thrive. Nearly every inch of the grotto apart from the path teemed with delicate blossoms in every conceivable color and shade: blues deeper than the ocean, lilacs gentle and peaceful, reds so intense they seemed to shout, "Stop! Look here!"

Leticia sat gingerly on a plain wooden bench. It wasn't just the colors—a veritable bouquet of fragrances swirled around her on the breeze.

Some ten minutes had passed when Mama Dassa reappeared at the entrance. "Come in, my child, and have a seat." She proceeded to anoint Leticia with a drop of water from the purple bottle.

"How do you make so many flowers grow?" Leticia asked shyly. "Where did you find them all?"

"Eh? All over. All over from my travels, and I help them to grow by convincing them they want to grow." Leticia didn't quite know how to respond to this, and after a moment, the lady continued, "Ha. You are no longer hot. This is better. You can go in peace now. Do not fret. Things will be under control. This will make her twitch."

Twitch? wondered Leticia.

Smiling uncertainly, Leticia opened her wallet to pay Mama Dassa. She gave the lady three twenty-dollar bills, American currency. Mama Dassa spied the hundred-dollar bill in Leticia's wallet, and her expression shifted subtly, took on an extra gleam.

In fact, her eyes nearly came out of their sockets, landed on the desk, and bounced right back into place like a cartoon figure.

Leticia smiled ever so slightly, just a little upward curve at the corner of her mouth. She was on more comfortable terrain now.

Mama Dassa looked right up at Leticia and said, "Child, with that extra hundred dollars, I will give you some things with special instructions."

"Okay," said Leticia without hesitation. It was Melba's dirty money anyway, that Melba had given her before she left, and it wasn't like Leticia was hurting financially. She handed the bill to the mysterious woman.

Mama Dassa reached under her desk and took out a box. She withdrew three small sticks and handed them to Leticia. "These might resemble plain pieces of tree wood, but they are not. They are from a special tree."

Leticia looked at them from all different angles, but they looked pretty ordinary to her.

"Leticia, I need for you to listen keenly to what I am saying." The young woman met Mama Dassa's gaze at once; it was the first time Mama Dassa had actually used her name. "You must follow these direction just as I am telling you."

Mama Dassa took the three sticks back, along with the pillowcase, and placed them in the Ziploc bag. She then gave Leticia step-by-step instructions for using the sticks. She added that the damp pillowcase needed to dry in the sun.

"Finally, my child, with my instructions, these won't make her twitch. They will make her twitch twitch."

Twice the twitching, Leticia thought. She was torn between amusement, doubt, and wonderment.

"Now, go in peace," Mama Dassa concluded. Her voice was softer this time, like an echo floating through the wind.

But Leticia hesitated before walking out.

Mama Dassa seemed unconcerned. She said, "Ask me what you have to ask me, child. You aren't the first. You won't be the last."

"Urh, yes. Is this ... I mean ... this ..."

Mama Dassa chuckled, a reverberant sound that echoed around her chest and then exploded into the room. "Black magic?"

Leticia felt inexplicably humiliated and terrified that she had offended.

"Isn't it late to be asking?" But Mama Dassa laughed again, booming. But then she said, "What I do is not black, not white, not magic, not even mystery. It's natural law, child. It's gray, impersonal; it's a thunderstorm." She paused and let that sink in. "But 'tis true this, that what you put out circles round. You've got to really want to put this lady down. How bad do you want it?"

Leticia didn't answer immediately.

"Huh? No answer, doesn't work. It's your heart that powers it. Your heart doesn't know what it want, it doesn't work. So how bad do you want it?"

"Bad," Leticia whispered, her voice tiny.

Mama Dassa nodded serenely. After a moment, Leticia made her way out of the room and met her mother outside. They said goodbye to Estrella, who gave them each another cold tea to drink before departing. "You have to drink this for safety in your travels."

"This one is delicious!" exclaimed Mrs. Patrick. "What kind of tea is this?"

"Mama Dassa's secret blend" was all Estrella would say. Then she handed a small sachet of tea from her pocket and held it out to Leticia. "For your friend."

"Oh!" Leticia exclaimed. She had been so caught up ... She had told Mama Dassa about Evanne's plight with a plea for help, but then forgotten. Estrella smiled secretively. "It's Mama Dassa's secret blend, too."

Leticia thanked her profusely, and then the ladies mounted Horse and Donkey and headed down the steep hill with JoJo and Kevin. Leticia could almost sense the presence of the pillowcase and sticks in her handbag the whole way, but she figured that was just her imagination. She felt unaccountably tired, though, almost exhausted.

As they were leaving, JoJo said, "Good day, ladies. I am now waiting for Mama Dassa's noon appointment."

Clearly dismissed, mother and daughter smiled at each other. They said farewell to the two men, and then drove down the hill. As they turned onto the main road, they saw a brand new Mercedes Benz sweep past them and go up the hill.

"Well?" asked Leticia's mother finally.

"Sorry, Mama, but I can't tell you."

"Letty!"

"No, Mama, I can't tell you anything at all!"

"Well, that's all right, my child. Denver was told not to reveal anything about his meeting. He wouldn't tell me no matter how much I begged, and see how everything worked out for him?"

Leticia nodded.

"And now it will work out for you," Mira added. "When you called and told me that woman had you doing her laundry …! You don't know how angry that made me." Leticia could tell; when *she* got upset, her Jamaican twang intensified. When her mother got angry, the effects of her British-based education came out, and her words took on a soft, genteel, heart-chilling tone. "I had been wavering whether to get involved, or stand back and let you deal with the situation in your own way. That is the reason you are in America now: to learn your own way. I did not wish to intrude."

"Oh, you could never!" Leticia protested.

Her mother offered her a brittle smile. "If only that were true. At any rate, I initially decided to let you handle the situation. Indeed, I was curious to see how you would. But then! Then … that *woman* … treated my baby girl like … like a … like a servant! Like some sort of ordinary, common person! My extraordinary baby girl! That's what convinced me. *No one* treats my children like they're common laundry maids."

"Thank you, Mama."

Mira nodded sharply. "And when you mentioned that you still had her pillowcase, how even after being so kind as to take her laundry to the cleaners for her, she still berated you for forgetting the pillowcase, I knew I had to get it. I was going to get it to Mama Dassa one way or another. Thank the good Lord above that you came back home so you were able to bring it yourself. My only fear was that it would have gotten lost in the mail. I knew Mama Dassa would need some kind of tangible connection to *that woman*, which makes that pillowcase as precious as diamonds for our purposes. I trust you can at least tell me that she made use of it?"

77

"Yes, she did." Leticia had to stop herself from going into more detail.

Again, Mira just nodded sharply. "Good. I knew she would."

The women stopped at a gas station not far from Mama Dassa's. They ducked into the bathroom and emerged wearing their original outfits. Mrs. Patrick had even refreshed her makeup.

They made a more leisurely journey back home. They stopped at a nearby iced-cold jelly stand to buy some cool, refreshing coconut water. After that, they pulled into the first seafood restaurant they could find and ate lobsters and conch in butter sauce. They reminisced together about Leticia's childhood and told jokes and laughed with one another. Leticia found she was feeling almost jubilant.

CHAPTER 10

ONCE HOME, LETICIA PROMPTLY TOOK the pillowcase to the backyard and hung it in the sun to dry, just as instructed. She regarded the off-white cloth, dancing a little in the soft breeze. Under the sun's strong light, it looked so innocuous. Ordinary even. But according to Mama Dassa, it would make Melba "twitch twitch."

Whatever that meant.

Fala saw Leticia. He ran over with a deep growl and started barking at the pillowcase. Astonished, Leticia looked back and forth for a moment. Fala kept barking, even after Leticia told him to hush.

She looked again at the pillowcase. Well, apparently Mama Dassa had done something to it.

Feeling more confident, she returned inside to join her mother.

That evening during dinner, Mr. Patrick said, "Leticia, if things are unbearable in New York, come home. You have a home and a job here. Neville is learning the business, but I wouldn't mind if you would take part, too."

Neville nodded solemnly, chewing his jerk chicken.

"Down the road sometime, Daddy," Leticia said truthfully. "But let me learn some more and then we can talk."

Mrs. Patrick didn't say anything, but she nodded approvingly. Leticia remembered a conversation she'd had with her mother about survival camps before she'd left for New York. People went to survival camps to learn to survive in the wilderness, and frequently, the camps literally dumped their students in the middle of nowhere so they could practice their skills.

"That's what you need to do, baby girl," her mother had said.

"I need to go to a survival camp?" Leticia asked, confused.

Her mother had a good, long laugh at that. "Not exactly, sweetheart. I mean, the world is a wilderness, and it's really about more than surviving. You want to thrive, right?"

Leticia nodded.

"You have the skills," Mrs. Patrick continued. "We've made sure of that. But you've never really had to use them. You've never been tested. If you want to thrive in the wilderness of your life, that's what you have to do."

That conversation came back to Leticia now as she took another bite. At other times, Mrs. Patrick had commented how much easier her children had it than she did as a young woman. Leticia's mom didn't talk much about her past, but Leticia knew it had been hard. Well, perhaps up until she had met Mama Dassa.

"It's important for me to be as successful at Lexhouse as I can. Then I can transfer that success back here."

Her father laughed, a hearty belly sound. He waved his fork, a piece of meat still skewered on it, toward Leticia's mother. "See? And you fret if she's okay up there in New York! We taught her all we could, and listen to that—she picked up on everything we said."

"I never had any doubt Leticia would be successful. I worry about her being alone up there."

"I'm not alone, Mama. I have Auntie Martha and Uncle George."

"I know, but you don't have us."

"It's important to get off on your own," said Neville around a mouthful. "It's the only way you know if you can stand up on your own two legs."

"Right!" said Leticia. "How would I know if my success was really mine, if I didn't do it myself?"

Her parents burst out laughing. Her mother reached over and grabbed, squeezed Leticia's forearm. "Right you are, girl; right you are! In our family, we succeed by our own wiles."

"But sometimes with just a little help," added Leticia wickedly.

"Sometimes," agreed her mother with a conspiratorial wink.

Mr. Patrick looked back and forth for a moment, and then heaved a dramatic sigh. To Neville, he said, "Women. Always with their mysteries."

"That's right," said Mrs. Patrick. "But now, now is not the time for worries," she added, turning back to Leticia. "We've done everything we can do. You're on vacation now!"

Leticia smiled. "Yes, Mama."

"Yes!" agreed Mr. Patrick. "We should do something fun. I'm on vacation now until Monday, too!"

Neville and Leticia started throwing out some suggestions, but then Mr. Patrick said, "How about a midweek pantomime?"

"Oh, yes," said Leticia. She loved plays.

After dinner, the family loaded into Mr. Patrick's SUV, and off they went.

On the way to the theater, Mr. Patrick listed several activities that he planned for his family for the next few days.

Once they arrived at the theater, Leticia and her mother headed straight for the ladies' room. "Mama, it's a good thing we went today," Leticia commented. "With Daddy's plans, we would not make it at all!"

"I know, my dear." They both laughed, and then went to rejoin Neville and Bill Patrick for the play.

It turned out to be a surprisingly entertaining comedy about a man making a complaint to a well-known gentleman in the community. "Sir," the man said, "Mi use yuh bredda da witch doctor to ridda a ghos'. Bu' im cheated me, uhn ayuh wan' me pig back."

The man explained that he kept hearing the ghost almost every night. The witch doctor, who was the gentleman's brother, accepted the task of exorcising the ghost in exchange for a large pig.

"Im come tuh mi house uhn prayed uhn talking somethun bangarang, uhn im danced all over. Den im tol' me tuh go inside t' lock da windows an' doors."

"Did you?" asked the gentleman.

"Aye, mon." The witch doctor then proceeded to pull out a large machete and chop some limbs from a lime tree that was rubbing against the house every time a breeze rocked it.

At first, the man thought the witch doctor had completed the task and offered the pig. But when the homeowner realized all the witch doctor had done was cut some limbs from his tree, he got angry. He hoped by approaching the witch doctor's more intelligent brother, he could secure the return of his pig.

"Are you still hearing the ghost?"

"Nah, mon."

"Well, my brother deserves his payment. He got rid of the noise that was keeping you awake."

Leticia watched the performance attentively. She had her own ghost back in America to exorcise. She wondered how Mama Dassa's solution would work, but then realized it didn't matter, as long as it did work.

First thing the next morning, Mr. Patrick shouted from downstairs, "Everyone packed?"

Each family member echoed yes one by one.

"I want an early start; we are going to be busy today," Mr. Patrick stated.

Just then, Peggy called her employers to breakfast. She had laid out a buffet of fried plantains, bread with butter, liver stew with boiled green banana.

As the family sat down to eat, Mr. Patrick asked, "Coffee for me, Peggy?"

The maid nodded and looked around at the rest. "More coffee, anyone else?" she inquired.

The three remaining members looked at each and said, "Chocolate," at the same time. The family started to laugh.

As the meal wound down, Mr. Patrick asked Peggy if she was ready to join them.

"Yes eyeyah," replied the delighted maid. "All I have t' do is put de dishes in de dishwasher, sweep de dining room an' de kitchen, an' I, too, be ready for Negril."

"Is that all?" asked Mr. Patrick dryly.

While Peggy took care of those chores, the rest of the family brushed their teeth and piled their belongings into the SUV. Mr. Patrick put in a CD with some smooth gospel reggae for the trip.

The beaches of Negril lay on the far side of the island, but the drive passed quickly for the family, and as soon as they arrived, everyone jumped out of the car. As her father checked into the rented bungalow, Leticia ran right into the sea with her clothes fully on. She yelled, "This feels good, the sea, the Caribbean Sea! This is the life!"

She thought of New York's lingering winter, cold and dreary. She thought of the silvery steel skyscrapers rushing into the sky to meet iron-colored clouds. Instead, she relished in the warmth of the Jamaican sun and all the blue: the cloudless azure of an endless sky and the electric blue of warm water rushing to meet the sky on a distant horizon.

In fact, the group spent most of the day in the water and lying on the beach. Only Peggy interrupted, and then only to serve the meals. While the Patrick family ate, she would go swimming herself.

As evening fell, the colors shifted and muted, and the Jamaican fragrances—the salty tang of the ocean, the fresh green smell of lush vegetation—seemed to grow stronger.

Everyone dressed up, especially Mrs. Patrick. They loaded into the SUV and went to Rick's Café for dinner. They watched the famous sunset, a splendor of gold and burnished brass tones settling into the darkening waters. They danced and drank a bit of everything behind the bar that night. Leticia smiled to herself as she saw her parents slow dancing with her mother's head laid against her father's broad chest as they held hands while swaying to the music. As she watched her parents, an image of Paul and herself dancing flashed through her mind. Leticia chuckled at the thought.

It wasn't until 2:00 a.m. that everyone piled back into the SUV, and Neville drove back to the three-bedroom bungalow. He had to physically help his father to bed since Mr. Patrick was drunk as a skunk.

The next morning, everyone got up late. "Mama, you look tired," said her daughter.

"Yes, last night I danced so much I must have lost at least five pounds."

"I don't think so, Mama, because you had about four sunset breezes and two pina coladas!" Leticia teased.

Mrs. Patrick just sighed.

Peggy had already laid out a breakfast of omelets and toast with Anchor butter.

Leticia talked and ate at the same time. "God, I've missed Anchor butter," she said. She savored the rich creaminess.

"Where is dat Mr. Patrick?" asked Peggy. "Im coffee ready."

"I'll take it to him," Neville chuckled. He took the steaming cup gingerly and went to his dad.

"Mama, Daddy won't wake up!" Neville shouted at the top of his lungs.

Leticia looked up in alarm, but Mrs. Patrick just smiled wanly and shook her head. "Leave him be, darling; let him sleep it off."

Neville stepped back into the room. He didn't seem any more worried than Mrs. Patrick, so Leticia went back to her hot chocolate.

Mrs. Patrick checked her watch and added, "Neville, it's nearly noon already. Would you put your father in the car and then go check us out? We girls will load up the vehicle."

"Yes, Mama," said Neville obediently. He managed to pull Mr. Patrick out of bed. Only half conscious, Mr. Patrick stumbled out of the room blearily. Neville half supported, half carried his father to the car, and then strapped the older man in the passenger front seat and clicked the seatbelt.

"Whew!" he said and wiped his sweat-slicked brow. Panting, he turned to check the family out of the bungalow while Leticia, Peggy, and Mrs. Patrick loaded their belongings into the SUV.

Mr. Patrick, still wearing the same clothes from last night, slept the entire way from Negril to Dunn's River Falls. The three-hour trip took them from the far western point of the island to the northern coast, a little over halfway to the other side of Jamaica.

During the drive, the family mostly kept quiet, each recovering from the late night in their own way. After an hour of Mr. Patrick's snores, Mrs. Patrick did lean forward to knock him in the shoulder. He didn't wake, but he snorted in his sleep, shifted position, and breathed more quietly after that.

"And to think this man makes his living selling alcohol," she said under her breath.

Leticia chuckled but continued to lean her head against the window as she watched the landscape sweep by. How she enjoyed all the bright colors of the island, sorely missing in New York. Yes, the city had the crowds and the simmering chaos of the island, and nothing could compete with its sheer scope. But with its sterile towers and gray skies, New York seemed so much more vacant and empty. It cared more about carrying people from point A to point B along the subway, or about people sitting at the desks in those monstrous buildings scratching out a living with their pens and computers, than about actual living. Leticia couldn't deny that New York had its own magic, its own vitality, but so different, so alien from the lush and vibrant warmth of Jamaica.

Maybe it wasn't Melba versus Leticia so much as Melba versus Jamaica … or Leticia versus New York … or New York versus Jamaica …

Her eyes drooped shut, and she drowsed as Neville steered them toward their destination.

Every so often, Mr. Patrick would crack open his eyes and croak, "Where are we?" Only to return to sleep before anyone had a chance to answer. The rest of his family would giggle without answering.

When they had nearly reached the falls, Mrs. Patrick instructed Neville to stop at the next restaurant and wake his father, who shambled into the restaurant half awake and asked, "Where's the toilet?"

As he went to relieve himself, a host guided the rest of the family to a table. Mr. Patrick emerged and took his place at the table. Quite sober, his rich baritone perfectly steady, he said, "I would like a cup of coffee and toast, please."

Peggy beckoned to the waitress and passed on the request, and everyone else ordered their lunch.

"Daddy, you are so lively; you slept the whole way," Leticia teased after the waitress has walked off.

"Princess, I import booze for a living; there is knowledge in managing your liquor. And by the way, when I ask 'Where are we?' please don't ignore me and laugh. That was rude."

Everyone was shocked, but Mr. Patrick smiled to take some of the sting out of his rebuke. He turned to Leticia and said, "Tell me, baby girl, was your quality time with your mother day before yesterday fruitful?"

"Yes, Daddy, very fruitful." Leticia glanced at her mother, who was regarding her husband with a surprised and puzzled expression.

Mr. Patrick said, "What did you ladies do?"

"Yes, what did you do all day Thursday?" interjected Neville.

"Never you mind," said Mrs. Patrick forcefully.

"Mama—"

"Don't you 'Mama' me. Never you mind."

"No matter," said Mr. Patrick. "I expect you wouldn't have been in such a good mood if it hadn't gone well."

Mrs. Patrick looked as if she was dying to ask her husband just to see how much he knew, but couldn't quite bring herself to do it.

"I knew you both would be on a dangerous shopping spree," Mr.

Patrick said dismissively, but he looked mightily proud of himself. As if he knew they were lying. He sucked in a great big breath and expanded his chest out.

Leticia and her mother exchanged a look.

Mr. Patrick watched the two of them and burst into loud guffaws. "You two lovelies have got shopping and spending money in your blood, you know." He tapped the side of his head with a meaty finger, as though he had them all figured out, and he laughed again.

Neville watched them all with pursed lips.

After their late lunch, the group finally reached Dunn's River Falls. Neville parked the car, and everyone filed out with their respective bags from the back of the vehicle. They passed through a makeshift park of snack bars and souvenir stands to come to the entrance. The attendant looked up and broke into a toothy smile. He recognized Mr. Patrick right off and said, "Ayuh dere, sir an' missus Patrick." He opened the gate and let the group in for free.

They headed down the stairs to an area with lockers where they were able to pull off their regular clothes in favor of bathing suits and then stow their belongings. From there, they headed for the falls.

First thing everyone did was stand at the end of the falls for a thundering hard massage of water smashing into them.

"Lawd dis place cris," sighed Peggy, marveling at the beauty and sensation of the water.

"I couldn't agree more," added Leticia. She closed her eyes and smiled. The air was cool and moist with spray. The water roared in her ears; the sunlight fell in dappled patterns on the layered falls as white-crested water cascaded along an oversized stairway of rocks and stones.

"Right now, I wish my twin sister was here; she loves this place," Mrs. Patrick shouted over the din of rushing water.

"Me, too," said Leticia, suddenly missing her aunt and uncle.

"Mira, I remember the last time Martha and George came here with us. The mischief you and Martha got into was too much!"

Mrs. Patrick laughed, but Neville and Leticia just looked at each other.

Mr. Patrick continued, "Instead of climbing with everyone hand in hand, oh no, you and Martha decided to make your own route walking up a different way, and all you did was bounce against the rocks."

Mrs. Patrick smiled indulgently at her husband even though she heard only every third word, thanks to the roar of water. "You and your twin sister make a dangerous pair! Thank God your parents only had you two." He smiled fondly at her.

Neville, eager to get started on the upward climb through the falls, beckoned to his family to start holding hands. The worked their way along the rocks through the flowing water, climbing up to the next level, and then repeating the process all the way up. Mr. Patrick went first, holding Leticia, who held Peggy, with Mrs. Patrick and Neville at the end.

Leticia always forgot just how slippery the rocks could be, and how powerful the torrent of water, as she waded through. She started to lose her footing, and then her hand slipped out of her father's. She fell and slid into a pool with some hard rocks. Peggy, Mama, and Neville went crashing with her against the falls. Mr. Patrick just stopped and looked back with a quizzical expression, and then shook his head and continued up the falls alone, laughing all the way.

The remaining four struggled to regain control of themselves. The falls weren't dangerous, but they were treacherous, and they defied visitors to make their way up the watery way without falling. Like a circus act gone bad, the four fought against the falls to get back onto the rocks. The more they struggled, the more they thrashed and bounced against the huge smooth rocks. Thoroughly drenched and even a little chilly, the group laughed at their mishap.

If anything, this was what Leticia loved and missed most about her family. It was full of laughter. Nothing was too serious; everything was funny. Life was just an ongoing sitcom, and it was a lot more entertaining that way.

With the help of a falls employee, one by one, they emerged from the shallow pool and headed up with this guide. Thankfully, they didn't have to traipse up the entire length of the falls. A discreet exit nearby allowed the family to escape back to dry land under cover of trees with tall, narrow trunks.

They returned to the dressing area at the bottom of the falls. Mr. Patrick awaited them, already fully dressed. He greeted them with a wide grin. "Bit slippery, eh?"

"Oh, you," his wife chided.

"I didn't notice so much myself."

"Oh, look at that!" Mrs. Patrick muttered. She lifted a leg to show the group. "Bruising already!"

The remainder inspected themselves. The falls had managed to leave its imprint on all of them except Mr. Patrick. Leticia, in fact, had the most, all along her legs and arms.

Neville looked at his and muttered, "Daddy, you'll have to drive."

"Bet they don't have anything like that in New York!" Mr. Patrick commented.

"No, Daddy."

"You should come back home. What do you need in New York, anyway?"

"She needs to learn to fend for herself," answered Mrs. Patrick on Leticia's behalf. "Needs to learn what a big world it is. It's a lot more than just Jamaica!"

"True, true. Well, you know you always have a place here, princess. No need to put up with any foolishness if there are problems up there."

"Yes, Daddy," Leticia said automatically, but when she glanced over, she noticed her father was staring at her, no trace of a smile on his face, perfectly serious. A little surprised, she met his gaze and held it.

And she realized, with something of a start, that her father had just landed her at a crossroads. Did she even want to go back? Maybe the best way to deal with Melba was just to leave her behind, forget about her, not even give her the time of day. Maybe this Mama Dassa thing was going too far, making more of Melba than the bitch even deserved.

But she looked over and found her mother looking at her, too. Was that the best way, to just run back home whenever she ran into difficulty? True, she could, but the question wasn't *could*, it was *should*. Should she?

"I know, Daddy," she said.

He nodded, and the family finished dressing in silence.

On the way back to the car, Neville quipped, "Letty, did Daddy tell you that Denver wanted to send him a brand new BMW SUV? And Daddy turned it down."

"I don't want anyone to say a word about my car; I love it!" said Mr. Patrick. "Now let's just get home so we can rest, and Letty can pack. We have church in the morning."

And home they went.

That night, Mrs. Patrick helped her daughter pack so the ladies would get some last private time together. "Precious, remember, don't tell anyone what you are doing; just do it. Peggy will have the fried fish and breadfruit for Martha in the morning. The plan is to load your things in the morning, so we can go straight to the airport from church," said a tearful Mrs. Patrick as she kissed Letty on her cheek.

"Mama," said Leticia, "Daddy surprised me today."

"Me, too, baby girl."

"Do you think I should stay? Not go back."

Mrs. Patrick didn't answer immediately, then: "You already know what I think. I could see it in your eyes. Honey, go back. You are from a family of fighters. Always remember that. Furthermore, no one—no one!—harms my child and gets away with it."

"I think I'm glad to know I have all of you, but I still need to learn to make my own way."

Mrs. Patrick nodded. "Then that's what you need to do. Doesn't mean you can't use some help on the way," she added with a wink.

"Yes? You don't think it's, um, cheating?" In other words, was coming home to use Mama Dassa's services against Melba really any different from just coming home altogether? This thought had been plaguing Leticia ever since they left the falls.

"Heavens, no! Letty, the good Lord above gave us free will, and we can either stand by and let the world happen to us, or we can reach out and make things happen for us. That's what I've done, and that's what I've taught all my children to do. That's what I hope you're learning to do in America."

"Does Daddy know anything about Mama Dassa?"

"I don't think that Daddy knows; those things are just not his things," her mother answered. She shrugged. "Sometimes, he surprises me, which is something I like about him. We all have our secrets, don't we? We'd be boring without them. But I don't think Daddy has any secrets like these."

Leticia laughed.

Mrs. Patrick kissed her daughter on the cheek again and whispered, "Good night, baby girl."

Leticia awoke the next morning to a huge breakfast Peggy had already laid out for the prodigal daughter's final meal: johnny cakes, fritters, ackee with salt cod fish, callaloo, fried fish, bread with butter, coffee for Mr. Patrick, and hot chocolate for everyone else.

"Peggy, please come join us for breakfast," pleaded Leticia. The rest of the family agreed and demanded that the housekeeper eat with them. Peggy had worked with the affable Patrick family for so many years she had grown into an integral part of all their daily lives.

Still, that didn't stop her from walking to the bus stop after cleaning up from breakfast to begin her two days off.

The rest of the Patrick family, meanwhile, set off for church. Leticia's father held her hand as they entered their favorite pew and sat, right at 10:00 a.m. on the dot. He proudly smiled up at his wife as she took her regular seat up at the church organ.

"Your mother is such a good Christian woman," he whispered to Leticia.

Leticia almost started giggling at the thought: her mother, playing the organ at her church one day, taking Leticia to see an old mystery woman another.

Mrs. Patrick started playing as everyone rose to begin the service. The minister, at the conclusion of his service, even gave a brief mention of Leticia's visit.

Afterward, they raced for the airport. Neville unloaded Leticia's luggage and went to park the SUV. Mr. Patrick pulled his daughter's suitcase, while Leticia kept her purse and carry-on. With her parents on either side, they passed the huge sign indicating "PASSENGERS ONLY."

The three Patricks simply walked past the congested line of outgoing passengers. The attendant who verified Leticia's ticket just said, "Eyeyuh, Mr. Patrick!"

"A great afternoon to you, my dear."

The Patricks went straight to the American Airlines counter. Neville joined them there, and a supervisor came over to help Leticia check in. The entire family passed another long line of passengers moving through security screening.

The security supervisor belted, "Hello, Mr. Patrick!"

"Hello, Ivan, having a good day?"

Ivan nodded his head *yes, sir*, with a big smile. He came over himself as the family passed through an otherwise vacant metal detector. He didn't keep them but just waved them through.

The Patrick family took the elevator and went upstairs.

Leticia smiled through all of this. And to think, everyone back in New York thought she was poor Jamaican trash trying to eke out a living. Melba in particular. *Melba deserved anything Mama Dassa could dish out,* Leticia thought.

"Now Leticia, let me explain something again," Mr. Patrick began as they all took seats in the lounge area. "Denver is not planning to run our business. He's happy as an engineer. Neville is working with me, and he has his hands full already."

"I know, Daddy."

"You know I just want you to be happy."

"Yes, Daddy."

"And you can come home anytime."

"Yes, Daddy."

"But you still want to stay in New York."

"Yes, Daddy." *I have a plan,* Leticia thought. *I am going to take on Melba. Especially with Mama Dassa's help.* No one was going to deter her from this mission now that she'd set her course upon it.

Mrs. Patrick nodded, looking satisfied.

Mr. Patrick continued, "Good. Do not forget there's a reason you're there. You are to learn the practical side of the business world, how to deal with people—even those you don't like—and how to deal with people from different cultures. That's important in the family business, too. There's no better place than New York City to teach you all that."

Leticia nodded.

"Don't strive to be at the top; stay where you and just soak up everything you can learn. Executives have their guard down around the lowest level staff, so they will say and do things that you wouldn't otherwise ever see or hear. This is how you learn. Watch the office politics, but don't join it and don't vote."

"Right, dear," interjected her mother. "Don't watch the office politics. Control them."

Mr. Patrick smiled indulgently at his wife. "Now, now, dear. Leticia isn't there to take over Lexhouse."

"According to whom?"

The family laughed, although it was somewhat strained.

"Leticia has gone to learn. One learns by watching—"

"And doing."

"Watching how it's done."

"And then doing it."

Leticia's head swung back and forth between her parents. Their disagreements were rare, and even now, they were both smiling placidly at each other and speaking evenly. Any strangers looking on—and their public situation was surely the reason they were smiling, no altercations allowed in public view—would hardly notice anything amiss. It was only Leticia and Neville who noticed the sudden draining of laughter and warmth.

"How will Leticia learn to fly if we clip her wings?" She said *we*, but Leticia knew her mother was saying *you* to Mr. Patrick. "We taught our children to have big visions for their lives, to set ambitious goals and then do what they must to achieve them."

"And so she should. Her goal is to learn—"

"Her goal is to prove herself."

"Nonsense. Leticia has nothing to prove."

"Not to us, dear. It's to herself she has to prove it."

Her parents continued to stare at each other for long moments. Then, perhaps because they mutually realized they were at a standoff, her father turned back to Leticia and continued, "Always smile and say thank you—"

Mrs. Patrick interrupted her husband again. "Sweetness, we know you have your bachelor's degree in business, but with practical experience, you can move faster in this world and be a better asset to the family business."

"I know, Mama. I know, Daddy. It's going to be fine." When she had left for New York, her father had told her to lie low and learn everything she could. That was the goal, in his eyes. Her mother had told her to be the best employee she could be; she had advised Leticia to act with the dignity and power of the corporate boss she would one day become, inevitably. At the time, the two goals had seemed complementary; now, suddenly, they seemed irreconcilable.

Damn that Melba anyway! It wouldn't be like this if she hadn't be so awful.

"Plus, you are only going to be there for two years."

Leticia nodded.

A waitress from the nearby cafe wandered over. "'Ello, Mr. Patrick, whey yuh havin' t'day?"

"A cup of coffee for me and three hot chocolates for my family, please," replied the popular entrepreneur. "Anyhow, this was a good trip; I really enjoyed myself."

"Me, too," said Mrs. Patrick.

"Me three!" added Neville.

The family all laughed. Then they heard the announcement that Leticia's flight was boarding. Mr. Patrick led them to the gate, up to the "PLEASE PRESENT BOARDING PASS" sign.

"Mr. Patrick," nodded the ticket agent as the entire family entered the aircraft.

"Number 3, my seat is right here," said Leticia. "How nice, they bumped me up."

"Leticia Andrea Patrick,"

"Yes Daddy"

"Let me leave you with these words. *Always keep this in mind; as you try to climb that corporate ladder, be careful of the toes that you step on, because they may be attached to the foot to kick you in your behind on your way down.*"

She then gave her father a hard hug, a tight squeeze around her tearful mother, and a final embrace for her older brother. The rest of the family finally departed as passengers filed toward the plane doors. Leticia sat down in her first-class seat.

PART THREE—CONUNDRUM

CHAPTER 11

Uncle George and Aunt Martha both eagerly awaited Leticia's return. Leticia, with a smile as wide as the Grand Canyon, ran straight into their arms.

"Girl, I missed you!" exclaimed Aunt Martha.

"My God, you and Mama look exactly alike! The both of you are two peas in a pod."

Aunt Martha laughed, as they gripped each other so tightly that Martha's hat almost popped off her head. "Outside is freezing! Here is your coat; put it on, girl!" ordered the happy aunt.

Uncle George didn't say much, but that wasn't unusual for him, especially when his wife was talking. He smiled beneficently at Leticia and gave her another hug. "Everything all right, Letty?" he asked.

"Yes, all is well, Uncle."

Leticia noticed that he was wearing his deacon tag on one of his favorite suits with a bright yellow tie under his coat. And Aunt Martha wore her favorite purple and red dress with a matching felt hat, with a single bright purple feather standing straight up.

"Are you coming from church?" Leticia asked.

"Yes," said Uncle George. He chuckled. "That's really why I'm so glad you're here, before I drop dead from starvation!" He winked at her, and Leticia laughed. "All I've had for the day is a cup of coffee," he continued, "and your poor Aunt Martha has been waiting for her fish and breadfruit."

"Of course!" Leticia passed her hand luggage over to her aunt, who opened the bag.

"Yes! Wonderful! Dinner has arrived!"

"Good," said Uncle George. "Now we can go home and eat!"

He pulled Leticia's suitcase behind him while they went into the parking lot. Leticia sighed inwardly. It was still full winter here in New York. She missed Jamaica's temperate, verdant climate already. She could see the wind rocking people on their feet as it tried to snatch hats and scarves. A ceiling of gray swept across the sky. She could feel the icy cold before she even stepped into it.

She threw herself into the car as soon as they arrived and wrapped her arms around herself, still shivering. Uncle George climbed into the driver's seat and thoughtfully turned the heat up to full blast. "Th-th-thank you," she said through clattering teeth.

Once she had thawed a bit from her brief exposure to elemental New York, she began to tell them about all the fun she'd had with the family. She apologized that she hadn't been able to go see Cecil, Sonia, or Madge, but she explained that Mama would give them their gifts from Martha. Between Aunt Martha's questions and Leticia's stories, the two women did not come up for air the entire time. Uncle George just kept shaking his head and laughing whenever the ladies laughed.

Leticia did not mention Mama Dassa.

And Aunt Martha didn't ask, until later that evening, almost bedtime. She came into Leticia's room, closed the door, and asked, "How did the special thing work out?"

"I can't say anything about it, Auntie! I wish I could, but I have strict orders not to say anything. I cannot tell anyone. I couldn't even tell Mama." Leticia ironed Melba's pillow case, folded it neatly, and placed it in a plastic bag.

"That is all right, darling. I know how it is." She said this with a twinkle in her eyes.

Leticia was astonished, and then realized she had no reason to be. "Of course, of course. Mother said our family has always used Mama Dassa and her family."

Aunt Martha nodded. She sat down on the bed and smoothed the sheets with her hands. "How do you think I got to England, when I kept failing the nursing exam?"

"You *failed* the nursing exam?" Now Leticia was astounded. She knew Aunt Martha only as a successful charge nurse. And if *anyone* knew her stuff, it was Aunt Martha.

"Oh, yeah. Matter of fact twice my dear." She chuckled. "Mother—your grandmother—made me go to Mama Dassa's mother or grandmother, I don't know which, who was then a *very* old woman. Oh, your mother, Mira, she was so inquisitive, so very curious about it all. But Mama Dassa made me promise not to tell, just like she did you."

"But can you tell me, now that it's done?"

Martha laughed. "I told your mother, not at the time, but years later. So I suppose there's no harm. It's not as exciting as you'd expect, no elaborate rituals in the full moonlight or any such nonsense. She gave me a broth to drink before my next nursing exam. She said my nervousness at the test was letting all the knowledge flow away like water, and the broth would turn my mind into a steel trap that would keep everything I know in easy reach."

"Did it work?"

Martha nodded deeply. "Oh, yes. I earned the highest score in my class. But it was no pleasure drinking."

"What was it like?"

"Like boiled seaweed made into a powder."

Leticia grimaced. "Urgh."

"I don't know what it was. It was powdered something that I was supposed to mix into hot tea. But the tea turned thick like sludge, and it tasted like ... well, it tasted like dipping a teacup into a toilet after using it."

Leticia stuck out her tongue and made an expression of disgust.

"You think that's bad? You're just hearing about it. Think about poor Uncle George, who kissed me after I finish the exam."

"Did he taste it, too!"

"You should have seen the look he gave me! '*What* have you been eating?' he asked." Aunt Martha laughed with the same ease as all the rest of the Leticia's family.

"What did you tell him about it?"

"Sort of the truth. I told him it was a superstition, a tea made from the bark of some Jamaican tree, but that it tasted terrible. I went to brush my teeth, but the taste didn't go away for weeks. Uncle George got so he wouldn't kiss me!"

"He must have started again sometime," Leticia teased.

"That he did. At any rate, it is a good thing you went yourself rather than mailing the pillowcase to her."

"Oh, yes, Auntie! In person was better. Suppose the pillowcase had gotten lost in the mail?"

"Well, good night, my dear. Get some sleep, because I am sure tomorrow you will be very busy!"

"Good night, Auntie!" Leticia replied as Martha went off to her own bedroom, and Leticia closed the ironing board and set the iron in the corner to cool.

Leticia then went into the kitchen and took three round Jamaican buns out of their store-bought boxes. She wrapped them individually with aluminum foil and placed them in her bag.

Next she put some black pepper on an individual paper towel, folded it carefully, and tucked it into the corner pocket of her bag. She paused thoughtfully. This was her own plan, not Mama Dassa's, whose instructions she would begin implementing tomorrow. She wondered what was going to happen to Melba. What did "twitch twitch" mean?

"But!" she said to herself. "Now I am ready for Monday morning!" She laughed quietly as she turned off the lights and went to bed.

She went in earlier than usual on Monday morning. Before she entered the building, she took out the paper towel and inhaled the black pepper directly. Her eyes instantly went misty, and she rubbed them on and off for a full five minutes before going to Frances.

Mr. Foles's secretary got up and gave her a hug. "How is your mother?" she asked gently.

"That is what I want to talk to Mr. Foles about before his regular staff meeting."

The person in question stepped out of his office. "I thought that was your ocean breeze voice," he said. He smiled with surprising tenderness and hugged Leticia briefly. "Welcome back, but more importantly, how is your mother?"

"That is what I want to talk to you about, sir."

Mr. Foles expression went grave. He nodded somberly.

Leticia reached into her bag, grabbed a bun, and handed it to Frances. "This is for being so kind to me," she said warmly.

"You are welcome, and thank you."

"This one is for you, Mr. Foles," Leticia said, almost shyly.

He took the aluminum-wrapped bun and said, "Well, young lady, that was very thoughtful of you." He asked Frances for a knife and

100

some coffee. Then he turned back to Leticia. "Come in and sit down," he ordered.

Leticia followed him in and sat down across his desk. She sat on the edge of the chair, her back very straight. She cast her eyes about his paper-strewn desk, looking uncertain and demure.

"How is your mother?"

"Well, sir, that is what I want to talk to you about. I know I have a lot of work to catch up on. In order not to get a lot of interruptions with concerns about my mother, may I please have five minutes of everyone's time? Maybe Frances could use the PA system to announce to all employees to come to the conference room a few minutes before your regular meeting so I can tell everyone at the same time about Mama's condition?" She took a deep breath. Then she continued before Mr. Foles could speak, a plaintive note in her voice. "Please, sir, I just need five minutes, so I do not have to repeat everything to everyone."

"Of course, Leticia. That sounds like a fine plan. Frances!" he yelled. "At nine fifteen, call everyone over the PA system to come to the conference room." He turned back to Leticia, and his voice softened. "Leticia, I don't plan on revisiting our last conversation, from before you left. I spoke privately with Evanne, and she confirmed verbatim what Melba instructed you to do."

Leticia nodded, wide-eyed. "Thank God Evanne was there. Mr. Foles, I would never manipulate her expense account. I love my job here, and I have nothing to benefit from submitting an incorrect expense report."

"I understand, Leticia, and I do want to say again: if Melba is a problem for you, I will send you to Paul's group. He would be happy to take you."

Leticia thought of Paul's handsome features, how his eyes twinkled when he made stupid jokes, of the way he'd run his hands through his light blonde hair. And here Mr. Foles was offering her a chance to work with him every single day!

But Leticia had a mission. Ironically, it was a mission Melba had given her, without realizing it.

"I am concerned—" Mr. Foles started, but Frances interrupted him with a fresh cup of coffee. While she delivered it, he cut into his bun and took a bite. "Oh! Oh, my! This is delicious!" he exclaimed.

"Best pastry I ever tasted." Frances nodded, and then left the office and closed the door behind her.

"Let's continue talking about Melba."

But Leticia said, "Sir, I have to learn to work with all personality types."

Leticia, her mother had said to her before she left Jamaica, *you have to learn how to manage all personality types. What buttons to push, what things to say, what actions to take. You want to be in control of every situation you're in, but control requires different actions with different people. You have to learn that.*

Mr. Foles nodded. "True enough."

"Whether good or bad," Leticia continued, "that's what the world is made up of. And I am a learner. I believe that I can be an asset to Melba and the company."

Besides, she thought to herself, *I need access to Melba to implement Mama Dassa's plan, and I can only do that if I stay with the bitch.*

"Well, I do admire your tenacity. But Melba has made two incorrect accusations against you now, about the money and about the expense report. About the latter, I spoke to HR, who advised me to have you report to someone other than Melba, while they … well, for the time being."

Leticia smiled. "I appreciate that, sir, but it is not necessary. I consider Melba a challenge. We have a saying in Jamaica. 'What doesn't kill you makes you stronger.' That's what I feel about Melba. She makes me stronger by learning how to work with her."

"You have high spirits and display confidence." He spoke through a mouthful of bun. "But most of all, I love this bun!"

"My cousin Madge made them for me as thank-you gifts for you, Frances, and Evanne."

"Well, you must thank her for me. In the meantime, please know that you are always welcome to revisit the question of working with Melba with me."

Once again, just like at the end of their last conversation before she left for Jamaica, Leticia had an eerie sense that there was more going on here, that some political current was bubbling just under the surface, between Mr. Foles, Melba, and maybe even Paul.

Mr. Foles dismissed her, and Leticia returned to her cube. She found her desk nearly hidden under a cascade of sympathy cards, notes of good wishes and prayers. She was so shocked, she almost felt guilty. It wasn't her intention to take advantage of innocent people.

Then she heard Melba's voice. Her guilt vanished like a puff of hot breath in the frigid New York air. She remembered that she had a purpose.

She hurriedly put away her winter gear, barely putting everything—heavy coat, scarf, hat, gloves, and warm winter boots—in their proper places before Frances made the announcement. Everyone rushed to the conference room, abuzz with questions why they were being called in early.

Leticia rushed to catch Melba in her office before the meeting. She opened the plastic bag and said, "Good morning, Melba! Here is your pillowcase. I am so sorry it took me so long to return it to you."

Melba's overly red lips wrinkled and twisted, as though she wanted to say something spiteful and nasty. But then, she remembered the circumstances. She tried to paste on a sympathetic expression, but it barely fit on her face amid the dark blue eyeliner and foundation, so thick they were almost crusty. Her bleach-blonde hair was crinkly around her face, the roots dark. "I understand," she said and walked past Leticia as if the young woman were merely a statue.

Well! thought Leticia. *She didn't even ask me about my mother!*

In the conference room, Mr. Foles said, "Good morning, everyone!" A few people murmured good morning back. "I've called this impromptu meeting as we all know the tragedy of Leticia's mother. Well, Leticia is here to give us an update."

Frances filed in last, eating the last of her bun.

Almost everyone hugged Leticia. She was almost out of breath.

Then she addressed the group. "Oh, everyone, I want to thank you all so much and personally for the donations, cards, and sincere sympathy," she gushed. "First thing I have to ask everyone here, if you are a member of a church, please put my mother on your prayer list. Her name is Sonia Patrick."

A number of heads nodded somberly.

"When I left the doctor, he upgraded my mama to stable condition. Her pain medicine is very expensive. My three younger brothers have been working, cleaning people's yards, and doing everything they can, to help pay for the medicine."

No one spoke, but Leticia could see expressions of "Oh, you poor, literally poor, thing!" This irritated her as much now as the first time she'd encountered the attitude upon arriving in New York. Well, yes, she was pretending to be poor, but why did everyone just assume it before they even knew? Was it not possible, in the mind of an American, for a Jamaican girl to come from an educated, successful, and influential family?

"The doctor plans to release her next week, and her sister, my Aunt Peggy, and her husband, Uncle JoJo, will take her to their house. They live closest to the clinic.

"One of Mama's church sisters, Miss Fala—" Leticia paused briefly for breath, and momentarily pictured the dog Fala dressed in Sunday finery. She had to suppress a giggle. "Miss Fala will take Daddy's produce to sell at the market so they have some income. I have been in the country almost five months now, and you people are so good to me. Thank you again."

Her eyes turned red and watery—perfect timing!—and she almost started crying.

Paul said, "What happened to your arm, Leticia?"

Leticia nodded and pulled up the legs of her pants to show additional bruises. Although bruises were never fun to sustain, she thought of how much she had enjoyed that day with her family at Dunn's River Falls. The bruises were worth it.

"My Lord!" exclaimed someone.

Leticia said with her Caribbean lilt, "Oh, that's me being clumsy. I fell at least four times. Our house is up a steep hill, and the lane is full of jagged rocks. When it rains, it gets so slippery I keep losing my balance and keep falling. And it's Jamaica, so it rains almost every day. Again, everybody, thank you so much!" At that point, her Jamaican accent permeated the room as she just kept saying thank you to everyone who touched her as Leticia stepped out of the room so they could begin their ordinary staff meeting.

The other cube drones followed Leticia, and Evanne approached her friend. She took Leticia's hand and said, "Oh, you poor thing."

"Come to my cubicle," Leticia whispered. "I have something for you."

Once she could retrieve it from her bag, she handed Evanne the bun. She explained how her cousin Madge had made it.

"Oh, Leticia, thank you! I don't eat pastries, of course; I am watching my figure." Evanne said this with a perfectly straight face, as if Leticia hadn't seen the bags and bags of potato chips at her house, nor helped Evanne with her grueling clothing regime. "I will give this to Tony. He will gobble it up, I'm sure. But thank you for thinking of me! You didn't have to do that." The two ladies hugged. "I'm glad your mother is stable. Did you get to see other family, too?"

Leticia nodded somberly. "It was good to get home, even if it was under such circumstances. But I have to tell you about something that happened! One day, I went down to the seaside to think and pray for my mother. The sound of the surf is so soothing, and the sight of endless ocean—that's what God must be like, right? So, I went there and wandered along the water's edge, and I wasn't paying any attention, and I crossed from the regular beach into a nude beach."

"No! What happened!"

"I passed by a large rock, and on the other side, I heard a conversation between an American and a Jamaican. So I climbed to the top of the rock, sat down and I had a good look at them."

"Were they *naked?*" Evanne asked.

"As the day they were born. The American had the initials W and Y tattooed on his private parts."

"No!"

Leticia nodded again, perfectly serious. "The Jamaican had the same letters on his, too."

Evanne's eyes narrowed. "You're making this up."

"No! For real. The American was saying, when his private parts got … you know … it spelled out his girlfriend's name, 'WENDY.' And then he asked the Jamaican fellow if he had a girlfriend named Wendy as well.

"The Jamaican looked at the American and said, 'Nah mon, when my rod get hard it spell out '**WELCOME TO JAMAICA AND HAVE A NICE DAY.**'"

Evanne burst out laughing. She whooped and hollered and said, "I'd never have guessed you telling a dirty story like that!" She shook her head, still chortling. "Wait until I tell Tony. Well, until lunch today."

"As usual," Leticia replied, almost cheery. "But I'm not done yet. I have something else, too."

She pulled out the sachet tea Mama Dassa's assistant had given her. "A special Jamaican recipe just for, well, you know."

But Evanne shook her head, apparently confused. She didn't know.

"Your condition," Leticia whispered.

Still, Evanne looked perplexed. She looked from the sachet back up to Leticia's face.

"The cancer," Leticia said, even quieter. She didn't want to offend Evanne by spreading her news around. She actually felt honored Evanne had shared with her.

"Oh!" exclaimed Evanne. She took the sachet from Leticia and peered at it. "What's in it?"

"A special Jamaican recipe," Leticia repeated. "Remember, Evanne, my family is poor, and we can't afford expensive medicine. So from one generation to the next, we have different teas and bushes that we use for different ailments. Besides, all the modern medicines doctors make, they were derived from natural plants. This is the real thing we poor people use back home for recuperation. It's meant to restore good health, energy, vitality, good condition ..." She fell silent. Now that she thought about it, she realized she didn't know what precisely the tea was supposed to do.

Evanne looked up and smiled back at Leticia. "How thoughtful of you! To think of me while your mother is hurt."

Leticia shrugged shyly.

"What does it taste like?"

Leticia had a sudden flash of panic, remembering Auntie Martha's tale of having to drink toxic stew. "I don't actually know. The ingredients are rare. It's only for people who have been sick."

"Well, thank you, sweetie." Evanne wrapped her arms around Leticia and gave her a bear hug. "You're good people. I knew that the first moment I laid eyes on you. Good people."

Leticia smiled into Evanne's shoulder. Evanne was "good people," too. She treated Leticia like a little sister to watch over.

"Mm, excuse me." They looked over and saw Melba standing a couple of feet away. "I'll be in the staff meeting for a while, but when I return,

Leticia, you and I will have a talk about your duties." Without waiting for a reply, she scurried toward the conference room with her laptop in her hands.

Leticia just realized she hadn't seen Melba in the room, so Melba still didn't know anything about Leticia's mom. And she still hadn't asked! What a selfish—

"Oh, Lordy," Evanne said. "That woman just don' let up, do she?" She walked away shaking her head.

She returned a short time later, while Leticia was still trying to get caught up on e-mails and the files stacked on her desk. Apparently, no one had taken up the slack while she was away, so she had an entire week's worth of work to catch up on, in addition to her regular Monday duties.

"'Ticia!" Evanne whispered urgently. "Just thought you should know. It's just James and Melba in the conference room now. And Melba's face is red as the meat of a ripe Texas watermelon!"

"Leticia," said another sharp voice. Evanne straightened and found Melba standing right behind her, glaring.

"Oh, Melba," said Evanne airily. "Leticia and I were just discussing the watermelon I brought for lunch today."

Leticia stifled a sudden giggle.

Melba ignored her. "Leticia, I need to talk to you. Now. My office."

Leticia and Evanne made eyes at each other as Leticia rose to follow. Leticia mouthed, "More like a red beet."

It was obvious whatever Mr. Foles had said to Melba, she didn't like.

"Let me tell you—" Melba started. "Oh, close the door, will you? Then have a seat."

Leticia obeyed. She smoothed out her blouse and then sat across from the tyrant. Files were scattered across Melba's desk, including a disorganized stack in one corner. She also noticed that Melba hadn't removed the pillowcase from where she put it earlier. Melba herself sat down and let out one of the longest sighs Leticia had ever heard.

Then Melba took up a sheet of paper and showed it to Leticia. "These were going to be your new duties. That won't happen now." She literally ripped the page in half, forcefully and angrily. She rolled each piece and threw them, one by one, into the trash can.

"Mr. Foles did not accept my proposal for you to be my private secretary. But that is okay!" She didn't sound like it was okay, however. In fact, she was livid, so angry she was nearly crying. She turned, picked up her handbag, and placed the pillowcase right into it.

Leticia watched all of this in silence.

"Anyhow, I still expect you to keep a catalog of my presentations, just like you did for Paul. And assist with research for them." What Melba really meant was to do all the research for all the presentations, in addition to her regular duties. But this was something Leticia genuinely did not mind. She learned a lot that way, and she knew as much about Melba's clients as Melba did. Maybe more.

"And you will get me coffee each morning. If you agree to it." She glared at Leticia as if daring the young woman to disagree.

Leticia didn't say anything.

This seemed to unhinge Melba even more. "You will not tell anyone!" Melba exclaimed, much louder than she had probably intended. Melba's gaze darted past Leticia, to the cubes outside her office. She scowled. Leticia didn't turn, but she imagined some of the cube workers must be looking over to see what had made Melba yell so loudly.

Leticia said, "Okay."

Melba didn't say anything. She looked uncertain. She probably hadn't expected Leticia's quiet acquiescence. "Well," she said after a moment. She sounded much calmer. "That's it then, I guess. Oh, and those files." She waved in the direction of the stack on her desk. "I need them catalogued and organized."

Leticia bit her tongue. If Melba actually did her job, her files wouldn't reach such a state. But Leticia didn't say that aloud. Melba would get her due. As she struggled out of the office with the armful of file folders, Melba shouted, "Keep the door open!" Again, much louder than necessary.

The young Jamaican complied in silence. She noted that Melba had zipped her handbag and deposited it in her desk drawer. Perfect. Mama Dassa had just said the pillowcase needed to stay with Melba.

As Leticia hefted the weight of the unkempt file folders, overflowing with papers, she mused that she didn't even realize Melba did so much work. So much focus went to BALI, she forgot that Melba oversaw other, less important accounts as well. In fact, come to think of it, BALI was her *only* important account.

Maybe Melba was right about Lexhouse overlooking her. On the other hand, maybe if Melba didn't let all these files sit like this, and then thrust them in one giant unorganized stack at Leticia, Lexhouse would be willing to give her more accounts of increasing importance.

Her thoughts thus occupied, Leticia didn't notice the snag in the carpet until she fell forward. She was able to catch herself in time, just falling to one knee, but the file folders scattered all over the hallway between cubes.

"Oh no!" she cried. Then she sighed. It wasn't exactly Melba's fault, she thought angrily, but it was.

Grimly, she started gathering up the files. She picked up several sheets of paper that had flown out of their files. She glanced over them, trying to determine which papers belonged to which files. She couldn't. She shut her eyes and sighed again. The files were already going to be hard enough to organize for Melba; this would take forever.

"Leticia?" a soft and familiar voice whispered.

She looked up suddenly, her heart fluttering. "Paul!"

"Are you okay?" he asked, bending down.

She nodded and laughed ruefully. "Melba asked me to organize these." She gestured at the mess of papers and folders.

Paul surveyed the scene for a few seconds and then said, "Well, this does look like Melba's system of organizing."

Leticia burst out laughing, and Paul chuckled along with her. He got on his knees and started helping her shuffle and sort papers into the proper folders and stacks. For a few minutes, they worked in silence, Leticia keenly aware of Paul next to her and wondering if she should say something. And if so, what?

Then Paul asked, "What's it like in Jamaica?"

"Warm," Leticia said. She shivered dramatically, and Paul smiled.

"It does get chilly up here, doesn't it? It's probably a big adjustment. But I'm from Minnesota originally, so cold weather isn't exactly new to me." He laughed slightly. "Have you only been here, in New York, since you came to America, or have you visited other places, too?"

"Just here. This is the heart of America, isn't it?"

Pete, one of the other cube drones, stepped out of his cube into the hall. "Had a little accident, eh?" He grinned. "But it looks like you two have things well in hand."

"Er, yes," said Paul.

Pete stepped gingerly past them, over the piles of files. After Pete turned the corner, Paul started gathering files again. "What was that you asked? Oh, yeah. In some ways, New York is like the heart of America. But don't forget that New York isn't all of America. You can always find a place that feels like home somewhere in America. I don't know what place would be like Jamaica, though. Maybe some place in Florida, with the beaches and tropics and stuff."

"Mmm."

"How do you like living in the city?"

Leticia shrugged. "It's okay. I live in a boarding house with other people from other countries."

"That sounds exciting! Being exposed to all kinds of people, all kind of cultures."

"It gets old."

"Yeah. When I first came to New York, I was totally wide eyed at, well, at everything. All the buildings. All the different kinds of people. It's lots different from Duluth, Minnesota."

"What's Duluth, Minnesota, like?" Leticia asked.

Paul sat up for a moment, his gaze looking into space. He smiled, and little laugh lines crinkled around his eyes. Leticia just watched him. Then he started answering her question, and asking more of his own, and before Leticia knew it, she had a neat stack of files on the floor in front of her.

Paul picked up about two thirds of the stack, and Leticia took the rest. They carried them together to her cube and set them on her desk.

"Thank you, Paul," Leticia said sincerely. "You actually saved me a lot of work."

"Great! See, this is why I don't believe in bad luck. You never know when something you think is bad is going to turn into something good!"

Leticia nodded eagerly but, unsure how to respond, didn't answer.

This left Paul standing awkwardly in the entry to her cube for a minute. "Um," he started. Then he lowered his voice and leaned forward. "So, have you seen much of the city? Like the Empire State Building?"

"No," said Leticia, shaking her head.

Paul feigned mock outrage. "Well, that won't do! You can't live in

110

New York and *not* see the Empire State Building. It's the first place I went when I came here! I have to take you there." He fell silent suddenly, as though surprised at his own assertion.

"I'd like that," Leticia said shyly.

"Oh! Well, great! How about this weekend?"

"That would be great!"

Paul's face lit into a giant grin. "Where can I come get you?"

"Oh! No, it's probably not a good idea." Paul's face fell. "I mean, my landlady is very snoopy and doesn't like men meeting me there." Paul frowned. "But I can meet you there."

"Then can I call you?"

"I don't have a phone."

"What about your cell phone?"

"I don't have one of those, either."

"You are the only person I know without a cell phone. Okay, no problem. At the Empire State building? Great. We can meet right out front. If that's okay?"

"Yes!" Leticia nodded enthusiastically. In fact, she couldn't wait!

CHAPTER 12

Leticia sat down, a smooth expression on her face, but she was whistling on the inside.

Events were already moving better than expected. She'd gotten a free trip back home, she apparently had only to say a few words to Mr. Foles to be transferred to Paul's group if she wanted, Paul had just asked her out—that was him asking her out, wasn't it?—and best of all, Melba seemed on the verge of going crazy.

At lunch, Evanne said, "Time can really fly. The faster it flies, the faster I will get to my Tony." Evanne actually blushed at this, and Leticia smiled shyly.

"I need to tell you about the man I met in Jamaica."

Evanne looked up with interest, already half listening. Today's wig was short black braids, and it swung from side to side with every walking movement.

"That naked one?"

Leticia laughed. "No, no. This one was a fortune teller. My brothers dragged me to him to see what was going to happen to Mama. The fortune teller said if I'd go out with him, he'd intercede with the Fates to make Mama better."

"What did you tell him?"

"I told him the Fates obviously didn't listen to him because if he had that power, he would have stopped them from chopping off his hand."

"What!"

"Girl, he only had one hand. Someone caught him stealing some coconuts that they had gathered to take to the market, and they used a machete on him. He was a one-handed thief turned fortune teller."

Evanne stared at her open-mouthed. Then the corners of her mouth stretched upward. "A one-handed thief turned fortune teller?" she repeated.

Leticia nodded solemnly.

Evanne, obviously having no idea how to react to this story, merely opened her plastic container filled with chunks of honeydew melon. Leticia went to toast her bread. After, she opened her paper bag and pulled out some raw almonds. She placed the almonds between the bread slices and began to eat her nut sandwich. She didn't notice that Evanne had stopped eating and was eagerly watching her. "What are you doing?"

Leticia paused mid-chew. She looked up at Evanne, and then down at her sandwich. She swallowed. "You've never had raw almonds on toasted whole wheat bread?"

"No!"

"Well, don't knock it till you try it. It's very good for you." Leticia invited her to take a bite, but Evanne refused.

"I'm watching my figure, girl; you know that!"

Leticia didn't argue. She figured Evanne had as much right to her stories as Leticia had to hers. That's what people were like: they were the people they were, the people they wanted to be, and the people they pretended to be, all wrapped into one package. But other people could only see the last, the people they pretended to be. If God had meant it to be otherwise, he'd had given people the power to read each other's minds.

Evanne asked for more details about Leticia's mom, and she seemed genuinely concerned. Leticia took pity on her by whispering, "The doctor said he was very hopeful she'll make a full recovery."

Evanne sat back. "Good! I've been praying for her, you know."

"Thank you."

Then Evanne launched into the office gossip. In fact, she was nearly bursting at the seams to relate to Leticia everything that had happened during her absence. "There were so many rumors that you would be Melba's protégé, admin, personal secretary, bag carrier, hand holder, personal chef."

"Personal chef!"

"Well, okay, I made that one up. But just about everything you could be, people were talking about it. I know that's hardly shocking, but you do need to know that she and Paul are battling. Well, she's battling. Paul just laughs it off." Evanne paused. "My boss, Tim, thinks it's pretty funny, too. Do you think they know something we don't?"

Leticia thought about it. Mr. Foles, Paul, and Melba. She trusted her gut that something was afoot between the three of them. But what? She shrugged.

"Well, I just don't want you to get caught in the crossfire," Evanne concluded.

"No, I am here to work, and that's all. Whatever I'm instructed to do, I will, until I don't work here anymore."

Evanne's lips scrunched up as she studied Leticia. "Look, Leticia, I'm just saying this because I'm your friend, and I care for you, and I don't want you to get hurt."

"Okay?"

"But I think you're being awfully naïve."

"Oh."

"Maybe it's different in Jamaica. It sounds like you come from a much different background. But this is a cutthroat business in the middle of Manhattan. It's dog eat dog here. If you don't take care of yourself, you'll get chewed up and spit out. That's just how it works here in New York."

"Oh."

"You've got to take steps to protect yourself," Evanne went on. "Sometimes, you even have to be hard hearted."

"Oh."

"I know that will be hard for you; you're such a sweet girl." Leticia looked up, but Evanne just nodded back at her, wide eyed and open faced. "And that's why I'm your friend. I'm just telling you all this so you can watch your back, you know? You can't let people walk all over you."

"What should I do?" Leticia asked in a tiny voice.

"You've got to stand up for yourself. You've got to tell Melba, 'Hell no, I ain't doing that! It's not in my contract, and if you try to make me, HR will have your head on a platter!' You've got to take control of the situation."

Leticia spent a minute thinking about this. "Maybe I should try to get some edge on Melba," she whispered. She looked from side to side as if afraid someone would hear her.

"Yes! I'm sorry to say it, you're such a sweetie, but you've got to toughen up. That's all."

"Okay, Evanne. I trust you. I'll try."

Evanne smiled. "Good. So, let's talk about Jamaica. I'd love to visit someday."

Leticia launched into some concocted tales of the trip, but her mind wasn't on it. For a moment there, Evanne had sounded nearly like her mother.

That day, Leticia worked later than usual in order to catch up on cataloging many of the accounts from last week. Plus, Melba needed more assistance in preparing for her next presentation for the BALI account.

* * *

The following morning, the Tuesday wind blew in from the water, carrying its icy temperatures. Leticia arrived at work, missing Jamaica, and started removing her winter layers. She placed the apparel on the makeshift rack she kept in her cube.

Melba marched up. Without a single good morning, she said, "I forgot to tell you, your hours will be from eight thirty a.m. to five p.m. with thirty minutes for lunch. I am working with James Ass to get you two ten-minute breaks as well."

Leticia frowned. Weren't breaks required by law? But instead, she asked, "What about the overtime I'll have to do to catch up?"

"You will not get overtime pay. That is your job, and you are catching up."

Leticia's frowned deepened. She noticed that Melba *still* had not asked about her mother. "Is that legal?"

Melba dismissed the question with a wave. "I am not approving you for any overtime."

Leticia didn't say another word. She passed Melba and headed straight for Frances. But Melba caught up with her, grabbed her by the arm, and said, "Leticia, you are correct. I was not thinking clearly. You are an hourly employee, and therefore, you are entitled to overtime pay." Melba glanced over at Frances, who was watching the interplay with interest, and said, "Question resolved." She smiled for Frances's benefit.

"Thank you, Melba," said Leticia quietly. She smiled at her boss.

Frances asked Leticia, "You don't happen to have any more of those Jamaican buns, Leticia, do you?"

"No, I'm sorry, Frances. They are all gone."

"Oh, please tell your relative to make and send some more. I told my husband, Greg, and he wants to taste it. You know I ate all of mine! I'll be happy to pay for any shipping costs."

"Okay, Frances," said Leticia.

Frances turn to Melba. "Is your lip okay, dear?"

Melba glared. "It's fine." She looked like she wanted to say, "Mind your own business," but didn't quite dare.

Leticia took another look. She was surprised she hadn't noticed before. It looked like Melba had a cold sore on her upper lip. She wondered if it was just coincidence, or if this was Mama Dassa's plan starting to work. She frowned. How long would it take before Melba started to "twitch, twitch"?

Leticia excused herself to return to her cubicle. She did have a week of work to catch up. But she had barely gotten started when Melba came barreling into her cube again. "Here is five dollars. Go the drug store and get me something for this cold sore."

"I can't," said Leticia. "I promised Paul I would have this catalogued by nine thirty this morning. I can't leave until it's done."

Melba stared at her as though a third eyeball had opened in Leticia's forehead. "You're working for Paul again?"

"He needs it for a presentation at ten a.m.," said Leticia meekly. She tried to sit smaller in her chair, as though she were withering under Melba's anger.

"I will deal with Paul. Go now." Melba's words were clipped.

Leticia sighed and reloaded all her winter gear. She headed for the elevator. It opened, and Paul spilled out with his sunny smile. "Morning, Leticia! Where are you going?"

Leticia explained her orders for Melba.

"Do you want to go?" Paul asked.

"Not really. But she is my direct report, so I am going. It will be all right; Melba said she would talk to you."

"And so she will, I'm sure," Paul replied. He didn't seem bothered in the least. His eyes positively sparkled.

He moved aside so that Leticia could shuffle under Eskimo-like clothing onto the elevator. She vanished behind the closed door.

When she returned with the medicine, she ducked first into the lunch room. Now it was time to put part two of Mama Dassa's instructions into play. If the cold sore wasn't Mama Dassa's work to begin with, it might soon become part of it.

She grabbed a foam cup and half filled it with water. She nuked the water for about twenty seconds, and then reached into her hand bag and pulled out one of the sticks Mama Dassa had given her. She dipped it into the water, waited for a full minute, and then placed several paper towels into the cup, enough to absorb all the water. She then methodically wrang them out.

Now she pulled out the box of medicine from the store bag. She wiped the box with the damp paper towels for a good thirty seconds, and then tossed the cup and paper towels. She blew on the box to make sure it was dry.

She replaced the box of medicine in the store bag, put the stick back in her purse, and went directly to Melba. But Melba's office was empty, so she had to hunt her boss down. She located Melba in the conference room with many of the management staff.

Leticia opened the door, apologized for the interruption, and went to directly to Melba. The cold sore was already looking worse, red and swollen. "I hope this works," she whispered and handed the store bag to Melba.

"Thanks," Melba said, embarrassed, as she licked at the cold sore.

Leticia left, closing the door behind her, and smiled. In fact, she almost laughed.

The day was a busy one. Paul was sympathetic, and he helped Leticia to catalog his work. "You're a great worker," he commented by way of explanation. "Don't want to lose you."

After her meeting, Melba came to Leticia's cube. "James Ass instructed me not to send you out again, so I will not be sending you on any more errands."

Leticia nodded.

Melba applied some of the medicine to her sore, and then asked, "Where is my change?"

"Um, there wasn't anything. It cost about six dollars."

"I gave you a ten dollars."

Leticia stared at Melba in shock. "You gave me five dollars," she said.

"I gave you ten!" Melba cried angrily. "You owe me four dollars."

"You only gave me five dollars," Leticia repeated.

"Listen you, you give me my change, or I'll go to HR and let them know you've been stealing from me. Accounting already thinks you falsified my expense reports."

"Stealing!" shrilled Leticia. Not this again. She nearly erupted then and there, but she controlled herself. "Stealing from you on an errand you weren't even supposed to send me on? Well, I have the receipt, and it says I gave them six dollars in cash, your five-dollar bill, and one dollar of my own."

"I gave you two five-dollar bills. Ten dollars."

Leticia couldn't believe it. She was nearly in tears. She wanted to stand up and beat Melba over the head. She wanted to shove Mama Dassa's sticks right down Melba's throat. But that thought reminded her of something her mother had once said. *Sometimes you've got to swallow a bitter pill when you're taking your medicine.*

Leticia could feel her heart pounding. Her face was hot with rage. But she reached into her purse and pulled out four dollars. Melba snatched the money from her hands, triumphant. She stood over Leticia as if to exclaim, *Yes, that's right; you belong to me now! I have you cowed. I own you.*

Leticia turned back to her work, still on the verge of tears and completely unable to concentrate. When Evanne wandered in a few minutes later, she started talking about how much Tony enjoyed the Jamaican bun, but then noticed how upset Leticia was. "What happened?" she asked.

"M-M-Melba," Leticia mumbled.

Evanne's face hardened. "What did she do?"

But Leticia couldn't get it out. She was just so upset. She tried to get a hold of herself. She imagined her mother there with her. What would her mother say? She would probably just laugh and say, "Don't you worry about her! She's going to get hers. We already made sure of that."

So, Leticia forced herself to turn to her friend, plaster on a smile, and said, "Frances." She swallowed past the lump in her throat. "Frances already asked for some more buns. Would you like me to ask for some for Tony, too?"

Evanne studied Leticia's face for another minute or so. "You want me to put a hit out on her?"

It was the perfect thing to say. All of Leticia's frustration and anger burst out as laughter. "Oh, yes, could you?"

Evanne's expression relaxed. "Consider it done. And yes, I'd love if you could get some more Jamaican buns for Tony. We'll pay shipping and cost. My man is in love with your pastries. Don't you go getting any ideas now, though!" She grinned at Leticia good naturedly.

"I'll have to write a letter to Madge to see if she can do it, and then I'll tell you."

"What about this bun?" asked Paul as he walked up. "No one asked me if I wanted one?" He smiled and winked at Leticia, who explained what the pastry was. She apologized for not bringing him one.

Paul chuckled. "You didn't bring one for Melba, did you?"

"Oh, God! No!"

All three laughed, and Paul said, "No problem then. As long as I get to taste your buns before she does." Then he froze as he realized what he had said. A red blush crept over his features. "I mean, that is—"

Both Leticia and Evanne laughed, and Paul's fair features turned even redder. "I meant the pastry," he said hastily, and Leticia and Evanne laughed harder.

"I'm going to go away now before I get myself into even more trouble," said Paul. "I have my presentation anyway."

Leticia wished him good luck. She silently thanked Paul. Her good mood was now entirely restored. The whole episode was well worth four dollars.

At lunch, Evanne hadn't even sat down when she said, "Wait until I tell you, Leticia! I was on my way here when that bitch almost knocked me into the wall on her way to the bathroom. I followed her in to give her a piece of my mind."

Leticia nodded eagerly as she started to eat her warmed can of chili mixed with corn chips.

"Now, that is something I can relate to," Evanne said, staring at Leticia's food.

"Melba? A piece of your mind?" Leticia reminded her friend.

"Oh, yes." Then Evanne started laughing.

"What!" Leticia asked, dying to know.

"It's the sore on her lip."

"What about it?"

"It's gotten bigger."

"Oh? I saw it this morning. It was just a cold sore."

"Well, now it looks like God has pasted a dried cherry on her lip."

Evanne laughed again, and after a moment, Leticia joined her, thinking, *You mean, Mama Dassa.*

CHAPTER 13

L ETICIA COULD NOT WAIT TO get back to the office area to see Melba's "dried cherry." She took the longer hallway that would have her pass Melba's office. Unfortunately, her boss wasn't there, but the medicine was out of the box, and she could see that it was being used.

Rounding the corner, Melba almost ran smack into Leticia. Melba had her hand covering her mouth.

"Excuse me," replied Leticia timidly.

Melba didn't respond, barely even acknowledged the young woman. She just went into her office and closed the door.

A slow smile spread across Leticia's face as she returned to her cube to work.

The following morning, Leticia went to work and removed her winter wardrobe. Amazingly, for the first time during her entire stay in New York, she almost felt too warm in the winter wear. She was glad to get out of it, and then fire up her computer to get to work.

She hummed quietly to herself. Her aunt and uncle had invited her to a church concert to listen to some gospel music that night, and she was looking forward to it. She consistently refused their invitation to attend services, but she loved gospel music.

She didn't notice Melba's late arrival. "Why is this folder still on my desk? Why did you not give it to Mr. Foles? Now he is in Salt Lake City without my input?" Melba demanded as she stormed into Leticia's cube. "You have really screwed up this time." The force of her anger was undermined by her mumbling, though, as though she couldn't pronounce every word clearly.

"What are you talking about?" Leticia asked, thoroughly confused.

"Don't play stupid with me. I told you to give the folder to James Ass. I told you yesterday."

"No, you didn't."

"I sure did. At the same time you tried to steal my change."

Leticia stared at Melba. So this is how it was going to work. Melba thought she had beaten Leticia down, and now she could get away with anything. Melba herself made a mistake, and she was going to make Leticia take the blame.

"This is the first time I've heard of this."

"I guess you were too busy telling lies yesterday," Melba said. She grinned nastily at Leticia, and then took off for Paul's office. Leticia stood and watched over the top of her cube wall. When Melba realized Paul wasn't in his office, she yelled for his personal assistant, Berlina.

"Whoever is calling me, please come to me. I cannot leave right now," Berlina bellowed right back with her distinct fast-talking Spanish accent. She sounded irritated.

"My assistant, Leticia, ignored my instruction to give an important file to Mr. Foles," Melba shouted.

The entire office heard.

Other people had stood to peek over their cubicles. Now they turned to look at Leticia, who turned to head to the bathroom, where she could have a moment of privacy to collect herself.

"Well, you'll just have to take it up with Paul and James when they return from Salt Lake City," Berlina snapped loudly. "And by the way, the bandage from your lip is peeling off."

Furious—whether fake or not—Melba stalked back to Leticia's cube, but obviously Leticia wasn't there. "Trying to hide from me?" she shouted over the entire office. She called for Leticia again. "Let-eee-sha, where are you?"

Leticia emerged several minutes later from the bathroom. She was struggling to control herself, but she tried to channel her mother. Nothing ever got to her mother. Her mother, when insulted or upset, just pulled herself together, organized her plan of attack, and went on the offensive. So that's what Leticia was going to do.

Evanne saw her and waved for Leticia to come over. "What the hell was that about?" she asked. "Melba's sure on the warpath."

"Yes," said Leticia tightly.

Before Evanne could say anything more, Melba screamed at Leticia, "Get in here now."

Leticia walked into her boss's office. "Melba, what is that on your mouth? It looks like a dried cherry." She kept her tone sweet and concerned, but she was still a little annoyed at herself. She hadn't meant to give in to her fury quite so readily. Her mother would never approve.

"Do not worry about my mouth. Worry about your job."

"My job?"

Melba nodded once, staccato. "And maybe even your work visa," she added nastily, although Leticia was pretty sure Melba had no idea what she was talking about.

"I was just concerned, Miss Melba," Leticia said softly. "What can I do to help you?"

This seemed to be the right tone to take with Melba. She calmed down noticeably and said, "Plan on working late tonight."

Leticia swallowed. Of all the nights! She had been so looking forward to the church concert!

"I am going to call James Ass and have you e-mail the entire folder to his hotel late this afternoon," Melba continued. "Make sure you include an apology for you not getting this to him in time."

"I cannot work this evening," Leticia answered meekly. "And after you left yesterday, I was ordered by Mr. Foles to complete several filing projects for Paul."

"You don't work for Paul!"

"It was Mr. Foles who gave me the instruction."

"I need to get this to James Ass today. I am going to get this account at all costs."

"Melba, I have plans for this evening. I cannot work late."

"Since you have things to do, get out of my office and start your work. Maybe you'll finish in time."

Leticia walked to her office, almost in tears. Again. She was as angry about that as anything. Why was she letting Melba get to her like this?

Evanne was sitting in Leticia's chair. "You need to go to HR. I will be your witness."

"No," said Leticia sadly.

"Think about it. There is only so much one can take before breaking. You know Melba is already in their sights."

"Evanne, I am from a poor country. I am just happy to have a job. I can't jeopardize it."

"The way she treats you isn't right. Everyone would back you up."

"I have the situation under control," Leticia said, still tearful.

Evanne looked dubious but just gave her friend a good long hug. "It's going to be okay. Lunch is soon. I'll see you then."

Leticia smiled weakly.

The two ladies didn't speak much at lunch. Leticia told Evanne about her landlady inviting her to church, but now she wouldn't be able to go. Evanne's mouth and tongue were blue from her blueberries. Leticia had canned cream-style corn that she had placed in a bowl and warmed in the microwave, but she hardly tasted any of it.

She worked late into the evening catching up. She was bitterly disappointed to have missed the concert. She worked alongside her boss in Melba's office. "I am going to get one of my sodas from the refrigerator; do you want one?" Leticia asked.

"No, I'd like a cup of coffee."

Leticia paused. That wasn't what she had offered. At this time of night, she'd have to brew a fresh pot. But then an idea occurred to her.

She smiled brightly and said, "Sure thing, Melba."

Melba grunted in response.

On her way to the empty lunchroom, Leticia stopped at her cubicle to pull out her handbag, removed her change purse, and continued on her way. She realized the entire office was empty except for her and Melba.

"Time for you to shine, Mama Dassa," she whispered.

In the lunchroom, Leticia repeated her earlier ritual. She warmed some water in a paper cup along with one of the apparently special sticks. She dried off the stick, put it back in her change purse, and used the water to brew a pot of coffee for Melba. She served the coffee in the same cup.

She picked up an individual package of sugar and creamer on her way back to Melba.

"Thanks," Melba said absently. Leticia had to admire Melba's dedication to the project. She had half expected Melba to leave Leticia working late on her own, but apparently Melba really did want this new account, and she was willing to work for it.

Sometime later, Melba had finished her coffee, and she sat back from the papers on her desk. She was studying everything relevant to the account: spreadsheets of accounting numbers, previous advertising campaigns and more spreadsheets tracking their performance, new concepts for new campaigns.

"At least you will get overtime for this," she commented.

Leticia wasn't sure if Melba was being sarcastic or not. Her voice just sounded bored. She nodded silently and finished her own project for Melba. She was gathering her belongings to leave when Melba literally jumped up and ran to the ladies' room.

Powerfully curious, Leticia nevertheless resisted the impulse to run in after her. Instead, she went to the lobby and hit the button for the elevator. As it arrived, she heard a loud scream from Melba. She hesitated. Should she just leave, or go check on Melba?

Curiosity and concern intermingled with bitterness and anger. She stepped onto the elevator, and the doors slid shut behind her.

CHAPTER 14

To Leticia's surprise, her Aunt Martha had bought her a CD from the concert. Plus, Uncle George got her a small CD player. Her delight was offset by her anxiety over the incident with Melba. What should she do? She was still really angry about everything Melba had done, but the yells from the bathroom had shaken her.

She pulled Aunt Martha aside as soon as she was able to ask the older woman's opinion. "Have some faith" was her aunt's philosophical response.

"Do you think what I'm doing is wrong?" she asked, the first time self-doubt had crept into her mind. Up to this point, she felt Melba deserved everything she got.

"No! It's your boss who's in the wrong," Aunt Martha said. "Look, Letty, I don't know the details of the secret thing that happened in Jamaica, but I do know this. People like Mama Dassa exist to bring righteousness into form. Whatever Mamma Dassa told you to do is to help you and protect you from people like Melba. Don't fret about it.

"Just do as Mamma Dassa said, and don't discuss it with anyone, not even me. I am curious, but you have a goal. I repeat: it is very important that whatever Mamma Dassa told you to do is private. That is what will make it work.

"That Melba has the devil in her. Whatever Mamma Dassa told you to do will fix it. Let us not talk anymore about the subject until it is finished. Believe me, my dear niece, you will know when it is finished."

Leticia nodded. "I will just keep doing what Mamma Dassa instructed."

It was interesting listening to churchgoing Aunt Martha talk about the subject so easily, but her words did soothe Leticia.

The next morning, Leticia stepped off the elevator and paused. Everything seemed normal: people milling about as they started their day. No one paid any particular attention to her. She smiled and shook her head. What had she expected?

She walked to her desk and set up the CD player on her desk. She listened to the gospel CD softly while she completed her morning routine.

"That is nice music," Evanne commented as she wandered over.

"I know," replied Leticia. "It's from the concert I missed last night. Miss Martha bought it for me, and she even gave me this CD player that a previous tenant had left behind."

Evanne frowned. "The landlady who doesn't let you cook or keep stuff? I thought you said she was really stingy."

"Oh, she is!" Leticia said in a rush. Then she repeated herself slower, giving herself time to think. "She's just trying to make it up to me, because she wronged me, you know. She felt guilty."

"What'd she do?" Evanne asked, eyes wide.

"She caught me with a man."

Evanne literally gasped.

Leticia nodded, matching Evanne's wide-eyed stare. "A very handsome Jamaican fellow, tall and broad-shouldered with a brilliant smile. I was buying groceries, and you know how heavy canned food can be! He offered to help me carry them to my apartment."

"He didn't! Oh, my!" Evanne grinned. "Go on!"

"I invited him in for a cold drink, of course, some ginger beer, but just then, just before I was going to close the door, my landlady shows up. She sees him in there with me, and she threw the biggest fit you've ever seen. She yelled about not wanting visitors, especially men, and what kind of hussy was I to invite a strange man into my apartment, and on and on. My neighbors started poking their heads out their doors to see what was going on! 'You ain't married; you ain't married; it isn't right.' She wouldn't leave us alone!"

"As if Melba isn't enough drama in your life."

Leticia nodded. "The poor man got so fed up he left. I was completely humiliated."

"That … that …!" Evanne fumed, at a rare loss for words.

"But she felt guilty for embarrassing me, and she gave me the used CD player to say sorry."

"Well, she's better than Melba that way, at least. And who knows, maybe you'll bump into that man at the store again, and bump him again later." Evanne chuckled.

"Evanne!" Leticia cried, as though scandalized. But she was smiling, too. In fact, she had already started to think of Evanne as extended family, like a big American sister who had taken Leticia under her wing. They laughed so easily together, which was a Patrick family trait: they could all smile and laugh together at just about anything.

After that, Leticia settled in to get to work. She'd made tremendous headway in getting caught up, but she was still a little behind. So, she was oblivious to some of the events taking place. After a while, she noticed it was nearly mid-morning, and she hadn't heard anything from Melba.

She walked to her boss's office and found Mr. Foles in there, door closed. He was talking, and Melba was looking down. She didn't look happy.

Leticia went to get herself some coffee. As she returned to her cubicle, she found Melba waiting for her. "I asked you to send a note of apology to Mr. Foles, and to say it was from me and not from you."

"I don't—"

"That's right, you don't!" Melba shouted. "You don't think! You don't do what you're told! You don't do your job!"

Melba was shaking; she was so angry. A little spittle flew out of her mouth while she ranted.

Leticia just stared. Melba's face was as crimson as red cabbage, and her lips had swelled to triple their normal size. The dried cherry had also grown to the size of a small prune.

Any uncertainty or doubt Leticia had about her course of action evaporated. All of Melba's vindictiveness, all of Melba's petty cruelties and self-aggrandizing, selfish behavior came flooding back.

But now was not the time to stand up to Melba. Now was the time to have faith that Mama Dassa's orders would do what they were supposed to do. Goodness, maybe Aunt Martha was right: maybe Mama Dassa's plan was helping to draw the devil out of Melba.

"Miss Melba," Leticia squeaked in a tiny voice, "I don't remember you saying that; I'm sorry; I'm really sorry!"

Apparently, Melba had been expecting defiance. Leticia's seemingly sincere apology deflated her anger. She rallied for a final, spiteful, "Well!" before stalking away.

Berlina stepped out of her cube and stared as Melba walked away. Melba whispered something to her very quietly. Berlina responded, also quiet, and Melba slunk away back to her office.

Berlina turned toward Leticia and smiled sympathetically. She came over to Leticia's desk and whispered, "Don't take it personally, honey; I think she's having a rough time right now." Berlina pointed at her lip, at the same spot as the prune.

"Then she's always having a rough time," added Pete as he peeked over the cube wall that separated his area from Leticia's. "'Cause she's always like that. Glad I don't report to her. Sorry, Leticia."

"Well, Leticia's having a rough time, too; her mama almost died!" snapped Evanne, joining the small group. "But you don't see Leticia going around biting heads off!"

"I know that!" Berlina said. "No need to speak to me like that. I'm on your side." And Berlina swept around and returned to her desk.

Evanne turned to Leticia. "Guess I shouldn't have spoken so sharply, maybe. Lunch as usual?"

"Yes, please," said Leticia.

No one saw much of Melba that day. The woman sequestered herself in her office and avoided meeting with anyone. Leticia was terribly curious what Melba had said to Berlina, and what Berlina had said in return. But she heeded her father's advice and kept her head low in her cubicle.

The CD of gospel music had stopped, and Leticia started it playing again. Evanne asked for a copy of the CD.

"I don't know how to make copies of these things," Leticia replied apologetically.

"That's all right; I do. Let me have it for a few moments, madam, and I'll get it right back to you." Leticia nodded her assent, and within the hour, the original had been returned.

In the middle of her third listen to the CD, Melba returned to Leticia's cubicle. "Leticia, every time I step out of my office, I can hear your religious music. This is your workplace, not your home. This is not the place for that music."

Leticia thought, *What are you talking about? You've been locked in your office all morning with the door closed*. But she just said, "Yes, Melba," and turned off her CD player, leaving the area silent. Well, silent except for other workers' small CD players softly playing *their* music. Melba stalked back to her office and shut the door. Leticia stared after her. So, Melba was just being petty?

Well, it certainly fit Melba's MO. According to Melba (apparently), if Melba wasn't happy, no one should be.

At lunch, Leticia explained why her music had gone off.

Evanne rolled her eyes comically at Melba's behavior, and Leticia giggled. "You just need an earphone piece," Evanne told her. "So only you can hear the music. Then Melba can't complain. I have a few at home; I'll bring you one tomorrow."

"Great! Thank you!"

"Now, let's see what weird food you have today."

Leticia chuckled again. While Evanne peeled her tangerines, Leticia pulled out a jar of pickled pig's feet, popped it open, and started eating. Evanne stopped mid-peel and just watched Leticia eat for a minute. "Urgh," she said finally. "Some people have the weirdest eating habits," she said.

Leticia nodded. She almost said something about the potato chips in Evanne's pantry, but that was Evanne's secret to keep. She also sensed that Evanne was just teasing her.

Before returning to their respective jobs, they made a brief stop at the ladies' room. They found Melba applying some kind of powder to her lips and dabbing the prune with the cold sore medicine Leticia had bought for her.

"What're you looking at?" she barked when she noticed them looking. "Bitches," she muttered under breath, either thinking they couldn't hear or unconcerned if they did.

"B-b-" Evanne stuttered in outrage. "Now, you listen here—"

But Leticia grabbed Evanne's arm and whispered very quietly, "Evanne, don't. She'll just take it out on me."

Evanne steadied herself with noticeable effort, and then proceeded to treat Melba as though the woman with the swollen lips were invisible. Leticia followed suit, and thankfully, Melba left her alone for the rest of the day.

* * *

The next morning, Evanne greeted her friend by holding out a pair of earphones. She attached it for Leticia, who turned on her CD player and listened to the music pour out of the earpieces. "Oh, Evanne! Thank you! You are a true friend; you are a good person."

Leticia hummed along with the spiritual tunes, happily typing away, when Melba walked by. "Earphones! Leticia, how do you expect to hear anyone, if they need you?"

Leticia removed the earpiece. "Good morning, Melba. I can hear you and anyone else."

"I don't believe you."

Melba's attacks were becoming pettier, more personal, and more direct. But Leticia didn't want to meet Melba on her level.

"Melba, just tell me, what is the policy of music in your work area? Just about everyone in this office has a radio or something that they listen to while they work."

"They don't work for me; you do, and I do not want any damn music playing during work hours, whether anyone can hear it or not. Period."

"Is that company policy?" Leticia said very quietly.

"As far as you're concerned, I am the company."

Leticia didn't know how to respond to such a ridiculous statement. "I ... Melba ... but everyone—"

"No music." Melba stared at Leticia, as if daring the underling to challenge her authority.

Paul walked up. "Good morning, Leticia. Uh, Melba." He glanced at Melba's swollen face and looked away quickly. He seemed discomfited for a few seconds, and Melba looked away, as though trying to hide her face. Paul faced Leticia. "Um, Leticia, I asked Mr. Foles if I could have you help me again today."

Melba made a noise, and Paul added, "It shouldn't take too much of your time. Just finishing up."

"Sure, Paul."

Paul smiled brightly, and Leticia's heart fluttered a little. His teeth were so white and even, and his smile just made his smooth, tanned skin more appealing. "Thank you!" He nodded in Melba's direction without actually looking at her and then started walking away.

Then he paused. He looked back at Leticia and said, "I haven't heard your music today. I enjoyed it yesterday every time I walked near your cube. In fact, I walked this way a couple of times so I could catch some of it. You know the company lets you listen to music quietly at your desk, right?"

"I … um—" Again, Leticia had no idea what to say, but for an entirely different reason this time. She felt flustered and warm. Paul had walked near her desk on purpose several times yesterday.

He winked at her. "That's right. Company policy." Then he walked off.

Melba finally turned her head around to watch him. She sneered and looked as though she had swallowed something sour. "Fine. Listen to your damn music. Go get me some coffee, like a good assistant." She turned around and stalked off. Leticia was pretty sure she heard Melba mutter, "Interfering prick."

She felt her face darken, and she nearly yelled at Melba for calling Paul a prick. Instead, she just got up and obediently headed to the lunchroom to get some coffee for her boss. Unfortunately, the pot was empty, and Leticia couldn't find any packets in any of the drawers.

"We ran out," another office worker explained apologetically. "We put in a supply request. Should have some more this afternoon or tomorrow morning."

Leticia returned to Melba's office and explained the situation. "Would you like a cup of tea instead?"

"I asked for coffee," Melba said, as if she hadn't heard Leticia's explanation of the situation. "I do not like tea!"

"You don't have to shout," Leticia said softly.

"Then you need to not be deaf!"

"Melba, it's not my fault—"

Melba just hauled out her purse. "Go to Starbucks and get me a large coffee." She handed Leticia a five-dollar bill.

"I don't know where Starbucks is."

"'I don't know where Starbucks is,'" Melba mimicked. "It's just on the opposite corner. Are you blind? It's there every single morning when you walk into this building."

Leticia didn't take the money. She turned around and closed the door. "Melba," she said very quietly, almost whispering. "Melba, you told me that you would not be sending me on any personal errands."

"Let me explain this once more," Melba said loudly. Apparently, the quieter Leticia got, the louder Melba felt she had to speak. "You work for me, and getting my coffee is not personal."

"Would Frances agree?" Leticia snapped, grabbed the money, and left the office before Melba could reply. She returned to her cubicle to don her winter clothes. Her heart beat sharply in her chest. She wanted to slap the bitch upside the head. She sucked in several deep breaths to try to calm herself. She reminded herself, this wasn't at all how her mother would handle the situation.

In fact, her mother would probably say the situation was going very well. Every day, Melba was coming closer and closer to crossing a line that the company couldn't ignore. She was hanging herself with her own rope. All Leticia had to do was stay demure, just like her daddy said, and let events play out. She couldn't let her temper get the better of her, or she'd end up in the same situation as Melba.

And it was kind of like what Aunt Martha said, too. This was the devil in Melba. If Melba would just be nice to her, Leticia wouldn't have to draw the evil inner bitch out.

Nevertheless, it took considerable effort for Leticia to calm herself, and she was still hot with anger as she went to run Melba's petty little errand.

At the Starbucks, she gathered the appropriate condiments for the drink. The place was packed with office workers trying to perk up their day. Then Leticia took a second look. She wondered how many people were there not to get coffee for themselves, but for their own tyrant bosses. She watched a few minutes as people collected their coffee, added condiments, and then started drinking.

In fact, *everyone* else seemed to be getting coffee just for themselves. Leticia grimaced. That damn woman was treating Leticia like her own personal slave.

She did not return immediately to Melba's office with the coffee. Instead, she detoured back to the break room. She removed the lid from the coffee and microwaved the coffee with Mama Dassa's stick for two minutes. She then removed the stick from the steaming coffee, replaced the lid, and dried the stick with a paper towel. Leticia crammed the dampened paper towel into her pocket.

She walked very fast to Melba's office. "Sorry it took so long," she said in her best fake trying-desperately-to-please voice. "Starbucks is obviously popular. The line was almost out the door. It spilled on me a little," she added and pulled out the damp paper towel. "Can I toss it in your trash?"

"Sure, fine," said a calmer Melba as she took her first sip.

Leticia walked out of the office, but instead of heading straight down the hall back to her own cube, she took a left toward Frances's area. Melba noticed and immediately jumped up to follow. "Leticia," she said in a friendly voice that sounded unnatural coming from her, "you were correct; I meant to tell you, after you left, I did check with Frances, and yes, it is okay if you and I agree for you to get me coffee from our lunch room. However, you will not leave the office area to run any personal errands."

You mean your *personal errands*, Leticia thought. But she just smiled tremulously and nodded thankfully. Then she asked, almost whispering, "Did you double check about the music? I know you and Paul disagreed about the company policy."

Melba's fake smile slipped into a sneer. With the woman's grossly swollen lips, the ugly expression made her look as though she'd been in some kind of accident.

At that moment, at the end of the hall, Mr. Foles opened his office door. "Oh, there's Mr. Foles!" said Leticia. "He'd know, wouldn't he?" she asked sweetly.

Mr. Foles noticed the two women, and he greeted them with a smile and a nod. Like Paul, he avoided looking at Melba directly.

"No need for that either," Melba said quickly. "I asked Frances about that, too. It's okay."

"Leticia, good morning! Melba. Leticia, how is your mother?"

"She is progressing slowly, but that is expected; she was hit very hard."

Mr. Foles nodded sympathetically. "My own mother broke her hip a few years back. At a certain age, the body just takes its time to heal, doesn't it?"

Leticia nodded. "Yes, sir."

"Does the insurance cover her medical bills?"

"Oh. Well, ah, no. It turned out the driver and owner of the minibus had no insurance nor driver's licenses, so each of us—that is, my three younger brothers and I—we're helping with the medical bills."

"Living in a third-world nation must be hard," said Melba in a tone clearly intended to by sympathetic but which came across as condescending.

"Why are you in your coat?" asked Mr. Foles suddenly. "Is it cold in your area?"

"No, I had to—"

But Melba interrupted. "Leticia ran out to pick up a CD."

She looked as surprised as Leticia at the lie, as if she couldn't stop herself from lying to save her own skin. Leticia stared at the ugly, treacherous woman with the enlarged lips and huge cold sore, as if she were looking directly at a ghost.

"A CD?" frowned Mr. Foles.

"A religious CD," supplied Melba.

"I meant for Leticia to tell me," Mr. Foles irritably. He looked at Leticia for a long moment, and Leticia couldn't tell if he was going to rebuke her or not. She thought furiously for a moment: should she stand up for herself and tell Mr. Foles it was a lie, or should she still act as though she were completely cowed by Melba? She didn't want to be the one to hang Melba; she wanted Melba to hang herself. She knew Mr. Foles would be angry at Melba for lying, but she didn't think Melba had spun enough rope yet.

Before she could decide, Mr. Foles said, "Well, I can understand that you would want to find some comfort after such a difficult experience. You were on break, I trust?"

Leticia nodded hesitantly.

"Well, that's fine then. You need all the support and inspiration you can get in this time of family crisis. Go listen and enjoy your CD."

Melba looked as if she was ready to spit fire.

"Th-thank you, sir."

"By the way, Leticia, is there any way your family can make some more of those delicious Jamaican buns? I will pay for them, of course, including shipping."

Frances, who had apparently been listening from her nearby cube, piped up, "I've already asked for some myself."

"Matter of fact, Mr. Foles, I should be getting some from Jamaica next weekend. A lady that knows Mama said she could get them from my cousin Madge for me. So I should have them by next Monday."

"Oh, excellent!"

He beamed and walked away. Leticia shot Melba a vicious look. Melba almost looked confused by that, as if she couldn't quite believe that Leticia was angry. But it was fleeting, and Leticia was already returning to her cube and shucking off her winter wardrobe.

She placed the earphones in the CD player and turned the device on. She worked assiduously for the rest of the morning and actually managed to catch up on all the overdue cataloging, and she was able to get started on the current electronic filing.

She hummed along quietly with her music. The encounter with Mr. Foles had put her at ease; Melba could hardly contest Mr. Foles himself!

That day at lunch, Leticia recited the morning disaster piece by piece. She left nothing out. She mentioned her theory that Melba was terrified of Mr. Foles and couldn't stand the thought of looking bad in front of him.

Evanne spluttered in outrage. "That cow! Why didn't you tell Mr. Foles that she was a lying cow?"

"I didn't want to get her in trouble."

"You didn't … *you didn't want to get her in trouble?*" Evanne exclaimed in disbelief.

Of course it was completely untrue, but she didn't want to tell Evanne the real story. "It all ended up okay."

"But you didn't know that! You could have gotten in trouble! Mr. Foles could have gotten after you for leaving the office building during work hours—"

"I'm not a prisoner here," Leticia pointed out. "If I was on break, I can go anywhere I want."

Evanne continued as if Leticia hadn't spoken. "Or he could have gotten after you for listening to religious music. You never know with companies these days; they're all so sensitive about religion."

Leticia shrugged. "He didn't. He was very nice."

"Well. Well, I promise you, now that she sees Mr. Foles personally likes you, her attitude will change; take notice, my friend."

"She's a witch," Leticia replied between bites of her microwave-warm asparagus. "I hope the next time Melba goes flying that someone hijacks her broom."

Evanne laughed so loudly she couldn't eat her kumquats, and other employees turned to look at her. But Evanne paid them no mind. "I've never heard that before," she said between her great gasping guffaws.

"It's an old Jamaican saying," said Leticia, smiling.

Still laughing, they cleaned off their table and stopped by the restroom on the way back to work.

As they stood side by side at the mirror, prepping themselves to return to their work, Evanne looked slyly around the bathroom. She even ducked down to look under the stalls to see if anyone else was in there. Then she bent toward Leticia, who was watching her in bewilderment, and said, "I drank that tea you gave me."

"Oh! And?"

Evanne smiled shyly. She reached up and started pulled the wig back from the scalp, carefully peeling a section of double-sided tape back from the cap on the interior of the wig. She lifted the section up and invited Leticia to take a closer look, but Leticia didn't have a good view. She was only looking at a portion, and it was shadowed from the wig.

"I don't …?"

"My hair!" whispered Evanne excitedly. "It's growing back. Ever since the chemo, I haven't been able to grow it except in patches, and even those don't grow well."

"Oh!"

"And now it's growing back again!" Evanne giggled gleefully. She even did a little jig, and Leticia laughed and joined her friend with some rudimentary footwork of her own. The two women ended, hands on each other's arms, breathless and laughing.

"I'm so happy for you, Evanne!"

"Thank you for the tea!"

"How … how does it taste?" Leticia was almost afraid to ask.

Evanne's eyes widened, and she nodded appreciatively. "Deee-licious. Best tea I've ever drunk. Like the nectar of the gods."

"Oh, that's good! That is the same tea Aunt Peggy is giving Mama so she can recuperate."

"Oh really? I hope it works as well for her! Girl, I would drink mud if I thought it'd grow my hair out again. You know, I used to have the most beautiful hair, long and thick. I had given up hope." She sighed wistfully.

Just then, the bathroom door was thrown open. Evanne jerked away from it, back toward the mirror, and hurriedly adjusted the wig to make sure it was right in place.

Melba rushed to the toilet paper dispenser and grabbed some and started dabbing at her face with the paper.

"It burst!" exclaimed Leticia, looking at the prune-sized cold sore.

Melba's face turned an even darker shade of red than it already was.

"Is there anything I can do?" Leticia asked automatically.

"What have you put on it? Bovine growth hormone?" Evanne asked.

"Mind your own damn business," Melba shouted and grabbed a small clear Ziploc jammed with all sorts of topical medicines.

"Do you smell something?" Evanne asked. She sniffed at the air.

"It's a bathroom," Leticia pointed out.

Evanne insisted that they meet for an afternoon break later in the lunch room.

Leticia could not wait to hear what her dear friend had to say.

As they sat down, Evanne commented that she thought Melba was turning into a corpse before their eyes.

"She looks the same to me," Leticia muttered.

"No. The bitch is transforming into something, with that Swiss cheese face. Don't you smell the odor when she's around?"

"Maybe. What are you talking about?"

"Yeah, you smell it. Like dead flesh."

"That's gross, Evanne! We're eating."

Leticia had helped herself to a leftover bagel that was in the company's complementary bakery basket.

Just then, Evanne grabbed a pomegranate from her always filled bag of many fruits.

"Don't let that stop you from eating those bagels, because it sure won't stop me from enjoying this pomegranate."

Evanne ate in silence for a few minutes, while Leticia stared at the bagel in her hand. Then Leticia said, hesitantly, "You don't … do you think she's dying?"

Evanne just shrugged.

Leticia watched as Melba left the office to head to the doctor. She recalled something Evanne had said about her cancer, that sometimes the cure was worse than the disease. Leticia chewed on her lip, struck by sudden doubt.

CHAPTER 15

N EW YORK IS A STRANGE *creature*, Leticia thought.
She stood on the railing of a ferry, the *Zephyr*, coasting alongside Manhattan. Saturday's dusk was settling over the city; the sun set so early here at this time of year. The water was dark and murky, but then, it had started out that way, even when they first boarded. The slate gray shade of the water, its impenetrable depths, the occasional bobble of little bubbles amid the crests of the waves, all of it stood in such stark contrast to the clean, clear blue waters of Jamaica. It was as if even the water reflected the spirit of the cities.

New York was built out of steel and concrete and rose high into the sky; the city was humankind's willpower dominating nature, and even the waters of the Hudson submitted. The builders planted the seeds of industry and civilization, and they grew skyscrapers and retail. In Jamaica, Mother Nature still reigned; in fact, Jamaica had built its industry on harvesting the fruits and bounty that She sowed.

Leticia felt unbearably lonely in that moment, so far removed from home that—for a brief moment—she felt as though she could have been on Mars and felt no less alien. She had come here to make her own place. As that song went, if she could succeed in New York …

But she just felt cold and very far from home. Very uncertain. Leticia shivered. It wasn't that Jamaica was so pristine and clean, nor was her life there so perfect. And yet they were—Jamaica and her life there—in a way this place was not. She trembled a little more, and marveled at the uncomfortable diversity of the world.

Even as she thought these things, evening continued to fall. The sky turned into a deep charcoal blue, rapidly descending into a inky indigo. Lit bridges fanned out from Manhattan to the sides, and the endless urban forest of buildings glimmered brightly in the evening gloom. In the twilight shadows, the edges of buildings faded one into the other.

Prior to their ferry ride, Paul had taken Leticia to the 102nd floor observatory of the Empire State Building. She had marveled at the urban forest of buildings, broken only by the expanse of Central Park. But even that spot of greenery just seemed to accentuate and re-emphasize the gray tones of the city. But truth be told, her attention hadn't been entirely on the view. As Paul had indicated sites of interest, pointing with his right arm, his left arm had been draped across her back, his right hand on her shoulder. He had been warm and deliciously close.

As dusk struck, it transformed the city into a single, boundary-less, textured entity that shone bright even in the falling dark. It almost seemed to breath, to inhale and exhale, as the little lights of street lamps and office buildings and headlines filled the evening.

And Leticia marveled all over again. In Jamaica, when night fell, generally speaking, it *really* fell. Inky darkness covered the landscape. But here, the whole city twinkled aglow, full of a new kind of light and sparkle.

"Here you go," Paul said breathlessly. He held out a steaming mug of cocoa. "Sorry, there was more of a line at the snack bar than I expected."

Leticia smiled at Paul, and he grinned back. She took the mug, appreciative of the warmth in her hands. She took a sip and resumed her reflection on the view. She shivered again slightly.

Suddenly, she felt Paul slip up behind her, his arms around her. "It is chilly up here, isn't it?" he breathed into her ear.

"Mmmm," she replied. As he cradled her from behind, she leaned her head back against his chest.

And that was all it took, that single instant shifted a homesick moment into heaven. The cold wind couldn't touch her; the landscape of New York no longer seemed foreign; even the water was just water again. The differences no longer mattered. The strange creature of New York became like an old friend, winking indulgently at her and Paul.

The companionable feeling of contentment didn't fade as the ferry tour continued, with Paul occasionally murmuring comments about the skyline, and ended; nor as she and Paul walked hand in hand to catch a cab to one of his favorite restaurants. She felt perfectly at home as they slid into a booth, side by side. Music from a live band washed over them, as the waitress handed them each a menu.

After they had ordered, Paul looked nonplussed and said, "Um, Leticia, I feel that we need to talk about something."

The young Jamaican felt her heart hammer a bit in her chest, but all she said was, "Oh?"

Paul offered a brief smile and then said, "I just want us to be on the up and up."

"Up and up?"

He nodded. "What does that mean?"

"Oh," he said. "I mean that I want to be honest and clear with you." He cleared his throat. "My interest, ah, my interest in you is not entirely work related."

He looked so discomfited, blushing furiously and barely making eye contact, that Leticia was amused. And delighted. As if it hadn't already been obvious. But she didn't give an inch. She just said, "Oh," and nodded somberly with a soft wink of her eyes.

Paul bit his lip and then spoke in a rush. "At first, I told myself I was just being nice and showing you, someone new to New York, all the sights, and I didn't have any ulterior motives at all, uh-uh, not me." He flashed another brief, self-mocking smile. "But that's not true. And I just want to say that I, that is, I think you're very, um, you're special, and I'd like to get to know you better, but I totally respect whatever your feelings are. I told James that you were welcome on my team, but I'm glad now that you said no, so although we work together sometimes, you don't actually report to me. But we do work together, and I know, um, I know it can be weird or hard to have a relationship outside of work with a co-worker, and the last thing I want to do is put you in any kind of uncomfortable situation, and so I just wanted to tell you—"

"Paul."

The handsome man froze. He looked expectantly at Leticia, his lips still slightly parted and pursed, frozen on the next word he was going to say. He was flushed all the way to his ears.

Leticia paused, searching for the right words, but she realized she was in uncharted waters herself. It was uncomfortable and exciting in equal measure, and she savored Paul's anticipation of her response. She just said, "Thank you. I appreciate everything you just said." She turned her head, listening to the music from the live band, and noticed the dance floor with a handful of couples on it. "Look, they have dancing." She turned back again and looked Paul in the eye.

The man licked his lips and then grinned. "Would you like to dance with me?"

She smiled back and nodded.

Paul stood, held out his hand, and helped Leticia out of the booth. He led her to the dance floor. The song playing was an upbeat, jazzy piece with sultry vocals from the chanteuse.

Leticia didn't miss a beat. She and Paul joined hands, and she started rocking in time with the beat. Paul, unfortunately, danced like a white boy. He tried his best, bless him, but his legs and arms couldn't seem to agree on the proper movements, and none of his appendages could seem to keep up with the tempo of the music. Leticia watched him attempt to dance for a minute or two. Then, laughingly, she pulled him closer.

His arms swept around her. "Not my song," he chuckled into her ear. Conveniently, the piece ended and shifted smoothly into a slow-paced song. "Good. This is more my style."

His arm wrapped around her back and held Leticia closer; she sighed into his shoulder. Now that Paul wasn't trying to rock out, his body seemed to know just how to respond to the notes—and to her. They drifted across the dance floor perfectly in sync. She leaned into him. She could smell his delicious cologne, feel his heat. His cheek pressed against the top of her head, and they spun around.

The music faded into the background, and their dance slowed. Leticia lifted her head from his shoulder. His blue eyes twinkled down on her. He was not blushing now. A soft smile tugged at the corner of his lips. She leaned her head back, and he leaned in. Their lips met, lightly at first, just grazing. Then he pressed in more firmly, and their kiss deepened. The tips of the tongues touched, and it was electric. Slow, languorous, and intimate, they kissed in the middle of the dance floor. When he finally pulled back, it was like a gust of cold New York wind had suddenly swept into a warm, candle-lit room.

"So that's how New Yorkers stay warm," Leticia quipped.

Paul burst out laughing. "You have no idea," he replied archly. He winked but led Leticia chastely back to their table. She continued to buzz with the aftereffects of their kiss.

On Sunday, Leticia woke with thoughts of their kiss still on her lips. It was delightful to have discovered something so lovely and so unexpected. It was like walking down the street, the snow streaked black with dirt and grime, and finding a sole rose blooming.

Somewhere deep down, her consciousness buzzed with the thought, *He tried to be "on the up and up" with you; why aren't you with him?* But she pushed that thought away. What? Just because she told him she lived in a boarding house? That her mother was hurt?

She was true to her *feelings*. That was all that mattered.

She relayed all the events of the week to Aunt Martha. She felt her face grow hot when she talked about Paul, but Aunt Martha just chuckled.

"And then he asked me to go to Broadway with him!"

"What, to see the street?"

Leticia laughed. "No, Auntie, to go see a musical. *Wicked*. He said after Melba, I would appreciate it."

Martha looked mournful.

"Auntie! What is it?"

"Your uncle never takes me anywhere anymore."

Leticia didn't mention anything she did with Mama Dassa's stick. Uncle George drove the two of them to the Jamaican bakery in the Bronx, where Leticia bought eight freshly baked buns.

She could hardly wait for work the next day.

PART FOUR—LIKE A DUCK

CHAPTER 16

L ETICIA ARRIVED AT WORK ON Monday after having carefully wrapped each bun individually in aluminum foil. All of the management staff were settling in the meeting room for their Monday morning conference, while Frances went around passing out paychecks.

Leticia opened hers and saw with some surprise that they hadn't included overtime pay for the evening she helped Melba.

She approached Frances immediately, but Mr. Foles intercepted her as he stepped out of his office to head to the management meeting. "What's wrong?" he asked. "Is it Melba again?" he asked in a whisper. "Do you want to step into my office to tell me about it?"

"Okay," Leticia said. She followed him into his office. "I was forced to work late last Wednesday," Leticia said immediately, "and Melba told me I'd be paid overtime, but there's no overtime on this check." She handed it to Mr. Foles, who scrutinized the paystub.

He looked up and smiled. "I'll straighten this out. Don't sweat it, stay calm, and keep up that tropical enthusiasm."

Leticia smiled bashfully.

"I also wanted to mention you've done a great job catching up on your work after being out for a week. I noticed that Melba didn't make any effort to help keep you current. You must have had a deluge of tasks when you got back."

"Yes, sir."

"You know, Leticia, my door is always open. If Melba, well, if you ever want to talk, I'm here. We want all our employees to be happy."

"Yes, sir."

"As you know, I had some concerns about your performance before you left for home."

"Yes, sir," Leticia repeated again, so softly Mr. Foles almost couldn't hear her.

"But, well, let's just say I'm not sure I was looking at the right party."

"Sir?" Leticia's ears perked up. She wondered if this was part of Mama Dassa's intervention, or if Mr. Foles was just seeing Melba clearly now.

"That's all, Leticia. Just remember my invitation."

"Thank you, sir!"

At the door, Leticia paused. "Oh, sir, I almost forgot. The buns came this weekend; I'll give you yours after the meeting finishes."

"Excellent! Thank you."

As Leticia passed the conference room, she noticed that Melba was wearing a hat. Leticia thought of Evanne's wig collection and returned to her desk, somber. She kept right on schedule with all her cataloging.

An hour after the end of the meeting, Mr. Foles, Frances, Melba, and Paul all came to her cubicle. Paul beamed at her. Mr. Foles handed her original paycheck back, along with an additional check for the overtime. He also had a Virgin Store plastic bag. "Here are a couple of CDs."

"We all still feel really bad for your mother," Frances explained.

"We hope you like them," said Paul.

Melba said nothing but looked anywhere but at the group of people.

Leticia found genuine tears trying to force their way out. She blinked them back. "Th-thank you all," she said thickly. "I will listen to them today."

Finally, Melba spoke, still keeping her head down. The wide brim of her hat obscured most of her face. "Leticia, I don't know where my head is. When your timesheet was presented to me for approval, I just forgot to include your overtime."

Forgot, my ass, thought Leticia, but she just nodded and smiled. "I'm just grateful it got fixed," she said.

Melba's expression soured again, but everyone else smiled back at Leticia. "Also, I know you mentioned you had other plans that night. You only have to help me past your regular hours when you can." She spoke as if she were having to choke out the words.

"Thank you." Then: "Oh! The buns."

She pulled out the bag with the individually wrapped buns. She gave two to Mr. Foles, two to Frances, and one to Paul. Was it just her imagination, or did his fingers linger on hers as she handed him the bun?

Everyone thanked her, and the group dispersed—Paul clearly reluctant—except for her boss.

"Melba, I like your hat," she ventured.

Melba looked up, and then away quickly.

"Oh my Lord!" Leticia exclaimed. For a brief second she had gotten a good look at Melba's face, which was covered by red spots, breakouts, and small sores.

"Leticia, I am going to the doctor. I should return before lunch."

Melba walked away. On her way out, Leticia overheard her say to Paul, "Paul, I want to talk to you."

"Let's go into my office," Paul said through a mouthful of bun. From there, Leticia could hear no more.

Evanne wandered over, staring after the lady. Today's wig was a black afro so large it made Evanne's head take up three times as much space as usual. "What's up with the hat?" she asked.

What's up with your wig? Leticia wanted to ask. Instead, the young Jamaican just shrugged. "Oh, you missed it. That woman is as humble, as you Americans say, as humble pie."

Evanne laughed. "No, Leticia, we Americans do not say as humble as humble pie." Then she looked disappointed. "I'm late to the office and missed all the action."

"Where were you this morning?" Leticia asked curiously.

"I went to pay some bills before they came here with the handcuffs for me."

"But you didn't get your paycheck!"

"Oh, I have direct deposit."

"What is that?"

"You don't know about—? Well, I'll explain at lunch. But first, tell me what happened!"

But before Leticia could relate the morning's events, they heard shouting.

"Who is she shouting at now?" Evanne wondered with a frown.

"I don't know, but it's probably Paul."

Almost all the workers stood up to see what was going on, and some people gathered outside Paul's office.

"It's like she's having some kind of breakdown. If she keeps going nuclear on everyone's ass, they're going to fire her," Evanne commented. "Tim says none of the other account execs can stand her."

Leticia said nothing.

"I am causing you stress? I am causing you to break out?" Paul shouted from behind his closed door. The rest of the office was so quiet, straining to hear, that you could hear a pin drop. "Get the hell out of my office!" He sounded as if he wanted to add more but cut himself off before he said something he might regret.

He swung the door open and gestured angrily for Melba to use it. She stepped out and suddenly realized everyone was staring at her. For one terrible minute, she was frozen, her face upraised and staring back at everyone in horror. Everyone had a clear glimpse of her face. She looked like a cartoon witch.

"Someone's not having a good face day," someone muttered off to Leticia's right, a cube or two away.

Melba apparently heard, too. Whatever force was holding her frozen broke, and she ducked her head. "What are you all staring at?" she yelled and darted to the elevator.

"She looks awful," Evanne said conversationally. "Karma's a bitch, ain't she?"

"Yes," said Leticia. "Yes, she is."

As the office returned to normal, Leticia handed two buns to Evanne. "They came this past weekend. Tell Tony to enjoy!" She winked. Despite Evanne's protestations at work, she doubted Tony was the only one who would enjoy the pastry.

The next several hours passed peaceably. Once Melba returned, Leticia relayed a message from Frances that Mr. Foles wanted to see her. Melba didn't say anything but just marched over to Mr. Foles's office.

Evanne and Leticia went to lunch and speculated what Mr. Foles might be saying to Melba.

"You're fired!" Evanne guessed.

"You think?" Leticia wondered after a bite of her own Jamaican bun.

Evanne peeled her ruby red grapefruit. "Nah. But he's probably keeping a list, making a case against her. That's what you have to do these days."

"Really?"

"Yeah. You've got to have lots of reasons to fire someone, or one *really, really* good reason. Otherwise, they'll just come back and sue your ass."

"Oh."

"But I'm telling you, the power is falling. I am making sure I'm not in the way when it falls."

"I couldn't agree more," said Leticia.

Evanne handed Leticia a direct deposit form. "I picked this up for you. You just need to complete it and give it to HR with a blank check."

"I don't have any checks," said Leticia.

"No checks? They come with a checking account."

"I've never had one of those."

Evanne stared at her friend in disbelief. "You don't have a checking account? How about a savings account? No? How do you cash your check?"

"At the place next to where I live that says 'Checks Cashed.'"

"How do you pay your bills?"

"I only have rent, and Miss Martha takes cash and gives me a receipt." Leticia took another chew, and then added, "Most of it I send home for Mama's medicine."

"Well, I guess you don't need this." Evanne balled up the form and tossed it in a nearby trashcan.

The two coworkers returned to a very quiet office. As they passed Berlina's cubicle, Evanne stopped to ask what had happened between Paul and Melba. Paul's assistant whispered in a confidential undertone that she'd probably already used with everyone else in the office, "Melba thinks she's being ignored for accounts. She thinks she's more experienced than Paul because she holds a marketing degree. She says Paul is being treated preferentially while she is being overlooked, no matter how hard she works."

"How hard she works!" said Leticia before she could stop herself. "I do half her work for her!"

"Really?" Berlina asked. "Hm. Not surprised. Anyway, she said she's been so despondent for the past few weeks, but this past week has been the worst, and she blames Paul."

"As if it's Paul's fault that she's a bitch," said Evanne.

"I know, right? Well, Frances told me she told Mr. Foles that her doctor said she is suffering from acute stress, and that is why her face now looks like a monster's."

"She told Mr. Foles that?" Evanne asked, amused.

"Well, not those exact words, I'm sure. But apparently, she was hinting that she might sue the company for creating an unpleasant workplace for her, and maybe even discrimination. Mr. Foles wasn't happy with her. I'm sure they'd go ahead and fire her, but you know how careful companies have to be before they can let people go these days."

"Wow," said Leticia.

"Tsk, tsk" was Evanne's only response. "She's just digging herself into an even deeper hole. What a moron. If she just treated people decently, people would treat her decently back. Paul and Tim are the two nicest account execs, and that's why the best things happen to them. That's all it takes. Why can't some people learn that you get back what you dish out?"

Leticia didn't respond to this comment, but a new excited energy coursed through her. Mama Dassa's specialty was working! She was thrilled. It filled her with a sense of power and purpose. She said goodbye to Evanne and Berlina and immediately headed back to her work area.

Just then, Melba emerged from Mr. Foles's office. Melba came directly to Leticia's cubicle; she acted like a wounded puppy as she asked Leticia to compile a folder from several files in the file room. Leticia humbly complied.

It was time for the next step in Mama Dassa's plan.

She grabbed a large foam cup, filled it with water, and then stuffed it full of paper towels. She added one of Mama Dassa's sticks and placed the cup in the microwave. Everything brewed for the next five minutes while Leticia stood close by to make sure no one could see what she was doing.

After everything stopped cooking, she pulled out the stick with a plastic spoon, careful not to touch it, dried it thoroughly, and replaced it in her change purse. Then she poured out the liquid and squeezed the excess from the paper towels. She put them back into the cup and headed toward the supply closet.

She grabbed an empty three-ring binder and then went to her desk.

She looked around to make sure no one was watching her, and then took out the paper towels and wiped the binder all over. She accidentally dropped a damp paper towel on a contract page. To her amazement, the page was not smeared or wet at all. In fact, she wiped the damp towel all over the page, and it remained bone dry. She performed the same ritual with every single piece as she put together the research file she had prepared for the BALI account, at Melba's order.

When the complete binder was assembled, and every square inch had been wiped by the paper towels, she happily went to Melba and placed the folder in Melba's hand.

"If you could please review it now," she said, "I can make the changes. I know that tomorrow is very busy for you, and you've been having a bad day, and hopefully this will help you look good."

"All right, have a seat," Melba said absently. As Leticia waited, Melba flipped through every single page and scrutinized the text. Leticia's nose wrinkled at an odd odor in Melba's office, but she didn't comment.

At the end, Melba nodded and said, "This is fine."

Her response surprised Leticia. She had expected a litany of complaints. But Melba just handed it over.

Berlina poked her head into the office. "Melba, here are some revisions to the BALI account for you to work on." She noticed Leticia sitting in the office, she said, "Or should I just give them to Leticia to do for you?"

"I no longer have that account," Melba snarled. "Go see Paul."

Berlina rolled her eyes. "I work for Paul, remember? He said to give you the BALI account since it is female-sensitive, dealing with lingerie and all that."

"Huh. I'd think Paul would be perfect for it. He probably wears women's lingerie." Melba laughed at her joke, but Leticia just stared at her. Berlina frowned and walked away.

Melba looked up at Leticia excitedly. "Leticia, this is critical; I will definitely make sure you get overtime pay. I've got to get this account perfect. Stay late and help me, and you and I will deliver the pitch to the BALI headquarters in Detroit together. I'll make sure you get full credit."

Leticia did everything Melba asked of her, unquestioning. Privately, she was shocked the company was still sending Melba, given her physical state.

At the end of the day, Melba declared, "This is great. I am sure the client will see us. Make sure you're here at six a.m., so we can go to the airport together. Put on your best business outfit. You won't need a suitcase because we'll fly back on the same day."

The older lady ran her fingers through her tresses and came away with a clump of hair. She stared in astonishment at the long strands of hair in her hands. When she noticed Leticia staring, too, her face snapped shut like a bear trap, and she snarled, "Get out!"

Leticia got out. Thinking over Melba's invitation, she wondered if the woman had turned over a new leaf. Was that was Mama Dassa's plan all along? But that last "Get out!" still seemed pretty Melba-like, even considering the circumstances.

She returned to her desk, let out a very big sigh, and felt some of Melba's excitement herself. Her first business trip! She agreed with her father's advice, she just wanted to keep her head low and do her work, but she was enthused at the prospect of actually taking advantage of all the hard work she'd put into researching the BALI account for Melba.

Over the course of the day, she told nearly everyone who would listen that she was going with Melba to the BALI meeting. Everyone was shocked that Melba would take her, but Leticia was convinced the plan was just working.

She imagined Paul's face when they revealed that she had helped land the BALI account. How he would smile at her and compliment her. She could feel herself blushing at the thought.

"Six o'clock sharp," Melba reminded her on her way out.

"I'll be there!" said Leticia with true delight in her voice. Maybe the binder had worked. Maybe the coffee brewed with Mama Dassa's sticks were designed to soften Melba up, and the binder made her nicer. Leticia was the last person to leave the office that night.

Leticia arrived promptly at 5:45 a.m. the next morning. She sat on a sofa in the waiting area near the elevator. Six o'clock came and no Melba. Leticia wasn't worried. But then came 6:30. Then 7:00. At 8:00 a.m., Frances arrived. "Good morning, Leticia, what are you doing here so early?"

"Melba told me to be here at six so I could go with her to Detroit."

"Oh. But Melba left on a redeye last night."

"What is a redeye?"

"A late night flight, dear. She'll be there this morning to deliver her presentation, and then come back. Melba won't be back in the office until tomorrow."

Leticia shook her head in disbelief. Was Melba really so evil? "Oh. I … Oh. Can … can I go pick up some lunch? I didn't bring anything from home."

"Of course, dear. You are already early. By the way, how is your mother coming along?"

"Oh. She's out of the hospital now," Leticia replied absently, her thoughts lingering on Melba's treachery. "She's with Aunt Peggy and Uncle JoJo."

Leticia felt embarrassed. She had been so excited, telling everyone. And now, she'd have to face everyone's questions why she wasn't with Melba. She felt humiliated and angry.

As she walked to the store, the wind was biting cold in her face. It was pointless to be angry with the wind, but Leticia was. Another one of her mother's favorite expressions sprung to mind: "Wha' noh poison, fatten." In other words, if it doesn't hurt you, it can help you. But Leticia was ready to put a world of hurt on Melba.

Her father had told her to lie low, soak it all up, and her mother had told her to take control of the situation. That's just what she was trying to do, but all this time, she'd felt torn about it. Maybe Daddy was right, and she needed to let go and just go with the flow. Grin and bear it, as the Americans say.

But it was one thing to grin and bear it when someone is rude. When someone is out to *get you*, you have to stand up for yourself or be steamrolled. Up to this point, Leticia hadn't been really, really sure what was going on with Melba. Maybe she was just a wicked witch of a woman, destined just to become an unpleasant memory, and then a funny one when one day Leticia sat in her own corner office at her father's business. Melba would become a story she'd tell at cocktail parties. That crazy American lady.

And Leticia had begun to wonder if her punishment against Melba was disproportionate to the crime. She was driven, not merciless. So she had wavered, gone back and forth.

But now, Melba had made it easy. Melba wasn't just a mean person. She wasn't playing some game with Leticia. She had declared war on the young Jamaican. And who knew why? Threatened by Leticia's competence? Confidence? Youth? Maybe she was just a racist old bat.

It didn't matter anymore. This was it. Leticia had had *enough*. No more doubting, no more uncertainty. Melba wanted to mess with Leticia? Fine. Leticia was going to mess with Melba but good.

Leticia went to the corner store and bought a microwaveable thirty-two-ounce insulated coffee cup with a secure lid. She also bought bagels for her lunch.

I know what Daddy said, Leticia thought to herself. *But he's not here. He doesn't understand the situation. I know what I want, and Melba isn't going to get the best of me. She's not going to make me look like a fool. I'm going to do what it takes to put things right and put* her *in her* place. *Watch out, Melba. It's on.*

She returned to the office, went to her cubicle, and repeated her daily routine of disrobing and preparing her computer for her input.

"Good morning, sweetie," said a bubbly Evanne. "I thought you said you were going to be in Detroit today?"

"Melba left without me."

Evanne didn't say anything for a long moment, and then let out a low "That cow."

Leticia just nodded sharply, not trusting herself to speak.

"Well, you look really great."

Leticia glanced down. It was the best business suit she had with her in New York.

"Thank you. My nicest outfit, and I wore it for nothing! That woman actually left me," Leticia mumbled.

"Sorry. Melba's a real piece of work, isn't she? Oh, by the way, how's your mother doing?"

"Out of the hospital, with Aunt Peggy and Uncle JoJo."

One hour later, Leticia took the insulated coffee cup she had bought and her change purse and headed for the lunch area. Luckily, it was empty. Leticia removed the lid from the cup she bought, and she placed all three sticks in it. She filled the cup with water and covered it with a paper towel and put it in the microwave for five minutes. When the microwave was done, she replaced the paper towel with the lid and shut the lid tightly. Leticia placed the moistened, steamed paper towel into her pocket. Then, she pulled a chair to the cabinets and placed the cup with the sticks and water on the highest shelf. She climbed down from the chair, put it back, and went directly to Frances.

"Hi, Frances," she smiled. "Could you open Melba's office for me? I left something in there last night by accident."

Frances didn't even hesitate. She pulled a bunch of keys from her desk and handed one over to Leticia.

Leticia used it to enter the office. She closed the door behind her. The blinds were already closed, since Melba had been trying to hide her face. Leticia went on to wipe everything in the woman's office: computer, telephone, clock, pen holder, the knobs on her drawer. Finally, she dropped the paper towel in Melba's trash can.

As she exited the office, she smiled grimly to herself. And this was just the beginning.

CHAPTER 17

L ETICIA ARRIVED EARLIER THAN USUAL the next day, early enough that she and Frances were once again the only two people present. Leticia volunteered to make the coffee.

"Sounds good," Frances yelled back as she went through her own morning routine.

Leticia grabbed her change purse and headed into the lunch room. She took a chair and climbed back up to the top shelf to retrieve the concoction she had left to stew for a day and a night, according to Mama Dassa's instructions.

The young woman methodically replaced the chair. She poured water from the cup, dried the sticks and replaced them in her change purse. She brewed three pots of coffee, poured a cup for herself, and returned to her cube.

She eagerly awaited Melba's return. After a while, she noticed Melba skulk silently past her cube. Trying to avoid Leticia after her deceit, probably.

Leticia grabbed something off her desk, immediately jumped up, and ran to Melba. "Good morning, Melba!" she said cheerily.

"Uh, good morning, Leticia." Melba seemed startled. She didn't look at Leticia directly but kept her swelling face down and hidden under her hat. Leticia could still see a thick layer of pancake makeup two shades darker than her skin, however, and Melba's blonde hair seemed stringier than usual.

Melba unlocked her door and entered the office with Leticia on her tail. She didn't say anything about Detroit, didn't even attempt a feeble explanation, certainly offered no apology. Leticia didn't bring it up either.

"There is something I have to tell you," Leticia said confidentially. "When you are ready to hear it, let me know."

"Okay," said Melba uncertainly, apparently not expecting this kind of greeting from Leticia the day after Melba's betrayal. Then her tone hardened and said, "You could get my coffee."

"Okay," said Leticia.

"Good. Well, hop to it," said Melba. She seemed back to her normal self, back into bullying mode now that she realized Leticia wasn't going to fight about Detroit. It was like some schoolyard bully had kicked another kid and then warily waited to see if the kid would fight back; when he didn't, the bully resumed kicking.

But of course Melba didn't realize Leticia *was* kicking back.

"And I have a gift for you."

"A gift?" Melba asked suspiciously.

"Sure thing. I'll show you in a minute."

Leticia returned with the new thirty-two-ounce mug filled with coffee, along with some sugar packets and creamers. "Here you are, Melba," she said. "I got you this mug. It's kind of a gift for me, too. I usually burn my hand when I get your coffee, and I know it burns you, too. So from now on, it will be steaming hot with a cool cup to drink from."

"You are right," Melba acknowledged. "It does burn my fingers. If the company was smart, they'd give each employee one of these mugs."

"Mm-hmm. Why don't you suggest that to Mr. Foles?"

"James Ass is too cheap for that. Now what is it you have to tell me?" Melba sipped from the mug. Leticia noticed Melba never said thank you.

In the privacy of Melba's office with the door closed, Leticia told her, "Some news I heard yesterday while you were out. Tomorrow, all the account executives are preparing for a conference call with headquarters. They'll be giving their own synopses of each of their accounts. Many of the executives are planning to come in early for a dry run. Some are coming in at seven o'clock. Do you have a key?"

"Don't worry about that; I will get in," replied the ungrateful bitch as she continued to drink her coffee.

Leticia returned to her cubicle. She shook her head. Not even a thank you from Melba for the heads-up.

Evanne wandered over to say good morning. "Whew, that smell is back again."

"Well, yeah," said Leticia. "Maybe I smelled something before; I wasn't sure, but I definitely did this morning. It was faint, though."

Twenty minutes later, Melba ran from her office to the ladies' room. Leticia watched her go but stayed calm, still humming along with a CD. As Melba returned a few minutes later, she passed Berlina's cube, and Berlina blurted out, "What stinks so bad?"

The whole office went quiet as Melba ducked toward Leticia's cubicle. Leticia had to cover her nose and mouth with one hand as Melba whispered, "I need you to meet me in the ladies' room as soon as possible." Leticia, who was in the middle of a phone call, nodded. Melba slunk away back to the bathroom.

Wide eyed, Leticia ended her call and followed her boss to the restroom. Along the way, she heard Evanne shout, "Frances, you need to call maintenance. Something must have died. Whew! It smells like rotten cabbage."

Two women exited the restroom just as Leticia reached the door. "My God," one of them said, "someone needs to see a gynecologist now! That is a hell of a stink."

The other woman concurred. "I can't use this bathroom; I'm going to the one upstairs."

The two women headed for the elevator, and Leticia pushed her way into the restroom.

The stench was nearly overpowering. Just as Evanne said, it smelled like a compost pile. Leticia covered her nose and mouth again and observed that only one stall was closed, but she didn't see any feet on the floor. Still, she knew that Melba was in here. She almost giggled to herself when she imagined Melba on the commode with both legs raised so she couldn't be identified by her shoes.

"Melba? Melba, you said for me to meet you in here."

Melba slowly opened the door to the stall. If Leticia thought she looked like a clown before, it was nothing like this. Melba's face was caked in makeup. It helped cover up the spots and breakouts, but she literally looked like a circus performer with her face painted on.

"Leticia, I know that I am not supposed to send you anywhere for personal errands, but I … I don't know what else to do. Here is forty dollars. Would you please go to the drugstore and get me a vinegar douche and a triple action Monistat."

"Okay," Leticia said through the hand covering her nose and mouth. "Of course."

Once outside the bathroom, she started humming under her breath. She grabbed her change purse from her desk and went to the drug store. When she returned, she went straight to the lunch area, repeated her usual Mamma Dassa procedure, and wiped the items Melba had requested with the damp paper towels.

She went back to the restroom; Melba was still hiding there. Melba accepted the items once again without saying thank you.

As Leticia turned to leave, Melba whispered, "My husband no longer sleeps with me."

"I beg your pardon!" Leticia was shocked that Melba would share this confidence with her.

"First, he was coming to bed with me with a surgical mask. Now he sleeps in the guest room."

Leticia just couldn't believe the wicked witch of the office was confiding in her.

"You've seen my husband. He is such a handsome catch that any woman would die for."

"Uh …" Leticia was stunned by Melba's appraisal of her husband. "Right."

She left the restroom and then started laughing to herself. "I must have given the cake to the wrong person," she mumbled.

At lunch that day, nearly everyone in the lunch room was discussing the odor that consumed the office. They confirmed it was coming strongly from Melba's area, especially when Melba's door was open. Everyone was also discussing Melba's deterioration.

"Let's not talk about that stink stuff again," Leticia asked as she sat down.

Deep down, she wanted to tell Evanne about the errand she'd run for Melba, but she wanted to enjoy her lunch without getting into any disgusting details about Melba.

Over the rest of the day, Melba made ten trips to the ladies' room. Leticia had counted and observed by the sixth trip, none had taken less than ten minutes. Some had taken twice that. So after Melba ducked into the ladies' room for the seventh time, Leticia casually slipped into Melba's office.

It smelled so bad Leticia had to breathe through her mouth. She stood over Melba's desk authoritatively, as though she had every right to be there. She shuffled papers as though sorting them for Melba. She glanced over at the computer, and her suspicion was confirmed: Melba had left so quickly, she hadn't actually locked the computer.

Leticia smirked.

She got into Melba's e-mail and sent a message to one of Melba's accounts. "I'm thinking of leaving Lexhouse to start my own firm. You in? Other clients here are getting more work for less money; I'll offer you best price, and you still get me."

As if anyone would want her, Leticia thought.

She clicked "Send," returned to the document Melba had been reading, and sauntered back to her desk. No one had even looked twice at her, and Melba never noticed.

She repeated the process after the ninth bathroom trip and managed to send three e-mails to three separate clients. She wasn't sure yet how she'd use this. Maybe casually mention to Evanne or Frances or Berlina—any one of whom would spread the news like wildfire—that Melba was sending e-mails to clients asking them to leave Lexhouse.

Satisfied with her efforts that day, Leticia decided to treat herself. That evening, she went shopping for a dress to wear to the theater with Paul.

"I don't know what to wear here, Auntie," she complained in the department store. "What's the right thing for the theater?" She held up a slinky sky-blue dress.

"Leticia Patrick! Your uncle and I are not allowing you out of the house in that ... that ... you can hardly call that slip of fabric a dress!"

Leticia replaced the dress on the rack. In truth, it wasn't very sensible for a New York winter. "I wonder what Paul would like."

"Hmmmm," Martha mused. "A dress that says, 'Keep your hands to yourself, mister.'"

Leticia laughed. "But your lips are still welcome."

Her aunt gave her a mock-severe glare. "Don't make me call your mother, young woman!"

Leticia laughed harder. "I wonder what Mama would think of Paul if she could meet him."

"She'd say, 'He's not good enough for our Letty,' and she'd be right."

"How do you know, Auntie? You haven't met him either," she reminded Martha.

"I know because *no one* is good enough for our Letty. How about this one?" She held up a billowy, flower-print hausfrau dress with ruffles along the collar and sleeves.

"Oh, Auntie!"

* * *

The punctual Leticia arrived at work the next morning, her thoughts still on the gorgeous evening gown she had finally settled on. The long, flowing ivory dress fit her like water. Spaghetti straps suspended the dress gracefully from her shoulders, and the satiny material almost shimmered like mother-of-pearl as she moved in it. Her aunt had tsk-tsked at its form-fitting cut and plunging neckline but otherwise offered no comment. Leticia couldn't wait to wear it to the theater with Paul.

As she made her way to her cube, the young Jamaican noticed that Melba's door was still closed.

"Ha," said a now vicious Leticia.

She stripped off her winter wardrobe and put on her music. She had been listening to one of the CDs Mr. Foles gave her, over and over. Now she slipped the other CD into the player. Surprisingly, it turned out to be a reggae CD. It started with a popular Bob Marley song, "Three Little Birds." She glanced at the CD cover and was surprised that she hadn't noticed it was *Popular Reggae Artists Greatest Hits*. She was a little surprised Mr. Foles even knew about reggae music.

On her way to get coffee, she ran into Evanne. "Sweetie, I brought you something. I was hurrying to get here before you got your coffee." Evanne winked at her.

Leticia smiled and asked, "What is it?"

"A piece of cheesecake!"

"Oh!"

"Yeah. Let me get rid of the Eskimo stuff, and I'll go with you to get a fresh cup of c-o-f-f-e-e."

"Evanne," Leticia said slowly. "Spit it out. You're dying to tell me something; I can tell." Evanne laughed a little. "So I insist you spit it all out."

"Okay," Evanne whispered conspiratorially. "Tony and I had the best sex last night, and I am still tingling."

Leticia burst out laughing.

After getting their coffee, Leticia left her friend and went past Melba's open office door. Leticia could smell the stench of rotting flesh. She found Melba in the conference room with her laptop and folders of all her small accounts and the major BALI account.

Leticia started laughing again as she headed straight to Frances.

"Good morning, dear," said Frances as she walked up.

"Good morning! Oh, Frances! I have some very good news about my mother, and everyone always asks me about her condition, so I was hoping I could tell the entire office at one time. All I need is about three minutes?"

"That's no problem. Everyone here at Lexhouse is concerned about your mother. What time would you like?"

"About nine a.m. should do."

"That would be great. Consider it done," Frances assured the young woman.

Leticia stuck her head in the conference room where Melba sat alone with all her accounts and laptop. "Good morning, Melba," greeted Leticia. Melba said nothing but drank her coffee from the special mug that Leticia had given her. The disgusting odor was stronger than ever. "What time did you get here? You sure have beaten the crowd," said a gleeful Leticia. "This is going to be great for you."

Sure enough, at that time, Frances used the PA to assemble the office in the conference room; Melba was still there. She was stuck as every person in the office rushed in, even Mr. Foles.

He was the first to speak. "Good morning, everyone!"

Leslie interrupted by muttering, "What is that funk? It smells like a dead animal."

"Uh, Leticia has some news about her mother," Mr. Foles announced. His voice was very nasal as though he couldn't—or wouldn't—breathe through his nose. "Go ahead, Leticia."

At this point, every employee was covering their noses and mouths with their hands. Some employees were hanging their heads; others held handkerchiefs and scarves up to cover their lower faces.

"This will be brief," Leticia said. As she started to speak, she noticed that the employees closest to Melba had started drifting away from the repellent woman. "I received news that Mama is standing. She still cannot walk yet, but she is up. She can also use her right hand to eat with. That is from all the prayers. Thank you all so much for your kindness and prayers, and please, continue to pray for Mama." Almost everyone responded with a nod and a smile at Leticia.

"That's it," said Leticia. "Thanks again!"

Everyone made a mad dash for the exit, eager to get away from the awful smell.

"James," said Tim, Evanne's boss, "get maintenance, will you? We might have something dead in the vents. Maybe a dead rat or something."

"It's especially strong over here," said another worker, pointing in the direction of Melba's office.

Mr. Foles relayed the order to Frances to call maintenance. "Tell them to come and do something before I lose all my staff!" he joked before he, too, rushed out of the room.

Leticia glanced at Melba. It was hard to tell if the woman was embarrassed or not. Her face was again covered in heavy makeup. Leticia walked out with Mr. Foles and thanked him for his consideration.

Melba jumped out of her seat and hurried over. "James, when?"

Mr. Foles looked at Melba with a contorted face. "Excuse me?"

"When is the headquarter account blitz?"

"There's no blitz scheduled for today, and furthermore, with the unpleasant odor from the conference room, we wouldn't be able to hold any meetings in here right now." He turned on his heel and walked away.

Melba stared after him for a moment and then gathered her laptop and all her papers.

Later that morning, Melba came to Leticia and asked the young Jamaican to join her in her office. Leticia turned off her CD player and followed Melba into her office.

"Close the door and sit down," said Melba. Leticia did as she was asked, even though she could barely stand to be in close proximity to her boss. "You're the only one I can talk to," Melba said.

CHAPTER 18

"MY HUSBAND PRETENDS I DON'T exist, and everyone else here is out to get me," Melba told the young Jamaican.

"Oh," said Leticia, unsure how to respond but appreciating the irony nonetheless.

"It's hard work being a female account executive here," Melba said. "I even had to put off having children so I could further my career here! That's how bad it is. These men here are so vicious."

Right, thought Leticia. *The* men *here are vicious.* She stared pointedly back at Melba, even though she knew the oblivious woman couldn't see past the end of her own nose.

"I was ready to explode with the BALI presentation and feedback," Melba continued. Leticia noticed that Melba's left hand was under her desk, resting on her left thigh and making a scratching motion. Leticia bit her lip. She couldn't believe that Melba was still drinking her coffee with one hand and scratching her private area with the other. The odor was now reeking.

Leticia kept a stoic face through all of this.

"But I'm going to get them," Melba said.

Oh, Lord, thought Leticia. She knew that Melba would never think the naïve assistant could deceive her with the idea of the blitz meeting. This made Leticia snicker silently.

"They're all going to get their comeuppance."

There was no way Melba would think that Leticia could come up with a plan to embarrass her. In fact, Leticia had already put such a plan into play for the next day.

Leticia nodded sympathetically. She was rather astonished, however, that Melba was starting to confide in her as though they were friends. If she was the closest thing Melba had to a friend, that was pretty sad for Melba, because Leticia was just shy of considering Melba to be her mortal enemy.

"By the way, the prep work you did for the BALI account sucked."

"What?" Leticia sucked in an outraged breath.

Melba didn't really notice; she just nodded absentmindedly as she continued to scratch her itch. "Yeah, the presentation didn't go so well, but it was because the materials you gave me weren't up to par."

"The materials—that I—! Melba, I gave that information to you to review before you left. If there were any problems, you should have said something then."

Melba just shrugged again and grimaced as she scratched.

Leticia just stared in open-mouthed wonder. First, Melba said Leticia was the only one she could talk to, and then she turned around and berated Leticia's work. After never asking about Leticia's mother. After never thanking Leticia for anything. After throwing Leticia under the bus for Melba's own mistakes. After humiliating and deceiving Leticia repeatedly. After …

Well. "Is there anything else, Melba?"

"More coffee. And don't forget to complete my expense report for Detroit. I need it done today."

Leticia resisted the urge to scowl as she fulfilled Melba's order. Instead, she tried to focus on what she knew was coming the next morning.

At lunch, Evanne took the reggae CD from Leticia to make herself a copy. As she returned it, Melba burst out of her office and flew down to the ladies' room as though she had been thrown by a mini-tornado.

Evanne looked back at Leticia and arched an eyebrow. "When ya gotta go, ya gotta go."

Leticia nodded solemnly, and then both ladies burst out laughing. Pete peeked over the cube wall again. "What's so funny?"

"Melba," they chortled together.

He rolled his eyes. "All right then, don't tell me." He ducked back down.

As they headed to lunch, Evanne said, "Melba is losing weight."

"I think you're right," replied Leticia.

"That lady didn't have much of an ass before; now, her backside looks like a deflated balloon. I wonder if she has cancer."

That brought Leticia up short. "You think?" she asked.

They crossed paths with Melba, who was returning to her office. Melba clutched at Leticia's arm. "Do you have any powder?"

"No, sorry. Are you all right, Melba? You've gone to the doctor; what did they say?"

Melba's eyes flicked over to Evanne, and she sniffed. She pulled Leticia toward her office, and Leticia called over her shoulder, "I'll see you in the lunch room."

Melba started rummaging through her office, apparently trying to find powder. "I spoke to the nurse earlier, and she said all my test results came back. They asked me to come in."

"Oh," said Leticia. That didn't sound good. She didn't know what to think, but again she wanted Melba to get *her* comeuppance. She peered more closely at Melba. The cold sore looked like a solid mass attached to puffed-out lips on a swollen, stretched, splotchy face.

"Yes, I'm going to the doctor this afternoon, so I'll be leaving early."

"Does Frances know?"

"No, but I'll go and tell her."

"Okay. Well, good luck, Melba."

Melba nodded.

Leticia and Evanne shared a quiet lunch. Leticia thought for a moment about Melba's doctor appointment, and her mixed emotions gave way to one certain truth: she wanted Melba to get everything that was coming to her. And Leticia had strong confidence in Mama Dassa. Look what Mama Dassa's plan had already wrought! Look what Mama Dassa had accomplished for Denver and the rest of her family!

Leticia's mother and aunt seemed to think Mama Dassa was some kind of spiritual figure, but as far as she was concerned, Mamma Dassa had acted more like a witch doctor. Her plan was doing something terrible to Melba. Each day brought greater visceral satisfaction to Leticia, even though she displayed an outwardly placid personality.

"Girl, follow me to the bathroom," beamed Evanne.

"What's up?"

"You will see and feel."

Evanne made sure no one else was in the bathroom. She pulled her wig away to display her hair with less bald patches.

"Girl, this tea works; it's working gradually. But, I will take gradual over nothing. I can't thank you enough. If your mother is drinking this tea, I am sure she will recover. This is not a tea; this is a potion."

As they returned to the work area, they immediately heard a hissing sound. Following the noise, they found Frances in Melba's office, keys in one hand, air freshener in the other. She was literally spraying every surface in Melba's office while covering her nose. Melba was nowhere to be seen.

She looked up when she noticed Evanne watching her. She smiled guiltily. "I just left the bathroom, and it smells strongest in there."

"That's the smell of Melba's personality," Evanne said.

Berlina, who had walked up behind them, started laughing. "The smell of a decaying bitch," she said. Leticia gave Berlina a stern look. "Oops, sorry, Leticia, I know she's your boss, but she is a bitch."

Later, Melba came to Leticia's cubicle before leaving for her doctor's appointment. Leticia had to consciously struggle not to gag, and her own voice sounded nasal as she breathed carefully through her mouth.

"I need you to take care of my remaining work—it's on my desk, in my office," Melba said. She gestured vaguely in that direction, distracted.

"Sure, Melba."

The older woman scratched at her temple, and another clump of hair fell to Melba's shoulder, where it seemed to catch on her blouse, and then shifted and fell as if in slow motion to the ground. Both women watched the hair descend, and then Leticia looked back up. Melba's hair did seem thinner, patchier.

"I have to go," Melba said. Her voice was thick. She turned on her heel and practically sprinted out of the office, leaving Leticia with a clump of Melba hair on the ground in her cubicle. Leticia grabbed a tissue, used it to pick up the strands of hair, and deposited the whole mess in her wastebasket as a Cheshire smile adorned her face.

Before her mad dash to get to the doctor, Melba had thrown an envelope on Leticia's desk with her expense receipts.

Leticia started filling out the expense reports, and then with meticulous precision crossed out several receipt totals and handwrote extra money. She signed each paper with Melba's initials, perfectly imitating Melba's handwriting.

Leticia went straight to Frances. The older lady greeted her with her usual smile. "What happened? You look like gloom and doom. Oh my, is it your mother!"

"No, Frances, I just don't want to lose my job," she cried. "I already had a problem with expenses from Melba before. And now!" She showed the altered receipts to Frances. "Melba gave me altered expense receipts *again*, and told me to do as she says or I will be fired. I don't want to lie on these reports. I'm not that kind of person! Please, Frances, I prefer not to do her expense reports anymore. She is making me lie, and I don't want to lose my job." Tears slowly rolled down Leticia's face as Frances could see the fear on the young lady's face.

"Don't worry; you are such a honest worker; just leave the everything with me. Go to the restroom and fix yourself up."

Leticia returned to her cubicle and sat down. She faced her computer monitor, with the rest of her office at her back, and she smiled.

* * *

Friday offered a break in the weather, which shifted from frigidly cold to merely uncomfortably chilly. Leticia didn't really notice so much; the winter weather hadn't been bothering her as much recently. It was like her internal thermometer had been edging up.

At her cubicle, she quickly removed her winter wear. In the office, she was actually too warm.

The atmosphere was festive. In fact, pretty much everyone was wearing jeans, except for Leticia.

"This is dress down day, Leticia." Evanne greeted her with a critical look at Leticia's normal work clothes. "Didn't Melba tell you?"

"No! When did this rule start?"

Evanne shrugged. "This week, I guess. All the managers forwarded to their staff the e-mail that came from corporate. Nationwide, we are now having Fridays as a casual dress day. They claim it promotes happier employees." Evanne certainly looked as if it was working; she was beaming. "Maybe Melba didn't read her e-mail. She's had a lot on her mind recently, having to face God's judgment and all."

"God's judgment?"

"Yeah, for being such an evil whore."

Leticia didn't know whether to feel angry at Melba for not telling her about the dress down day, or to feel amused at Evanne's matter-of-fact appraisal of Melba's situation. She chose to feel both. Even the comeuppance she knew was just moments away didn't soothe her anger.

She took her change purse out of her handbag and went to Melba's office. But Melba was not in.

So, Leticia returned to her cubicle and started her duties for the day.

She had lost track of time when she suddenly heard Melba's voice, ringing shrilly through the office. "She works for me, not you!"

"She works for Lexhouse! You don't own her!" Paul shouted right back.

Heads started poking out of cubes to find the source of the blow-up. Leticia stood up in her cube. The voices sounded as if they were coming from the vicinity of Melba's office, but she couldn't see anything. She heard someone whisper, "At least Melba's good for some drama. Work here's better than reality TV, I tell my husband."

Melba shrieked, "Don't think I haven't noticed those CFM looks you give her!"

Whatever Paul said was lost amid audible gasps, but Leticia frowned. *What* looks?

Melba continued immediately, "The entire office has noticed the way you look at her."

Leticia had a sinking feeling Melba was referring to herself. She didn't know what these "CFM looks" were, but she had a bad feeling about what Melba was saying. She thought she and Paul had been discreet. She thought she had so carefully compartmentalized everything. Besides, they'd only been out once! Magical though it had been.

But in fact, a number of the heads poking over the cube walls began to turn toward Leticia, who sat down. She turned toward her computer. Her face felt warm.

"I don't look at her any way!" Paul shouted. Leticia swallowed. She understood why he said it, but it didn't stop it from being almost harder to take than what Melba was saying, which was barely comprehensible.

There were a few more shouts and ripostes, but Leticia could no longer make out what they were saying. She thought she heard Mr. Foles's voice shortly after that, too, but she couldn't make out his words either. She had a sinking feeling that no good would come of it, but she was puzzled by what Melba meant exactly.

She decided she needed an expert point of view. She stood and resolutely marched to Evanne's cube. "Did you hear all that? What was that about?" she asked.

"Oh, hi, girl. Dunno. Melba being Melba, as usual."

"What do 'CFM looks' mean?"

Strangely, Evanne didn't make eye contact, but she answered readily enough. "Come fuck me looks."

Leticia face went from warm to hot. "Come … come … come *what* me looks?"

Evanne turned a gaze on Leticia that seemed almost pitying. She shrugged. "You know, looks that say, 'I can't wait to get into your panties.' Guess Melba thought that would push one of Paul's buttons. Who knows? I wouldn't worry about it, 'Ticia. You can't place any weight on the crazy things Melba says or does. No one else does."

Leticia nodded stiffly and began a long march back to her cube. She had been looking forward to today, because she had special plans for Melba, but this turn of events was souring the morning.

As she finally saw Melba for the day, the ire grew. Melba was casually dressed. Leticia realized that Melba did not tell her about dress down day on purpose.

She played her gospel CD to calm herself. It didn't work.

About ten o'clock, Berlina breezed by. "There's a flower box for Melba sitting on Corinda's desk," she said in a loud huff.

"Melba got flowers?" Pete asked skeptically from the next cube over. "She probably sent them to herself." Leticia chuckled. "Did Corinda say who delivered them?"

Berlina shook her head. "She found them lying there when she got in this morning." She dashed away to spread the word even further. Everyone within an earshot heard the loud announcement from Berlina. With utmost curiosity, everyone piled to the reception area to see these flowers for the most hated person in the office.

Leticia wasn't going to miss this for the world, especially after this morning. She sauntered over to the receptionist's desk. She had enlisted her uncle to deliver the box; she had asked him to pose as a deliveryman, but apparently, he was able to get in early and deposit the box without being seen. Even better. For his help, her Aunt Martha paid him a handsome romantic fee.

Leticia was not the only curious one. A small crowd had gathered around the receptionist's desk to gawk at the unopened box. Leticia went to stand next to Evanne. Corinda was unsuccessfully trying to shoo people away. "She's on her way to pick it up," she said irritably. "Nothing to see but a box."

But everyone had the sense that a show was about to play itself out. Even Melba, who arrived with a flourish, her personal problems momentarily forgotten. Not by the crowd though—everyone averted their eyes from her. "Flowers? For me?" Melba asked dramatically. "Oh, that wonderful husband of mine! That man loves me so much; he is my heart. Oh, I do hope they're not tulips. I do so prefer roses."

Leticia had to stifle a grin. Didn't Melba tell her that her husband was not sleeping with her anymore? *This woman can pretend anything,* Leticia mused to herself.

Melba untied the fancy ribbon binding the box and cradled it like a baby in her arms. Grinning triumphantly, she slid off the lid, positioning herself so she could show off her flowers. Instead, she found a box filled with tissue paper and hemorrhoid wipes, anti-bacterial soaps, Vagisil, and a variety of powder and liquid douches. Atop the personal hygiene products lay a note which, in large letters, spelled: "CLEAN YOUR DAMN SELF UP. WE HAVE TO WORK WITH YOU."

Melba stared at the contents of the box, her mouth moving without making any sounds.

Her entire face was crimson red. The embarrassment was too hard to hide. Then someone in the crowd started to laugh, quickly covered with a cough. Someone else followed suit. Other observers started whispering excitedly, looking at Melba out of the corners of their eyes and smirking. Melba flushed as red as Leticia had ever seen her and slammed the lid back on the box. She left the box right there on Corinda's desk. She rushed off to her office. Sporadic laughter spread through just about every cube in the office. Even giggles from some of the account executives.

Leticia followed. Her amusement at Melba's humiliation took backseat to a renewed sense of anger when she realized Melba had dressed to take advantage of the casual day herself but couldn't be bothered to mention it to Leticia.

Leticia swallowed her irritation—she was certainly getting used to it by now—and said, "How are you feeling? I said a prayer for you last night. Melba, some people can be so cruel. You did not deserve that." Leticia put all the sympathy she could manage into her voice.

"I need my coffee" was Melba's only response. She was still flushed.

"Sure, no problem."

Leticia headed to the lunch room and went through the usual ritual with Mama Dassa's sticks.

"Here we go," she said as she handed the mug to Melba afterward.

Melba started to drink her coffee when Leticia closed the door. "Did I tell you to close my door?" Melba snapped.

"Er, no, but this is sensitive and private. I want you to know that I prayed for you last night, and I asked for you to regain your health and the happy demeanor you once had. I hope the doctor had good news for you."

Melba took another swallow of coffee and said, "Nothing. All the test results were negative. They have never seen anything like this before. 'Cosmetic,' the doctor said. Cosmetic!" Melba's voice held the shrill note of borderline hysteria. "My body is falling apart, people here hate me, and he just asks if I'm under any stress!"

"So it's not cancerous?" Leticia asked hesitantly.

"No, he said it's not cancer."

"Good." Leticia meant that. She wanted Melba to get what was coming to her, but not send her to the afterlife.

"My doctor said he didn't understand it," Melba went on. "The fool mumbled something about writing a medical paper about it. I don't want him to write a damn effing paper about me; I want my good looks back!"

"Sometimes, illnesses are passed down in families. Maybe that's it?"

"The doctor asked that, too. No one in my family has ever had anything like this. Technically, they just don't know what it is. They said the most likely cause is stress. They're treating the symptoms, and they told me to try to take things easy. Take things easy! Everyone here is trying to get me fired, and he tells me to take it easy. Effing morons."

"Well, try not to stress yourself out. Anytime I can help, please let me know." And Leticia returned to her cubicle with a grin again befitting the Cheshire cat.

Twenty minutes later, she saw Melba run past on her way to the bathroom. Fifteen minutes later, another trip. After the tenth trip, Leticia started chuckling. It was kind of comical.

"What is wrong with your boss?"

Leticia swung around with a little gasp. She hadn't heard Berlina approach. "Berlina!" she said and put her hand on her chest. She could feel her heart pounding from the surprise. "I didn't hear you." To her surprise, a loud embarrassing laugh escaped from her, turned into a couple of coughs. "Berlina, I apologize, I don't mean to laugh, but I just read the funniest e-mail a friend sent to me."

"Have you been to the bathroom?"

"No, not since this morning. Why?"

Berlina leaned forward eagerly. *Ah, this is why Berlina came over,* Leticia thought. She had some good gossip, and if Berlina didn't share the scoop with half the office, she'd just explode. "Well, I just followed Melba in there, you understand. And Melba went into one of the stalls, right? And I swear she sounded like a freight train and smelled like a barnyard filled with manure. No one can use the bathroom; can you believe it? I didn't even think a person could produce noises and smells like that. Do you think Melba is the cause of the smell in the office? I mean, you spend more time with her than anyone; what do you think? It always seems to follow her!"

Berlina stopped and took several deep breaths after her rapid-fire speech. She blinked several times in quick succession, her plump bosom heaving, her small dark eyes focused intently on Leticia, who was apparently the office Melba expert.

"Oh," said Leticia. "I don't know. I hope she is okay. I was so busy; I was not paying attention."

"Hm. Someone has to tell this to Frances," Berlina declared as though it were an important duty.

"I will," said Leticia.

"Oh, no!" Berlina looked horrified at the thought that someone else might end up privy to good gossip first. "I'm going to ask Frances to check on Melba."

Berlina left, and Leticia started giggling. She was working in an office populated with crazy people. Evanne with her pantry of chips and closet of torture-wear, calmly talking about God's judgment on Melba and the smell of Melba's bitchy personality. Berlina absolutely delighting in the great juicy gossip Melba's odors produced.

A few minutes later, Frances went into the ladies' room. She didn't last a quarter of a second in there. "Whew!" she said with her hands covering her mouth. Leticia watched as Frances headed into the storage room and came out with three large aerosol cans of air deodorizers. She took a deep breath as if she was getting ready to plunge into a pool and then returned to the bathroom.

Then Melba stepped out of the bathroom. She froze and looked to the side. Leticia leaned forward, over her desk, and followed Melba's gaze. Apparently, a group of gawkers, Berlina at their center, had gathered to keep surveillance on the bathroom.

Melba slunk back to her office, but she hit the restroom no fewer than twenty times over the course of the day.

Shortly before lunch the same day, the phone rang, and Leticia glanced at the ID panel. Paul. Her heart beat a little faster. After the blowout earlier, which the entire office had heard, Leticia didn't know what to expect.

She picked up the receive and said, "Hello?" Her Jamaican twang sounded particularly pronounced in her own ears.

"Hi, Leticia." His voice was flat, distant.

This isn't good, Leticia thought. Her heart thundered.

CHAPTER 19

"P
AUL."
"Look, I don't want to make you feel awkward or anything. We should probably go ahead and postpone the play this weekend until another time." He sounded gentle, but firm.

Leticia licked her lips. "Is this—"

Paul interrupted. "You're a great worker, Leticia. Lexhouse is lucky to have you. We should probably leave it at that."

A moment of silence passed. Leticia didn't know how to respond. "Paul—"

He interrupted again, and this time, there was just the barest hint of pleading in his voice. "I've enjoyed showing you New York, and I hope you'll continue to see the sights of the city. But I need to really focus on work right now." He paused, then added, "I'm sorry."

Another awkward silence. Her thoughts flashed to the brand new dress hanging in her closet. "Okay, Paul," Leticia said. "Whatever you think is best."

"Thank you, Leticia. Keep up the good work."

Click.

Leticia sat for another moment with the receiver to her ear, before slowly setting it back down. Her thoughts churned, and thoughts of Paul washed into contempt for Melba. She remembered the screechy, horrible things Melba said to Paul earlier.

Melba did this. Leticia's heart pounded with anger. Melba did this to Leticia and Paul. Bitter bile burned in Leticia's throat. It wasn't enough for Melba to take Leticia's satisfaction and happiness just at work.

Leticia craned her head around, staring in the direction of Melba's office. She didn't stand, so she was actually staring at her cube wall, but her mind filled with a visualization of the scrawny, bleach-blonde woman sitting at her desk, grinning nastily to herself at the sorrow she sowed all around her.

Leticia's eyes burned with fury. *It's on, Melba,* she thought to herself. She had already decided that, of course, but this took things to a whole new level. *You've messed with the wrong woman's heart. You'll get yours now. A fake delivery is just a prank. Now it's time for justice and revenge.*

At lunch, Leticia felt doubly enraged when she realized she was literally the only person in the lunch room wearing work clothes: a nice pleated skirt and ruffled blouse instead of jeans.

"Evanne, please say something to cheer me up. I am so pissed that Melba didn't tell me about casual day. It makes me wonder what else she hasn't told me that's important."

"Okay. Here's a joke. On your way back to the work area, make a point to walk past Frances."

"Why?"

Evanne winked. "Trust me."

For the first time, Leticia noticed what Evanne was eating. "Pizza! I am shocked!"

"Well, Tony came home last night with two large pies. I thought about bringing you a piece, but I wasn't sure if you eat pizza."

"Yes, I do."

"What is that you're having?" Evanne inclined her head at the odd fruit.

"This is a jicama. You peel it and eat it raw. Would you like a piece?"

"No, thanks. It might spoil the taste of my pineapple pizza. But I learned something new today. Next time I'm in the supermarket, I'll pick one up."

"I learned something new, too," said Leticia. "I did not know that you can have pineapple on pizza." She thought of the sweet fruit mixing with tangy, acidic tomato sauce. It seemed like an odd combination to her.

"Yes, you can."

As they returned to work, Leticia followed Evanne's advice and detoured to walk past Frances.

"Hi, Frances," said Leticia.

"Hi, Leticia. Why aren't you dressed casually today?"

"Oh, that. I didn't know. No one told me."

"Oh, sorry, dear. Well, Melba. She has other things on her mind, doesn't she?"

"She came in dressed casually," Leticia couldn't stop herself from pointing.

"Well … yes." Frances couldn't seem to think of anything to say to that. "Well, James is letting everyone go home at three o'clock today, so it's not so bad, I hope."

"Really!"

Frances nodded. "Maintenance is going to inspect the area for, ah, for the source of the, erm, odor." Frances was typically a little generous with blush on her cheeks, but she reddened even more than usual.

"Oh, that's good," said Leticia with a smile.

Leticia walked into the restroom, where she found Melba almost waddling like a duck, as if she had something stuck between her legs.

"Melba?" Leticia asked with her hand covering her mouth and nose. "Frances said everyone is going home at three o'clock today."

"I know. But not me," said Melba. "I am an executive here. I have things to do." Despite her odd walk, distorted face and smelly body, Melba stuck up her nose and left the ladies' room. The horrible smell lingered, however, so Leticia went to use the restroom on another floor. She wasn't the only one.

At fifteen minutes to 3:00 p.m., Leticia noticed everyone leaving. She felt another rush of anger at Melba, who had said, "I know." If Frances hadn't told her, Leticia wouldn't have known. Since there was no PA announcement, Mr. Foles must have left it up to the managers to inform their subordinates.

Evanne came up to say goodbye. She stepped into Leticia's cubicle and slowly pulled her wig back a few inches.

"Oh my word, it's growing! Your hair! It's looking great!" Leticia whispered.

"Day by day, a little longer and a little softer. It is like that all over my head. I have hair!" Evanne was grinning ear to ear, her eyes shining with delight.

"Hey, do you mind waiting a minute?" asked Leticia. "I'll walk out with you."

"Sure, my true friend."

Leticia shut her system down and started layering on her winter clothes. As they left, they noticed Mr. Foles, Frances, and someone from HR entering Melba's office.

"What do you want?" they heard Melba snap. Not the smartest tone to use with your boss and an HR rep. Evanne and Leticia exchanged a glance.

The group closed Melba's office door and tightened the already closed blinds.

When they reached the lobby, Leticia and Evanne wished each other a great weekend and parted for separate transportation. Leticia quite happily left Melba to the mercies of upper management.

She just wanted to know what was happening.

PART FIVE—HOME BITTER HOME

CHAPTER 20

L ETICIA STEPPED OFF THE BUS on Monday morning and sucked in a great draught of fresh, cold air. Well, cold air, anyway. The diesel fumes and an odd mélange of food odors mixed with the faint hint of garbage permeated the atmosphere. Leticia paid little attention to those details, though.

It was one of the loveliest Monday mornings she'd yet faced in New York. Cold, yes, but the sky above the skyscrapers was cloudless blue, and the buildings themselves seemed more like gleaming silver than tarnished iron in the crisp light.

Last week had brought with it a pleasing sequence of events with Melba. The full scope of Melba's deeds and everyone else's certainty that Melba's inner ugliness was manifesting outwardly left Leticia feeling much lighter and excited to see what this week would unveil.

Over the weekend, Aunt Martha noticed a more contented niece. Apparently, Mamma Dassa was at work. It showed on Leticia's ever-smiling face.

Leticia arrived at the office to see two workmen each pushing a new executive chair, the pristine cushions still wrapped in plastic. She smiled at the two burly workers as they stood in the elevator. When the doors opened, they headed toward Frances, and Leticia moved to her own cubicle.

She peeled off her layers of winter clothing—fewer now than usual, but she just hadn't been feeling the cold as intensely the last week or two—and sat down. She noticed a sticky note on her computer monitor.

"Leticia, please come see me ASAP. —Frances."

Leticia rushed up. On her way to Frances's desk, she noticed Melba's office was wide open and missing a chair. Melba's personal belongings all remained, although the mug wasn't sitting on the desk.

"Good morning, Frances!" Leticia greeted Mr. Foles's assistant.

"Oh, hello, dear! Just give me a moment to direct these gentlemen"— she nodded at the two workers with the new executive chairs—"and I'll be right with you."

She went to turn on the light in the conference room and instructed the men to put one of the chairs in the open slot. Melba's usual seat, Leticia noted with an upticked eyebrow.

Then Frances turned to the other man and directed him to Melba's office. Both men removed the wrapping from the chairs while Frances surveyed their efforts. "Good work, guys." She dismissed them with a smile.

Then she returned to Leticia. "This is going to be a harried day. Mr. Foles and HR will be speaking with you after the morning meeting."

An unsettled expression fell over Leticia's face. Frances patted her arm. "No, dear, it's not bad news, not bad news at all. And it won't take long. I'll call you when they're ready. Just be prepared. It should be right after his routine Monday morning meeting, all right?"

Leticia was more curious than ever. She returned to her area and noticed, for the first time, that the unpleasant odor Melba had left in her wake last week was entirely gone. She went into Melba's office and sniffed surreptitiously. The scent was pleasant, reminiscent of evergreen trees and mountain streams.

More curious than ever, she went to get her coffee and ran into Evanne as the older woman stepped out of the bathroom.

"I had to go in there and see how it smelled." Evanne grinned at Leticia. "How was your weekend?"

"Wonderful! I can't wait to tell you about it at lunch," replied Leticia with buoyant spirits and a mischievous grin.

When Leticia returned to her desk with her coffee, she found a cheese Danish on her desk. "What is this?" she asked Evanne, who was still grinning from ear to ear.

"I was hoping you'd like it with your coffee. It's a cheese Danish!"

"I know. Good sex again?" Leticia asked, amused.

Evanne stood straight up and sang in her proudest, loudest soprano voice, "Yessss!"

Several heads poked up over their cubicles like gophers peeking out of their holes.

"Matter of fact," Evanne added, "when are you going to get some?"

"A lady never kisses and tells," Leticia replied with poise. Then she added with a throaty chuckle, "Until lunch."

"Ooh, I can't wait!"

Both ladies laughed, and Leticia thought, *This is why I like Evanne so much. I laugh with her so easily, as I do with my family. Even if she has unusual eating and dressing habits. But we all have our secrets, don't we?*

And Leticia chuckled some more.

They returned to their daily duties, until Frances finally called Leticia to Mr. Foles's office.

Leticia entered, wringing her hands nervously.

"Why are you so nervous?" Mr. Foles asked with a fatherly smile. "There is nothing, absolutely nothing, for you to be nervous about. Please have a seat."

As Leticia sat, another lady entered and closed their door.

"Hi! You must be Leticia! I'm Pamela from human resources!" The cheerful woman punctuated every statement with energy and enthusiasm. Her chestnut eyes matched her short hair perfectly, and she kept nodding as though keeping beat with some internal tune. If "perky" had a picture next to it in the dictionary, it would show Pamela from human resources.

"Nice to meet you," said Leticia shyly, her curiosity edging up with each passing second.

"This meeting is to clear up some things about your responsibilities!" Pamela said.

"Okay."

"But first, here are two paychecks for you. One is your regular check, and the other is for the overtime you spent last week working late with Melba when you came in at five thirty a.m."

Leticia looked shocked as she took the two checks. "But … w-why?"

"It appears Melba didn't submit your time sheet with your overtime, so we're remedying that for you!" Pamela gave her a rueful grin.

Mr. Foles added, "We had a talk with Melba last week, and it turns out she's been, ah, distracted, and hasn't been, um, appropriately communicative with you. We found out she had instructed you to come in early that day. Hence, the two checks. We're sorry for the, er, misunderstanding."

"Thank you so much," Leticia said, genuinely moved and grateful. She had never expected to see any overtime for the extra time Melba tricked out of her.

"We take care of our employees here," Mr. Foles said. "Or try to, anyway."

"Do you have it?" Pamela asked.

"Oh, yes, let me get it from Frances," Mr. Foles replied. "Frances! Please bring it in." He looked back at Leticia and added gingerly, "Leticia, here's the situation. Melba will be working from home for a while. We're giving you a document courier case with a lock on it. Melba has a key, and Frances has a key. Now, every day starting today, you will leave at three o'clock and take the case to Melba. You'll return the next morning and give the case to Frances. Frances will give you forty dollars each day for cab fare to Melba's place. Frances has the address and directions for you. Does all that make sense?"

Leticia listened seriously and nodded.

"Please make sure you get a receipt for the fare to Melba's. Then, take a cab from Melba's to your home. Comprende?"

"Yes," said a smiling Leticia.

"We don't need a receipt for the fare to your home from Melba's!" Pamela added.

Leticia sighed with relief, and Mr. Foles smiled indulgently. "Is that it?" she asked.

Mr. Foles let out a little laugh. "Yes, that's it. Easier than counting a barrel of monkeys. Starting today. Come see Frances at three o'clock to get the case."

Pamela stood and said, "And if there's anything you need from me or HR, please let me know!" She excused herself.

"Ah, Leticia," Mr. Foles added. "Before you go, did your family send any more of those buns?"

"No," laughed Leticia.

"Also, I just wanted to mention: As you may recall, we had a, ah, stern conversation before you left for Jamaica. How I regretted having to speak that way when you were leaving to attend to your badly injured mother."

"It's okay, sir," Leticia said neutrally.

Mr. Foles nodded. "Well, based on our conversation with Melba, I'm not sure we, er, fully understood the situation. I just wanted to let you know, we're very happy with your performance here. We wouldn't trust you with this important task otherwise. I just wanted you to know that you have my full confidence."

Mr. Foles put an odd emphasis on "you," and Leticia wondered what it meant. Maybe her as opposed to Melba, in whom Lexhouse was losing confidence? Well, how could they not? Melba was acting like a harpy who'd overdosed on crazy.

"Thank you, sir," Leticia said with real feeling.

"Very good. Enjoy the rest of your day."

"Yes, sir!"

As Leticia stepped away, Frances smiled up at her from her desk. "See! I told you it wasn't bad."

Leticia smiled, put her checks in her pocket, and returned to her duties.

Evanne was already waiting at her cubicle. *I'm popular today!* Leticia thought with a smile.

"I can't wait till lunch!" Evanne exclaimed. "My sources told me and Berlina that the entire office was fumigated. It took the crew, working twenty-four hours in shifts over the entire weekend, to get the stench out."

They both laughed.

Evanne was so excited by this bit of news, she didn't say anything more but turned on her heel to share with others.

It wasn't until lunch that she noticed Leticia's more relaxed and confident manner. "I am sure it is because of the witch," Evanne declared. "Without her here, everyone is happier."

And it seemed true. Leticia did feel more relaxed. But she didn't feel happier. It still felt as if Melba was winning, since the bitch had taken Paul from Leticia. But Leticia was still able to take grim satisfaction in the turn of events, and she felt more determined than ever to make Melba twitch twitch with Mama Dassa's instructions.

Leticia wasn't the only person who seemed more relaxed and carefree, even if it wasn't dress down day anymore.

"We won't talk about her," said Leticia.

"At least her funky smell isn't rotting the office anymore."

That was another change. It seemed as though last week, people were reluctant to attribute the odor directly to Melba. Instead, most of the workers conjectured that maybe a rat had died in the vents. But now they didn't hesitate to blame Melba, and everyone had their theories about what was going on. Most of them revolved around Melba's personality or vindictiveness, and Leticia learned a lot of things about Melba she hadn't known.

"She once took credit for a presentation I put together for her," Leticia overheard another assistant say at one point.

"She tried to blame me for technical problems with equipment she was using," someone else replied.

"I am sure she sabotaged a promotion for me," yet another person confided. "I'm not sure how, but you should have seen her. So ugly before, and then practically gloating after I didn't get it. I had to walk away from her before I started crying. I wouldn't give her the satisfaction!"

"It's karma, I'm telling you. The universe is bitch-slapping her for being such a bitch!"

"Whatever. That stuff's just hocus pocus. It's just coincidence."

"Whatever it is," Berlina declared, "she's getting her just desserts." Berlina told all kinds of stories about underhanded things Melba had done to try to undermine Paul. Leticia was shocked; except for their last argument, she had only ever seen Paul be polite, albeit distant, with Melba. But if Melba had done half the things Berlina now accused her of (and knowing Berlina, it probably *was* only half the things), well, Leticia felt a surge of righteousness for her actions. It wasn't just herself that she, with Mama Dassa's assistance, had helped.

"For one thing, she actually called Paul's clients, one by one," Berlina confided confidentially to everyone who would listen, "and tried to steal them all. I mean, not obviously, of course; otherwise, they would have fired her ass. But she called them and talked smack about Paul to them all. Some of his relationships with them never really recovered. Bitch!"

Berlina's stories about Melba always ended with "Bitch!" That's how the listener knew any given anecdote had ended. But she usually moved on immediately to the next story. "And I heard," she began in a conspiratorial whisper, "that management checked her e-mail, and she's been e-mailing clients about going off on her own and taking them with her! Stealing clients! And falsifying expense reports! Bitch!"

"Really?" Leticia asked in as shocked a voice as she could muster. "She didn't say anything to me about leaving Lexhouse."

"That was the final nail in her coffin, that bitch."

"'Final nail,' Berlina, I have never heard that term before," Leticia lied. She almost startled herself; the lie had just come out. But indeed, she well knew that she was the hammer that drove that nail straight into Melba's coffin and hopefully her career.

"You would have done a happy dance for sure!" Evanne said, laughing. "So what do you think of all this, Leticia? You work closer with her than any of us."

Leticia took a long, deep breath and looked somber. "She's hard to work for, but I wouldn't wish whatever's happening to her on anyone."

"You're a better woman than I am!"

Berlina looked skeptical. "But she's more horrible to you than anyone else. It's like she has it out for you."

"She's just very driven," Leticia said. "She'll do whatever it takes to succeed. Sometimes, that's too much."

"That may be," said Evanne. "Maybe. But I'll tell you this: in the end, people always get theirs back. Melba behaves like a witch, it'll come back and bite her in the ass. Mm-hmm." She nodded emphatically and poked her finger toward Leticia to make her point.

"She *is* starting to look and smell like a witch," said Berlina.

"Mm-hm." Evanne took a bite. "And her life will be filled with witchy people just as bad as she is. One after the other." Still chewing, she turned back to Leticia. "By the way, what happened this weekend?"

Relieved to have a change of subject, Leticia answered eagerly. "Well, madam, let me tell you! Miss Martha invited me to her church, and this man was sitting two pews in front of me."

"I hope this man did not try to make a move on you in church!"

"No, no. Eat your papaya and listen," Leticia said sternly. "No, he just kept turning around and smiling at me. He had these big broad lips."

"How old was he?"

"Around thirty. He was not bad looking. He was certainly dressed very well. Nice expensive suit. I did smile back at him, but only once, toward the end of the service."

"Playing hard to get," Evanne quipped.

Leticia continued, "After the service, Miss Martha and I were leaving, and he came up to us and said something to Miss Martha. I didn't hear what he said because his back was toward me. At first, I was very put off that he interrupted us just to speak to Miss Martha, with his back to me. I thought, *How rude.* But then I heard Miss Martha say, 'I will introduce you.'

"So Miss Martha turns to me and says, 'Miss Leticia, this is Frank; he is a member here, and since this is your first time, he wanted to welcome you.'

"I said, 'Okay.' Girl! I almost fell over. The man opened his mouth, and he had no front teeth. None at all! No front teeth! He had a toothless smile. We shook hands, and I could not stop staring at his mouth. That man was dentally impaired."

"At thirty?" Evanne asked. "Poor man."

Leticia nodded. "He must have realized, because he apologized and said he was waiting for new dentures. He went on to ask if he could call on me. I told him I don't have a private phone."

"No private phone?" interrupted Evanne. "Girl, no checking account, no savings account, no bills, no private phone." She shook her head.

Again, Leticia continued as if she hadn't heard. "All of a sudden, Miss Martha gave him her phone number. So far he has not called, so I am safe. But this was just yesterday."

"Lady, I bet he will call, as soon as he gets his teeth," Evanne said with a snicker. Then she paused and added with a wicked gleam in her eye, "But maybe it'd be better if he didn't wait."

Leticia looked at her quizzically.

Evanne explained, "You know how blind people have better hearing, that kind of thing? Maybe dentally impaired people have better tongues. Mm-hmm, I went there."

Leticia stared at Evanne for a few seconds and then burst out laughing. She couldn't remember when she had laughed so hard. "Evanne!" she gasped. "You are terrible!"

Evanne just grinned.

"I don't know if I can go out with him," Leticia said when she had quieted down. "I have a phobia of men without teeth."

After lunch, they stopped at the restroom, and Evanne breathed deeply and contentedly. "Ah! No rotting flesh. By the way, did you know that they had to replace the chairs Melba had used?"

"No, I didn't see that," Leticia said, thinking of the workman she had watched. "Really?"

"Yes, it's true. They replaced the one in her office and the one she mostly used in the conference room. Apparently they, um, absorbed the odor the most." She wrinkled her nose and made a face at Leticia, who laughed.

"That's gross, Evanne! Wow."

* * *

At three o'clock sharp, Leticia reported to Frances. She had closed out her work for the day and had mentally steeled herself to deal with Melba. She collected the carrier case and the forty dollars, and then she headed back into the lunch room.

She prepared some paper towels with Mama Dassa's sticks according to the usual method, humming as she waited. There had been a couple of moments last week when she wondered whether she was doing the right thing, but her faith was entirely restored that Melba was getting her due.

She retreated to the ladies' room and wiped down the entire carrying case with the wet paper towels. She put the paper towels in her pocket and left the building.

She provided Melba's address to the taxi driver. He used a GPS device to help him take Leticia directly to Melba's building.

"So, this is the famous Chelsea district of Manhattan that I have heard so much about," Leticia said to herself as she exited the taxi. The brownstone apartment buildings were more attractive than what she had expected. Some had bodegas and eateries on the ground floor with individual apartments on the high floors. Although the area held a trendy flavor, it would have been more cosmopolitan without those pronounced fire escapes in the front of every building.

Leticia was careful to get a receipt for the taxi before proceeding into the building. Melba lived on the sixth floor. Thankfully, there was an elevator. Leticia stepped into it alongside an elderly lady with a tiny Pomeranian who immediately started yapping at Leticia.

Leticia had the case in her right hand. When the door closed, the dog started growling and snarling at Leticia. "I am sorry, miss; I don't know what is bothering Dixie. She is usually so friendly," the woman apologized to Leticia.

Leticia shrugged it off. She remembered Fala's strong reaction to the pillowcase. Leticia placed the case in her left hand, and the dog started pulling toward Leticia's left side, growling and barking.

"Maybe he smells your lunch or something," the old lady suggested. She clearly felt very bad about her dog's behavior.

Leticia nodded and said, "Yes'm, maybe that's it." Leticia just smiled and waved it off. The lady and her dog left the elevator on the fourth floor. Dixie was still twisting and turning in the woman's arms as the dog tried to get at the case. The woman continued to admonish Dixie until Leticia couldn't hear them anymore.

Leticia grinned to herself. She knew without a doubt that Mamma Dassa's stuff was working. Sometimes, animals could sense things people couldn't, and if the sticks and paper towels and pillowcase evoked such intense reactions from dogs, Leticia assumed it meant they each held a powerful aura.

Before she knocked on Melba's door, Leticia retrieved the still-damp paper towel from her pocket and wiped Melba's doorknob for a good thirty seconds.

Someone from the neighboring apartment—a stooped, elderly man with a walking cane—exited his apartment at the same time. He noticed what Leticia was doing and nodded his approval. "I don't blame you for wanting to disinfect the door," he said. "I think someone in there is sick."

He turned around and walked toward the elevator, his walking stick click-clacking along the floor.

Leticia pocketed the paper towel and then knocked. She heard Melba's voice announce, "One minute!"

When she opened the door, Leticia's eyes widened in shock as a wave of the familiar stench rolled over her.

Leticia had been very curious to see Melba, but now she just wanted to hurry and get out of there. Melba seemed even skinnier than usual, and without her pancake makeup, the puffy redness covering her face was startlingly apparent. Leticia could barely stand to look at Melba directly. The woman was wearing a thin cotton nightgown, and she was walking with her butt up in the air and her legs at least two feet apart, waddling more like a duck than ever.

"How … how are you?" Leticia inquired politely.

Melba scowled. She went to the sofa and laid down on her side. "This is the only position where I can get some relief," she said.

Leticia noticed Melba was using some pillows, one of which was covered in a very familiar pillowcase. Leticia suppressed a smile. It wasn't hard: now that the door was closed, the foul odor was almost overpowering.

"Give me a few minutes; I'll get the stuff for you," Melba snapped. Her mood had clearly not improved at all. "Do you know," she continued, "I've been to an oncologist, dermatologist, gynecologist, and every other -ologist my doctor can think of, and you know what they all say? Every one of them? Do you know what they say ails me?"

Leticia just shook her head. She was terribly curious to hear the answer.

CHAPTER 21

"STRESS," MOANED MELBA. "STRESS! THEY think it's stress! Look at me!" the woman practically screeched. "My skin is raw and red and awful all over, and I have to wear an ice pack as a diaper all the time."

"Oh, bless your heart," Leticia said disingenuously.

"Every doctor has said they've never seen anything like this before. They've prescribed everything they can think. Now they think maybe I'm having an allergic reaction.

"And to make matters worse, my darling husband"—Melba practically spat this part—"thinks that I have had an affair and caught something incurable. He is threatening to leave me. I am totally faithful, Leticia! Well," she amended, "mostly. I'm as faithful as he is!"

Leticia wondered just how faithful that really was. "Does he have any symptoms?" she asked with insincere sympathy.

"No, he is totally okay." She sounded angry about it. She added in a low whisper, "At first, I thought he had given me something. Wouldn't be the first time, the rat bastard." Then she burst into tears. "But I love him, damn him. Why is he leaving me in my time of need?"

After learning that Melba had cheated on him, Leticia certainly had no sympathy. Although it did sound like the two of them deserved each other.

Leticia looked around and noticed photographs of the couple. She mentally confirmed that she had given the cake to the right man, at least.

"I will continue to pray for you," Leticia assured Melba. "Prayer can help. Prayer helped my mama, you know."

But Melba didn't seem to notice. She was lost in her pity party. "I'll get the files for you," she mumbled. She waddled over to her desk. Using her key, she opened the case and placed several folders in it. Then she snapped the case closed and locked it.

"See you tomorrow," Leticia said as she walked Melba to the door.

Melba didn't reply. She locked the door behind Leticia.

The young Jamaican kept the money for the other taxi and instead used public transportation to get home. Her meeting with Melba had not taken long, thankfully, so she actually got home earlier than usual.

* * *

On Tuesday morning, Leticia went straight to Frances without even shedding her winter clothing first. She handed the executive assistant both the courier case and the taxi receipt.

"Good morning, and thank you," Frances said. "Did everything go okay? You look more at ease."

"Oh, yes, everything went fine, and I do feel more relaxed."

"I don't blame you," Frances whispered, and then looked slightly abashed as though she had said something she shouldn't. Well, Frances was probably privy to a lot of private information through Mr. Foles, and her job was to protect confidential information.

Frances put the case on Mr. Foles's desk, and Leticia returned to her work area. She took off her coat and scarf, and then went to Evanne's area. "I was waiting for you before I went to get my morning coffee," she greeted her friend. "Just in case you had good sex again!" She looked around as if wondering where her morning pastry was.

"Sorry, sweetie, it's going to be just coffee this morning. Did Mr. Toothless call?" Evanne whispered. Today she was wearing a brunette wig that had been spiced up with some red glitter, so her head practically sparkled every time she moved.

Leticia peered closely at her. "Is something different about your eyes?"

Evanne looked pleased that she had noticed. "I'm trying some of those colored contact lenses. I was wondering if anyone would notice."

"It's a pretty big change from brown to purple," Leticia observed.

Evanne giggled. "I'm just a big chameleon."

"That you are!"

"So, Mr. Toothless? Did he call?"

"No. I guess he is still waiting on those dentures." They both hooted with laughter as they went to the lunch room.

"What is it?" Evanne asked after they had both settled down.

"What are you talking about?"

Evanne was eyeing her up and down. "You seem so free, not as uptight, timid, or scared as a rabbit as you used to be."

"Uptight!" Leticia protested.

"And timid and scared. Maybe it is the church service?" Evanne repeated.

Leticia thought for a moment. *It is called the services of Mama Dassa,* she thought to herself. Aloud, she said, "Yes, maybe it's the church service."

"No, no, it's something else. Hmm. There is a peace about you. Oh! I know what it is. It is not having that bitch of a boss here in the office!"

"Well, it's definitely not Mr. Toothless," Leticia replied with a snort.

The ladies returned to their cubicles, put on their music, and went to work.

Berlina passed by Leticia and heard the same music coming from both Evanne's and Leticia's areas. "Is this a deal or what?" she asked. "Listening to the same music. What's up with that? By the way, Leticia, you seem much calmer than usual, like a load of manure has been lifted off your shoulder."

"Don't use that word!" Evanne called from her area. "Remember that smell from last week."

"Right. Anyhow, I'd like to make a copy of your music, Leticia. You have good taste. Is it a tape or a CD?"

Both Leticia and Evanne said "CD" at the same time.

"What are you now, the echo twins?"

"Here, Berlina, take mine," Evanne said, walking over with the CD in hand.

"Thank you, mada—oof!"

Berlina was almost knocked down by Frances, who had zoomed around the corner to see Leticia. "Oh, sorry, dear! Leticia, did you see the BALI account folder?" Frances asked urgently.

"No, ma'am."

"It wasn't in the case."

"Oh! Well, I didn't see what folders Melba put in it. I didn't touch it."

"I can't find it!" Frances said with a high-pitched note of panic in her voice. "The client is going to be here in fifteen minutes. Can I use your phone?"

Leticia stood up to get out of the way, and Frances grabbed the handset. After dialing a few numbers, she asked sharply, "Melba, where is the BALI folder and pitch? Why not, Melba? Well, they're here now, and we need the presentation pieces." Frances was silent for a moment, but her face grew pinched and tight, like she was torn between panic, exasperation, and fury. "Bye, Melba," Frances suddenly interjected and slammed the phone down.

"Did I screw up?" Leticia asked fearfully.

"No, dear. She didn't give it to you. She said she forgot to put it in the case. I swear! That woman will do anything to sabotage this campaign." She looked stricken as soon as the words slipped out. "Ooh. You didn't hear me say that."

"No, ma'am," said Leticia. But she noticed both Berlina and Evanne were listening carefully with ears perked up.

"The team is supposed to do the presentation directly with the client in fifteen minutes," Frances continued. "I need to tell James and Paul."

Frances hurried away. Berlina and Evanne drifted off, and Leticia started typing. But not three minutes had passed before both Paul and Mr. Foles came to Leticia's desk. They moved so fast, they practically appeared out of thin air.

"Leticia, do you recall anything of the campaign, when you worked on it with Melba?" Mr. Foles asked.

"Of course she does," Paul said. "I told you; she practically … well." Paul fell silent, and Leticia wondered what he had been about to say. He didn't look at her, and she felt another pang of regret and sorrow at how things had turned out between them, and another stab of fury at Melba for being the cause of it.

Mr. Foles didn't respond to Paul. "Leticia? This is a crucial account."

"Yes, sir. I helped Melba put everything together. But I just know the outline. If Melba had anything else to present, I don't know it."

"That might do. Will you please present the outline to the client?"

CHAPTER 22

"**M**E, SIR?" LETICIA ASKED, STUNNED. "Sir, I thought Melba had already made the presentation, when she went to Detroit." *Without me,* she added silently.

"She botched it," said Paul flatly.

"Paul!" Mr. Foles turned back to Leticia and didn't notice the wink Paul gave her. "Luckily, the client is giving us another try, and this is it."

"Well, yes, okay, then," said Leticia, slightly flustered. "Do I look okay?"

"Very professional, as always," Mr. Foles affirmed as he guided Leticia to the conference room. They stepped in and he said, "Ladies and gentlemen, let me introduce Leticia Patrick. Leticia will give you the outline of our concept for the campaign."

He didn't introduce the three representatives from BALI to Leticia, but they all seemed friendly enough. They smiled and nodded at her.

Leticia swallowed. *Sink or swim,* she thought. She thought about Dunn's River Falls.

"Ladies and gentleman," she started. Her voice caught nervously. She cleared her throat and was pleased to find her voice firm and steady after that. "All of the ladies involved are aged thirty to thirty-five to appeal to your target audience. The scene appears to be a ladies' dressing room in a typical department store, with a redheaded lady standing in her undergarments.

"One by one, three more ladies appear, taking off their outer clothes to reveal their underwear. The first new lady says to the redhead, 'Are those Vassarette?'

"'No,' says the redhead.

"With some flattering remarks, the first new woman says, 'Whatever it is, it makes you look trim and shapely.' The camera pans over the garments, showing off how great they look on the model.

"The redhead uses one of the taglines we developed for the campaign—" Here, Leticia faltered. For the life of her, she couldn't remember the specific tagline.

Mr. Foles saved her. "All of the taglines were included in the package we sent you originally."

"Mm-hmm," a gray-haired gentleman in a dark pinstriped suit said. "Yes, we got that. We were impressed by them. In fact, that's why we decided to come back to see if you could do better than the last meeting," he added.

Mr. Foles nodded, and then looked at the young Jamaican. "Please continue, Miss Patrick."

"Okay. Well, the second new lady peels off the rest of her clothes and says, 'Are you wearing Vanity Fair?'

"'No,' says the redhead again with a little chuckle.

"'Won't you tell us what you're wearing?' the second lady asks. 'It fits you perfectly.'

"Then the third lady interrupts with another compliment, also a tagline for the campaign, and then says, 'It's definitely Victoria Secret; it just fits like a glove and shows off every curve you want and hides the curves you don't.'

"'No, no, it's not Victoria Secret,' the redhead says, laughing now. 'It is BALI.'

"Now the camera zooms out to see a gorgeous young man, wearing only a T-shirt, his socks, and a pair of boxers. He's happily smiling at the ladies, and he nods enthusiastically. As the camera zooms out, the viewer realizes that it's not a ladies' dressing room, but it's actually an airport security station, and the strangers are walking one by one through the airport metal detector, and everyone is watching them and making comments: 'Wow, I wonder what brand of underwear that is.'

"That is how I recall the campaign," Leticia concluded.

One of the clients chuckled, and then Paul laughed and Mr. Foles joined in.

"That is not what we got last week," the elderly gentleman said.

"Are there any questions?" Leticia asked.

"Yes, if I may. Where is your accent from?"

Mr. Foles answered for Leticia. "Oh, Miss Patrick is from the land of reggae."

"Ah! Jamaica," replied the client. "Beautiful island."

"Thank you," said Leticia.

"No, thank you, Miss Patrick," Mr. Foles said. "I think you can leave the rest of the meeting to us now."

Leticia left the conference room and headed to the bathroom. Frances followed. "I heard laughter in the room," she said.

"Yes, I think it went well," Leticia said, huffing a little. The adrenaline was still pumping, and she was breathing quickly. Frances grinned at her and returned to her desk, while Leticia took a few minutes to regain her composure.

CHAPTER 23

Paul came by Leticia's desk first. "You did a good job, Leticia."

"Thank you, sir!"

Paul stood there awkwardly for a minute, and then reached out to shake her hand. Leticia took it gingerly, and Paul pumped it up and down mechanically. Leticia remembered their slow dance, her cheek against his shoulder, his arms around her, how warm he felt, how nice he smelled with his mixture of cologne and spicy Paul scent.

Leticia noticed Paul seemed to be blushing, and he withdrew his hand abruptly. Still, his eyes kept flicking to hers, and then looking away shyly. "In fact …" he began but fell silent.

A few seconds of tender awkwardness followed before Leticia prompted, "Paul? Are you okay?"

He cleared his throat. If anything, his cheeks looked even rosier now. "Oh, yes, yes. Well, it just seems like we've seen a new side of you recently, so responsible and confident, now that you're out of her shadow." Paul jerked his head back to indicate Melba's office. "You'll do well at Lexhouse. And I just, well, I was just wondering—"

Leticia found her own heart racing a little bit faster as Paul nervously gripped the wall of her cube and looked anywhere but at her. Paul, suddenly shy? But it was adorable.

But alas, Mr. Foles chose that moment to join them. "Wonderful job, Leticia!" he exclaimed heartily. "For a pinch hitter, you did very well. We were certainly up a creek; I'm pleased you were as familiar with the material as you were. That shows some initiative, wouldn't you say, Paul?" Mr. Foles beamed at Leticia and clapped Paul on the back.

"Yes, sir, it does!" Paul agreed. "If you'll both excuse me …"

"Of course," Mr. Foles answered. "Whenever you're ready, Paul, we'll sit down and do a postmortem on the meeting."

Paul said, "Sure thing, James." He turned and left without another word to Leticia, who had to swallow her disappointment. Had they been about to reconnect, before Mr. Foles showed up?

Leticia watched him go. Paul looked back toward her over his shoulder. Twice.

"When will you hear back, sir?" Leticia asked. At least she was well practiced at projecting emotions different from what she was actually feeling. Her voice sounded strong.

"Thursday," Mr. Foles answered blithely. He didn't seem aware of any undercurrents. He left Leticia's area whistling.

She resumed playing her spiritual CD to help calm her down and worked through the morning, with no interruptions and no shrill cries of "Lee-teeee-sha!" echoing through the office.

At lunch, she joined Evanne. Leticia had brought a jar of pickled herring, and Evanne pulled out a clear bag of some exotic fruits. Berlina approached them almost immediately and brandished a couple of CDs. "Here you go, twins," she said happily. "I made you both a CD of mine. Enjoy!"

The "twins" thanked her, and Berlina slipped into a spare seat. She looked directly at Leticia and said, "So, what's the scoop, girl. Tell cousin Berlina all about it."

She patted Leticia's hand, but the young Jamaican looked confused. "Scoop?"

"Melba, of course! Is it perfectly awful going to her place? Does it stink?"

"No, no, her place is very nice."

"Not her place! The bitch herself! Is she about ready to keel over?"

"Well, I don't think so," said Leticia. "She says the doctors can't find anything wrong."

Berlina frowned a little, as though this tidbit disappointed her. But then she brightened. "Well, what about your meeting this morning?"

Evanne looked up at this statement. "Meeting?" she asked.

"Oh yes," Berlina answered on Leticia's behalf. "She met with the BALI representatives, since Melba effed the account up. Paul said you were simply marvelous. You know," she added slowly, "Paul has started blushing every time he says your name."

Leticia's dark skin hid her own blush at this news. "Oh, well, that's—"

Berlina leaned forward eagerly. "So you and he, hmm? You sly little minx—"

"No, no—" Leticia protested. She suddenly felt hot. Much to her surprise and chagrin, Berlina's comment managed to unearth a fresh new flood of anger and regret over the way her and Paul's nascent relationship had taken a nosedive.

"Oh, Leticia and Paul don't have nothing going on," Evanne drawled. "Leticia's hooking up with a dentally impaired gentleman."

Berlina frowned as she tried to work out this puzzling statement.

To distract her, Leticia asked Evanne, "What are those?" She gestured at Evanne's strange-looking fruit.

"Lychee," answered her friend. "A Chinese fruit. See, you pop one open and suck the flesh." Evanne demonstrated.

"I have never seen those before."

"They look scary, but they are sweet. Would you like to taste one?"

"No," replied Leticia, "I don't want anything to interfere with the taste of my pickled herring."

Evanne also offered a piece of fruit to Berlina, but Paul's assistant was not about to be distracted. "Well, tell me about the meeting!"

"It was nice," said Leticia. "I just went over the outline from Melba's presentation. Since I had helped prepare it, I already knew it."

"How did the BALI people react?" Berlina persisted.

Leticia shrugged. "I don't know. I left the meeting right after. I've already told you everything I know. Paul probably knows more. Frances might have some news," Leticia offered hopefully. "Mr. Foles was there, too; he might have mentioned how it went to Frances."

"Oh, right!" Berlina said. "By the way, did you hear about Melba's husband? He's leaving her! Guess he couldn't take her either. Bitch. Have you met him, Leticia?"

Leticia was astounded. How could Berlina possibly know that? She blinked rapidly and said, "No. Well, I guess I met him briefly when Melba made me get him a cake. He was a lot like her."

"Witchy people gather," said Evanne. "They attract each other, and then repel each other, and then attract each other."

"Because they deserve each other," said Berlina. "But Leticia, what did he *say* to you? Was he perfectly awful?"

"No, not like that. It was just like, well, like I wasn't really there. I was just an object delivering his cake, not a real person."

"And now Melba is an object to be discarded, too," said Evanne, "but she hardly has the right to complain. She treats you and everyone just the same way. That's how the world works. When you put nastiness out, you draw nasty people into your life, and you push the people who care about you away."

"Who'd ever care about Melba?" snorted Berlina. "Even her husband—soon to be ex-husband—doesn't!"

"But that's the point, girl. People never get to *start* caring about Melba because she's so bad no one can stand to be around her. It'd be different if she at least tried. Wouldn't it, Leticia?"

"Sometimes she does try," Leticia allowed. "She just doesn't do a very good job."

The three of them chuckled at that.

"I just feel sorry for her," Leticia said. "Because you're right, Evanne. She's the cause of all her own problems. She earned everything that happened to her."

"What happened to her just being driven, doing whatever it takes, all that stuff you said before?"

"It's still true. I feel sorry for her. But she's still responsible for her own actions, like being fair and nice to people, and not showing them up or lying to them or accusing them of things."

"Wonder if her husband is the same way?" Berlina mused. The question sounded rhetorical, but she was eyeing Leticia as if hoping for an answer.

"I don't really know," the Jamaican answered.

Berlina sighed, grinned, and then launched herself up, waving goodbye over her shoulder, and then took off to find Frances.

The "twins" watched her go, and once she was out of sight, they started laughing.

"That woman is like a heat-seeking missile for gossip," Evanne joked. "So how is it now that Melba isn't over your shoulder all the time?"

"I'm actually getting my work done! I have two more accounts to catalog today, and I think I'll get them done, even having to leave early. It is so much easier now."

"You mean, easier without Melba's presence or without Melba's stench, which one?"

"Both," laughed Leticia.

The two ladies cleared off their table and headed to the restroom before returning to work.

"Thank God we can finally use this toilet again," Evanne said.

At three o'clock on the button, Leticia was already standing in Frances's area.

"Hello, dear. I heard you did well today. Mr. Foles was very pleased."

"I hope so," said Leticia with a smile.

"Well, here is the case and your forty dollars. Could you please sign these forms for petty cash? I forgot to give you one yesterday, so please sign both for me."

"Sure," said Leticia as she complied with Frances's request.

Before Leticia left the office, she returned to the lunch room and performed her three-stick ritual and wiped the case thoroughly again. Again, she placed the damp paper towel in her pocket.

She hurried downstairs and got a cab immediately. She told the driver Melba's address.

"Eh?"

She repeated herself, but a language barrier prevented mutual comprehension, so Leticia gave him the piece of paper with the address.

The driver nodded, set his navigational system, and returned the paper to the young woman.

Once he had deposited her at Melba's building, Leticia ventured inside. At the elevator, a tall, thin man with a goatee and a ponytail joined Leticia. "This thing is as slow as hell," he commented genially. "Ah, but here it comes."

They both got into the elevator and both pressed six.

"Beat you!" said the stranger with a chuckle. Leticia smiled shyly back at him. "I have never seen you here before. Are you new? I know just about everyone in the building. If I had seen you before, I would definitely remember. I always remember pretty ladies. Sorry for my monologue. My name is Ron. And you are?"

"Jane," said Leticia.

"Nice to meet you, Jane!" Ron said.

The elevator doors popped open. Leticia nodded in Ron's direction and headed toward Melba's door.

"You know that stinking cow?" Ron ask, his nose wrinkling at the very thought. But he didn't wait for an answer; he just shook his head, muttering, and disappeared around the corner.

Leticia froze for a moment. What an odd experience. Melba had a similar reputation in her own building as her reputation back at the office. Leticia guessed the man just didn't want anything to do with anyone associated with Melba.

She frowned. How irritating. She had been fully prepared to give the man a fake phone number, and now she'd never have a chance. Stupid Melba.

She pasted a big smile on her face and knocked. To her surprise, Melba answered immediately. The woman was walking even worse than the day before, holding her buttocks even higher in the air, legs two feet apart and walking on her toes. She looked like a ballerina gone wrong.

Her hair was matted and unkempt. Her skin was red, splotchy, and inflamed all over, as if she'd not just fallen into some poison ivy but rolled around and fallen asleep in the poison patch.

"Good afternoon, Melba," Leticia said.

"Hmph," Melba grunted.

Leticia turned to close the door.

"Don't you close my door!" Melba shouted with surprising vehemence. Leticia turned to her with an arched eyebrow, but Melba was already stalking back into the apartment.

Frankly, the young Jamaican was perfectly happy to leave the door open. The stench in the apartment just about bowled her over. As she stepped forward to follow Melba, she noticed boxes stacked all through the room, neatly packed and piled atop each other.

"Are you moving?" Leticia asked.

"No. My husband is leaving me. These boxes are his. Dumb bastard."

"Melba! I'm so sorry. That's such a pity. He was, er, such a nice man."

"Yes, he is a nice man that is leaving his wife in her time of need. Who needs a nice man when things are down?" she snapped back. "He's a selfish ingrate. I deserve better than him anyway. Always thought so. Hmph. Here's the case. If there's anything not in there, that will be James Ass's problem."

Leticia's gaze wandered over the room while Melba packed the case. She noticed that Melba was *still* using the pillowcase she had given Leticia. *And* she was drinking from the mug that Leticia had given her.

Leticia took the paper towel from her pocket and pretended to sneeze into it. "Sorry, Melba, I think I'm coming down with something. Do you have a trash can?"

Melba gestured impatiently toward the kitchen, where Leticia deposited the paper towel in the trash. When she returned, she scrutinized Melba more closely. The older woman was scowling furiously and muttering under her breath. She looked different, though …

"Melba! The cold sore on your lip came off. You look better without it," she assured her boss.

Melba looked over at her and sneered. "I scraped it off, and it's left a scar for life."

And indeed, now that she was looking directly at Leticia, the Jamaican could see a ragged line that looked a little like a harelip.

"Oh," said the young woman. "Well, there are a lot of things on the market for scars these days, so don't worry; you'll find something. Again, you do look better."

Melba shrugged. "Here is the damn case. It is full." She waddled with Leticia back to the door. It looked even funnier than before, but Leticia kept herself from laughing. As she got outside the door, she turned to say goodbye to Melba, but Melba slammed the door in her face, and once again, Leticia could hear the lock clicking.

And once again, Leticia kept her portion of the taxi fare and used public transportation to get home.

* * *

First thing Wednesday morning, Leticia presented Frances with the case and taxi receipt.

"Thank you, you are so cooperative, Leticia. Sometimes I have to hound people to get what I need from them."

Leticia nodded and started to walk off, but Frances grabbed her arm. But Mr. Foles's assistant was smiling. "Just between you and me," she said in a low voice, "keep in mind that people notice things when you're not expecting them to see anything." She smiled again with a friendly nod and let go of Leticia's arm.

The Jamaican smiled and said, "Thank you," before returning to her desk. Frances's comment had left her puzzled. Was it some kind of veiled threat?

Frowning over the mystery, she performed her usual morning routine and waited for Evanne to arrive. She played the CD from Berlina. She was surprised to hear gospel music with Berlina doing a solo. She was shocked to realize Berlina was actually *really good*.

Her surprise carried her straightaway to Berlina's desk. "You sing?" she asked, wide eyed.

"I most certainly do! Matter of fact, I am in the church choir. One of these Sundays, you must visit my church."

Leticia was shocked. Berlina's favorite word was *bitch*, yet she was in her church choir?

People just never ceased to amaze her.

"Wow, I am impressed." Leticia noticed Evanne and waved her over. "Have you listened to Berlina's CD? She can *sing!*"

Berlina had turned back to her work, but Leticia noted that she was smiling to herself.

"Oh, yeah? No, I haven't had a chance to listen yet."

"You should!" The two friends then moved off to get their coffee. "No pastry?" Leticia asked.

"No sex. Phone call from toothy?"

"No call."

The ladies just chuckled.

The day passed by quickly and enjoyably. Multiple coworkers commented to Leticia how much more peaceful she seemed. Some actually described her as jubilant; others called her more energetic. Most just complimented her pleasant manner. Pete kept peeking over the cube wall to try to engage Leticia in conversation. He'd never really paid much attention to her before, but now, he seemed to want to talk every hour on the hour.

Berlina stopped by Leticia's desk and whispered, "Melba's departure was long overdue, wasn't it?"

"She's not gone forever."

"I know, but she's not here. That's the important thing. And I've heard some things, some very interesting things." She tapped her nose, winked, and walked away. Leticia stared after her, baffled.

Evanne got assigned a special project for two days. The project was early in the mornings, so it didn't stop the two friends from having lunch together. They each laughed at the food they brought. Evanne had chunks of sugar cane while Leticia dined on fried yucca.

Both women tried valiantly not to mention Melba or the impact of Melba's absence, feeling they had exhausted that subject, but they could not hold their tongues. Evanne was desperately curious and interrogated Leticia on every aspect of Melba at home, Melba's home décor, and Melba's behavior.

Leticia immediately heeded to her father's advice regarding gossip. Despite her eagerness to tell her friend about Melba's husband leaving her, she chose to keep quiet.

She was particularly shocked when Evanne herself came out with the news that Melba's husband was leaving. How did Evanne know? *This place is really a rumor mill*, Leticia mused.

"Took him long enough," she commented. "Don't know how he lasted with her. Must have low self-esteem."

"Evanne!"

"I only met him once, at an office party a couple of years back. He seemed as disagreeable as Melba. You should have listened to the two of them bickering! Neither could do anything right. They said some really awful things to each other. Melba called him worthless at one point; he called her a slut."

"Wow."

"Yeah, it was fantastic. Best office party I've ever been to. They didn't come again the next year. Very disappointing. I was all ready for the Melba show. Too bad he hasn't been there when you've gone to see her. I'd love to hear all about that!"

"Berlina was hinting that she knew something about Melba."

"Well, of course, she's Berlina! But, confidentially, according to my sources, Melba wants to be fired so she can sue the company."

"Really?"

"Yeah. Apparently, she thinks she has a lot of reasons, you know, with her health, with her being the only female account executive."

Leticia thought about that statement for a moment. She could totally believe it of Melba. "That bitch," she said finally.

"You said it, girl."

At three o'clock sharp, Leticia headed back out to Melba's. The taxi driver spoke great English and, once given the address, didn't even need his GPS device to navigate.

Leticia ran into the old lady with the Pomeranian at the elevator again. The older woman pushed the buttons for four and six.

"Thanks," said Leticia.

The dog started growling again, this time staring at Leticia's pocket, where she had once again deposited the damp paper towel. Leticia ignored him.

"Dixie likes strangers," the old lady assured Leticia. She frowned at the dog, and her brow furrowed as she tried to unravel the riddle of Dixie's odd behavior. "I'm so sorry he's like this toward you. I don't want you to think my dog is racist or anything."

Leticia turned an astonished stare at the old lady. She had no idea how to respond to that! Then the doors beeped and opened, and the old woman stepped out. "I heard that you visit that horrible woman on the sixth floor. Management here has been trying to get her to leave for years, but her lease was grandfathered in when the new management took over, so it's hard to put her out."

The elevator doors tried to shut, but the old woman put her foot forward to stop them.

"How do you manage the smell in there, sweetie? It permeates the entire laundry room when she does her washing, and the handyman said she just stinks." She looked eagerly at Leticia. Perhaps she was the Berlina of the apartment building.

But Leticia did not say a word. Disappointed, the old woman withdrew her foot and said, "Oh, well, have a nice day, dearie."

As the doors shut and the elevator lurched back into motion, Leticia asked herself out loud, "Does everybody hate this woman?"

She swiped the case absentmindedly with the paper towel a few more times until the elevator hit the sixth floor. For a moment, Leticia felt the strength of Mamma Dassa's instructions. She felt wonderful about her power and her ability to literally see the results of what she has done to Melba. Leticia felt great. After all, Melba deserved everything that Mamma Dassa had to dish out.

As the elevator opened on the sixth floor, that familiar foul scent was already noticeable. She was surprised to see Melba's door already wide open. "Melba?" she called out before crossing the threshold. "It's me, Leticia."

She saw mounds of packing boxes and noticed two swarthy men removing them. "Miss," one of them greeted her politely as they walked by.

Melba waddled up, moving even more slowly and awkwardly than ever. She winced, as though in pain, but Leticia didn't ask because of all the commotion.

Then Mr. Grossott came out of the kitchen. "Hello, Letisa," he said absently.

"Hello, sir. Um, actually, it's Leticia."

"Whatever." He went back to directing the moving men, barking out orders and berating the men for not moving quickly or gently enough with his belongings. Yeah, a real charmer, that one.

Melba wordlessly grabbed the case from Leticia's hand and slammed it down on a desk. She opened it with her key, didn't remove anything, but placed two folders back in it. She relocked the case. She returned the case to the young woman who continued to stand awkwardly in the entryway. She said nothing to Leticia, and Leticia didn't say anything to Melba. The young woman just hurried to the stairs and walked down a flight of stairs before getting on the elevator.

The next morning, she arrived early to present the case and receipt to Frances, and then went to her cubicle to peel off her outerwear to get ready for the day.

She had just started entering the information for a new account into the online filing system when she looked up and noticed Frances standing at her desk.

"Hello, dear. Mr. Foles would like to see you in his office."

"Is everything okay?" she asked, mildly alarmed. She remembered Frances's puzzling remark from the day before.

But Frances didn't answer. Leticia followed her back to Mr. Foles's office. Frances closed the door behind Leticia.

"Good morning, Leticia," said Mr. Foles. He was not smiling.

CHAPTER 24

"Good morning, sir," Leticia responded with a gulp. "Did Melba take anything from the case last night?"

"No, sir. From what I saw, she just added two new folders, relocked it, and gave it to me. I barely even got inside the apartment."

"What did she say?"

"Nothing, sir. I mean, not a word at all. But there were movers, and so it was kind of crazy."

"Movers?"

"Yes, sir. Sir, what happened?"

Mr. Foles shook his head. "There is some confusion. Nothing for you to worry about. That's all, Leticia." He saw the woman out of his office with a smile that was obviously strained. He closed the door behind her, and Leticia stood for a moment with a worried expression.

Frances said to her very quietly, "Don't worry; it is not you."

Leticia nodded, feeling a bit reassured. She returned to her work and put on her gospel CD. She sang along with the songs that she knew and messed up the ones she didn't. She sang to herself as she worked all through the morning. She missed Evanne, who was out of the office on assignment, but looked forward to her friend's return at lunch.

As a result, she greeted Evanne with greater than usual enthusiasm.

"Did you think I'd miss one of my favorite times of the day?" her friend said with a smile. Then an expression of concern stole over her features. "What happened?"

"Let's go the lunch room, and I'll tell you everything."

Evanne nodded. She brought out some prickly pears freshly bought from the market. "So, what's up?" she asked as she started on them.

"I won't even ask what those are," Leticia choked out.

"Girl, you can't pique my curiosity and then not tell me. What's going on!"

"Evanne, something big is going on, and I think it has to do with Melba."

"Oh, yes, everyone knows that," said Evanne with a wave of her hand. "According to my reliable sources, Melba hasn't touched a piece of work on any of her accounts that have been sent to her. Oh, maybe a scribble here and there. But she had an agreement with HR, you know, and she said she would continue to work from home. So they're not very happy with her. And apparently, she's made contact with some clients and, well, let's just say she didn't exactly compliment James or Paul to them."

Leticia was staring at Evanne wide eyed.

"Girl, you better close that mouth before a fly swoops in. Didn't you know all that?"

"No!"

"Why do you think they refer to her as the 'wicked witch of the working world'? But between you and me, she's just cooking her own goose. She already has a reputation outside these walls—"

That's for sure, Leticia thought to herself as she remember the reactions of the various people she'd met in Melba's building.

Evanne continued her harangue, "—and her talking trash just confirms her own reputation, not James's, not Paul's, no one's but her own. She's digging her own hole. She spinning enough rope to hang herself. We're all just sitting back and watching it happen. It was just a matter of time, you know. Actually, it's kind of entertaining to watch it happen. Couldn't have happened to a bitchier bitch."

"Wow."

"She's buried herself in this industry," Evanne continued. A little bit of juice dribbled down her chin as she bit into the fruit. She wiped it off with a napkin. "Now, she's playing the female card. Girl, no one's more sensitive to the proper treatment of the female of the species than me. I'm not going to take flack from no man, no way. But it's just a ploy for her."

"The female card? What do you mean?"

"She's saying that since she is the only female in the capacity of an account executive, she cannot be fired."

"Who told you all this?"

Evanne smiled mysteriously. "Let's just say I make it a point to spend time with the HR receptionist. I'm surprised Berlina hasn't said anything to you, though. It's all over the office, I thought."

"Wow. So she thinks she's irreplaceable?"

"Legally, at any rate."

Leticia hadn't touched a bite of her canned beef stew. As she returned to her desk, she found Mr. Foles, Frances, Paul, and Berlina all waiting for her. She stopped short and stared at the group while Evanne continued on to her cube.

"Come on, come on," Paul invited.

"You don't want us to shout this to the whole office!" said Mr. Foles.

Berlina jumped in. "Everyone in the office already knows."

Mr. Foles turned a frown on Berlina, and Paul turned red. Apparently, her loose tongue was not a quality upper management admired in her.

"I don't know," said Leticia as she approached. "I don't know what's going on at all."

Paul nodded. "Oh, it's good news, Leticia. You look like a lamb being led to the slaughter. No, it's good news—you'll like it. We're closing early tomorrow and my team—"

"Including me," Berlina interrupted unnecessarily.

"Er, yes. We're going to a Brazilian restaurant, can't think of its name right off hand."

"The Brazilian Experience," Berlina supplied.

"Right. It's all the meat you want, non-stop eating—"

"And it's *so good*," said Berlina excited. "The tastiest, juiciest, most succulent—"

"Thank you, Berlina," Mr. Foles said sharply, voice tinged with exasperation. "Leticia, thanks to your impromptu presentation on Tuesday, we have the BALI account signed, sealed, and delivered. So it is time to celebrate, and we definitely have you to thank for it."

"Mr. Foles! I almost fainted; I thought you were waiting here with bad news."

"No, darling," Frances said. "We all just wanted to see your face when he told you. We're all just so glad; it's the best thing really, that you worked with Melba that evening to complete the pitch. And with your good memory, it paid off!"

"Leticia, in front of everyone here, I really thank you," add Mr. Foles.

"Me, too!" added Paul.

Leticia started to cry, and Evanne darted forward from where she had been surreptitiously listening to give her friend a hug. They exchanged hugs all around. Leticia particularly enjoyed the hug from Paul. His cologne smelled spicy and appealing, and the muscles of his back were strong under her hands. She broke away almost reluctantly to find Paul was blushing beet red again, looking anywhere but at her.

"Leticia, close up shop, take the case, and go home early today. We'll see you in the morning. And don't forget that tomorrow is casual day!"

Leticia hastened to obey, though she did stop back in the lunchroom for her three-sticks ritual.

She arrived at Melba's door commensurately earlier than usual. Melba looked surprised to see her. The apartment stank like a sewer.

Melba didn't waste any time with questions. "Don't stand there so people will know my business," she snapped. "Come in and give me the damn case."

The apartment was virtually empty, and their footsteps echoed loudly in the empty chamber. "Where are all your things?"

"Mr. Grossott has them," Melba said bitterly. "Thief. Matter of fact, I was served divorce papers this morning."

"I'm sorry to hear that, Melba," Leticia said. She was nearly gagging on the smell in the apartment. "Um, Melba, I won't be coming by tomorrow. And I'm really sorry that things aren't going your way."

"Why aren't you coming tomorrow?" Melba asked, frowning.

"Paul's team is going out to celebrate the new account, and I get to go along with them. We're going to a Brazilian restaurant. It will be my first time!"

Melba was staring at her, her eyes looking darker and beadier, surrounded by the puffy and red flesh of the woman's face. They glittered with something that caused Leticia to take a step backward.

"What account did Paul get?" Melba asked slowly, her voice so low Leticia almost didn't hear her. Her eyes never left Leticia's face.

"Um. He got the international BALI account. They're letting his team off at noon to celebrate."

Melba stood frozen, still staring at Leticia. "You!" she hissed finally.

"Melba?"

"You!" Melba shouted.

Alarmed, Leticia took another step back. "Melba, why are you angry?"

Melba shook a fist at Leticia and took a menacing step toward the young Jamaican. Well, as menacing as someone walking like a duck could look. "You sabotaged me!" she shrieked. "I'll have you deported for this, you goddamn slut! We don't need trash like you in our country anyway! Just go back to your pig farm and live with the pigs like you deserve!"

Leticia's habit of dealing with Melba in a falsely conciliatory manner almost led her to try to protest meekly. But the reply died on her lips. Melba was practically writhing in rage, squirming, though whether out of physical discomfort or her fury Leticia couldn't say. The Jamaican regarded the older woman for a moment, and suddenly, it was as if Melba's fury infused her, as though it had lit some detonation wire that exploded inside Leticia.

Melba's rage was almost palpable; the air was electrified with it. Leticia felt her own body practically vibrate with the same feeling.

Leticia turned to leave the ranting witch. But Melba pulled Leticia's coat by the left sleeve and slightly ripped it from the shoulder. Without thinking, with an automatic reflex, Leticia doubled her fist, drew back, and launched, and it landed on Melba's boney jaw. It was only when she saw the scrawny woman lying on the floor with her legs wide open, revealing her red and blistered thighs, that she realized she had hit her.

She froze for a moment, shocked at herself, but then the fury took over again. Leticia started kicking Melba, hard enough to feel bone. Her punch had apparently split Melba's lip, and a thin line of blood dripped from the corner of her mouth. Leticia stood over her and grabbed Melba by her hair, which came off in the middle of her hand like an over-dried Brillo pad.

"Fuck you, Melba!" she screamed. She raised the hair high, brandishing it like some sort of trophy or weapon.

Melba was so shocked, she fell still and stared at Leticia. Strangely, her sudden stillness made Leticia alight with even more rage. Leticia snarled wordlessly, with her tightly-clenched fist, knocking Melba, hitting the dried-up pruned woman with every blow. Now, it was she who took the threatening step forward, and Melba seemed to shrink into herself.

Leticia's words were touched by her Jamaican twang, but she made an effort to speak very clearly and enunciate everything properly, so that Melba would understand her perfectly. "You're a stupid, shitty ass bitch, Melba!" Leticia yelled. "You are a frigging idiot. You low piece of shit!"

Melba's ghost-like pale face turned dark red. "You!—You!"

"Not me," said Leticia. "You. You did all this to yourself. Your husband left your ass because your face looks like an exploded mine, and you smell like a garbage boat. He left your tiny sagging tits because you have a heart made of shit, and shit for brains, and shit for a soul."

Melba tried to get up, and Leticia knocked her down again, this time on purpose. This time, Melba hit the floor with a loud thump. Leticia grabbed the woman by her flimsy nightgown, pulled her up a bit, and then just let her go. Melba's awkward position and movements caused her to fall to the floor with a crash.

Leticia made no move to help. She watched as Melba slowly, grunting, tried to pull herself up onto the couch. The anger in the air seemed to dissipate entirely. It left Melba looking like a shell of herself, and Leticia just feeling tired and dirty from having touched Melba. The Jamaican started to walk out the door, but paused and turned to Melba behind her.

"I know your kind," Leticia said. "Petty tyrants and asses." She took a step closer to Melba and knelt down. Melba seemed defeated. She looked away. Her face looked raw and red, her hair thinned and patchy as though she had been exposed to radiation. Leticia looked her up and down. "This is what you get," she said, gesturing at Melba's ruined body. She lowered her voice. "And when you come back to work, it's going to be different. You try to take me on, and I'll slam your ass into the ground, over and over."

"You did this to me," Melba said in a tiny voice, and then started crying.

"You did this to yourself. You disgust me." Leticia stood and turned around, no longer fearing the rage of a battered, wicked woman with no strength.

"Melba," she said in a voice not her own, "you have just gotten a Jamaican beat down, and I am ready to give you more."

Melba rallied. She started cursing a blue streak, jumped up, and swung an arm at Leticia.

Leticia screamed and grabbed at Melba's arms. Once she had a hold of them, she threw the older, weakened woman onto the floor again. This time, Melba landed with a clunk. Leticia grabbed Melba's hair again, and an entire handful just pulled away like before, leaving blank spots on her scalp. Leticia didn't miss a beat: she showed the hair to Melba and screamed, "This! This is the evil you've done to yourself!" She thrust the clump of hair into Melba's face.

Melba just lay there like an old, dismantled rag doll.

"You pathetic shitty cow." Leticia spit on Melba.

"I'll get you for this," Melba spluttered through her tears.

"You attacked me," said Leticia flatly.

"You did this to me," Melba repeated in an even smaller voice. She buried her face in her hands.

"What did I do? Defend myself against you? That's all I did. What, you think people are going to believe I made you sick? I'm the only one at the office who sticks up for you. Everyone else talks about what a bitch you are. They all hate you, every last one of them. Even your own husband. I'm the only one who says, 'No, she's not evil. She's just driven.' Ha! The joke's on you, you piece of shit."

"It's voodoo."

"That's Haiti, you dumb fuck. I come from Ja-mai-ca." She spoke with exaggerated slowness. She took a lurching step forward and stuck a finger in Melba's face. Melba flinched backward. "But I got friends." Leticia laughed. "I got friends who know how to make things happen. You mess with me anymore, maybe I'll give you cause to complain. Stupid fool."

And Leticia turned her back on Melba. She grabbed the case from the nearby table. "Have a nice weekend," she called over her shoulder as she left.

That seemed to enrage Melba all over. She stumbled up and after Leticia. She threw open the front door, which Leticia had closed, but Leticia was nowhere to be found. A strangled scream erupted from Melba's throat. "You!—You! You shiteater! You cunt! Thief! Immigrant! Help me! Someone help me! I've been attacked!"

But no one came out to help, and after a several moments of raggedly catching her breath, Melba shut the door and went back into her apartment.

CHAPTER 25

LETICIA WAS WAITING THE NEXT morning, sitting clutching her knees to her chest. She had arrived bright and early before the office opened. She was there as soon as Frances arrived, and Leticia was already crying—her eyes blazing red—thanks in part to a handful of pepper she had snorted earlier and some deep inhalations of raw onion.

Leticia leapt to her feet as soon as Frances came through the elevator door and ran to her, sobbing. "She went off on me," she blubbered. "I was just trying to help her, and she attacked me; she attacked me; please, don't make me go back there, Frances, oh, please, don't! You would not believe the vulgar things she said to me. She kept calling me a effing bitch. She tripped me several times as I tried to run. Look, she tore the entire sleeve off my coat!" Somehow, the minor tear that Melba caused to the coat apparently grew overnight. Courtesy of Aunt Martha and Leticia pulling it further apart.

"Calm down, dear! Leticia, dear, take a deep breath now. Come over here; let's sit down. Here's a tissue, dear. Now, what happened?"

So Leticia recounted events. She portrayed Melba's side of the encounter with only mild embellishment. She portrayed herself as simply trying to help Melba, who was facing physical difficulties getting up. Leticia's steady stream of tears did not abate; once she got started, she found it easy to keep going. "Please, don't make me go back, Frances; I don't want to get in trouble with Mr. Foles, but I just can't go back."

"Of course not, I will speak to Mr. Foles. I will also get you one hundred dollars to replace your coat. Just go now and get yourself a coat and bring me the receipt."

"Thank you." It did not take Leticia too long to find a coat; she returned in a couple of hours and gladly gave the receipt to Frances. Leticia felt victorious.

At her cubicle waiting for her were the rumor ladies.

Berlina beat a wigless Evanne to the first question.

"Girl, we heard about the fight; did you give a good Jamaican beat down?"

"Actually, I don't want to talk about it. I made up my mind this morning to look forwad to the restaurant and the weekend to recoup. Sorry, my friends, I just want to lie low on the subject."

"Okay, I understand," both ladies replied in unison.

Evanne returned with a slice of amaretto cheesecake for her friend.

Leticia started laughing immediately. "Good sex?" she asked.

"No," said Evanne, although she smiled. "I just wanted to bring you something. I must tell you this: I have had compliments on my hair and beauty while you were coat shopping," she said while rapidly winking her eyes.

The compliments were coming from every direction that morning. Evanne had a small natural afro and no contact lenses. Her real eyes were hazel brown, and she was a beautiful woman.

After that, Friday turned out to be a fun day at work. Especially since it was dress down day. Virtually everyone in the office had some kind of music playing at their own workstations, which lent a kind of party atmosphere to the workplace. While most of the employees used earphones, some just played their music softly. Leticia even went a step further: she sang along to her music.

The compliments about Evanne's hair lasted the whole day, especially at the restaurant.

"Oh! Well, thank you! Any calls from toothy?"

"No. Guess he's still waiting on his dentures."

"Leticia, this is one of the best days of my life, thank you for that tea."

"You are welcome."

For a moment, Leticia thought that for a fee, Mamma Dassa helped her destroy Melba who was wicked and mean. On the other hand, Mamma Dassa gave her the tea for free to help a kind, sweet person. They laughed together as they went for their morning coffee. The subtle spice of the amaretto in the cheesecake perfectly complemented the coffee.

But it only whetted her appetite for lunch. Paul's team gathered at The Brazilian Experience for their celebration. Mr. Foles, Paul, and a handful of others spoke briefly, but Leticia hardly paid attention. She was absorbed in the fragrances of roasting meats, the allure of a huge salad bar next to an enormous dessert bar, all while she watched attendants circulate around the dining room with slabs of meats on skewers, slicing off individual portions to diners who requested them.

The restaurant gave everyone a stop-and-go coin, which was red on one side to indicate the person didn't want any more meat, and green on the other to say, "Come offer me your delicious wares."

Evanne never put her coin on red. She happily ate every kind of meat they offered, like spicy garlic piranha, flank steak, filet mignon wrapped in bacon, tender pork ribs and roast pork tenderloin, lamb chops and leg of lamb, and every kind of chicken imaginable, all juicy, succulent, and delicious.

And that wasn't all for Evanne: from the side orders and salad table, she enthusiastically dined on a selection of cheeses, breads, potato salad, coleslaw, and anything else that looked fresh and appealing. She did not, however, sample any of the ample fruits the restaurant offered.

Leticia might have commented on that, but she was too busy following Evanne's example. Though she ate more slowly, a bit more selectively, and in smaller portions, she was generally too occupied with chewing to talk much.

That didn't stop Evanne, however. "Girl," she said around a mouthful of food. "That Paul keeps looking at you."

"I haven't noticed," Leticia said after she swallowed, although she had.

"Mm-hmm," said Evanne said disbelievingly before waving over a passing attendant with a skewer of spicy sausages.

The group eventually began disappearing one at a time. Evanne laid her hands on her belly and moaned pleasantly. "What a meal!" she exclaimed.

"You said it," Leticia agreed. She felt so full she could probably go for the next three days without eating. What a wonderful celebration experience!

Even better, everyone there knew her contribution to the company's success with the BALI account! Paul and even Mr. Foles both mentioned her in their brief speeches, and virtually everyone stopped by on their way out to pat her shoulder, congratulate her, or thank her. Evanne's boss,

Tim, even whispered, "Evanne's been trying to get me to add you to my team for ages. What do you think?"

Leticia simply blushed and grinned at everyone. She felt like the woman of the hour.

Finally, Evanne and Leticia said goodbye and gave each other a hug.

Paul saw them and said, "Are you two giving free hugs? I want one."

"Mm-hmm," Evanne said, with an I-told-you-so look at her friend.

He hugged both ladies. But after hugging Leticia, he was once again blushing bright red, and he mumbled his goodbyes and rushed off.

"It doesn't matter if he likes me," Leticia complained to Evanne. "He won't do anything because we work together. Remember that fight he and Melba had? Maybe he does like me, but he'll always do what he just did—rush off without even giving me a second look."

"He's just shy. It's a good sign! Being shy around the ladies means the man's not a player. You don't want a player; trust me. Besides, like you said, he's in dangerous waters, and he knows it—you both work at the same company. You don't report to him, but he's still higher in the organization. He has to be careful how he treats you. He doesn't want to get in trouble."

"I wouldn't get him into trouble! I wouldn't hurt a fly."

"Don't sweat it, 'Ticia. Patience is a virtue. Half the people at Lexhouse are dating the other half on the sly. Just give it some time!"

Leticia didn't say anything. Mama Dassa's work appeared to be paying off, but she had still lost Paul to Melba's interference. She didn't see how that would change, either. She suspected that Paul had been nervous about dating a coworker from the beginning, especially one who occasionally worked under him. Melba had shoved his insecurity in his face, and how could he recover from that, when it was still true?

Her heart full of sorrow, hurt, and anger, Leticia bid Evanne goodbye again. Even with the late lunch, she still managed to get home early.

She and Aunt Martha hit a discount mall in New Jersey that weekend. Leticia talked about her week, how despite her efforts with Melba, she had *still* lost Paul.

"That's almost the worst, Auntie," she said. She paused in flipping through the rack of blouses. "I can handle myself at work. But she struck at my heart."

"You liked this man that much?"

Leticia shrugged. "I think so. I think I really like him. I know I really enjoyed being with him. And then that evil cow had to get in the middle of it."

"The fruits of the heart are always the most satisfying, and the hardest to lose," Martha agreed.

"And Melba ruined it."

"Just keep up with the thing," Martha said. "Let Mama Dassa take care of it. She will, Letty. She did it for your mom, and for me, and for everyone in our family who's gone to her."

"It's already working," Leticia agreed grimly. "You can see it. At first, when it started working, I wasn't sure. I was starting to feel bad."

"You shouldn't," Martha said flatly. "She doesn't feel bad about you. The *world* doesn't feel bad about you. We take care of the people we care about, and ourselves. The rest just have to fend for themselves."

"Yes, Auntie. You sound like Mama when you talk like that."

Martha chuckled. She stretched out a knit scarf in her hands, ran her eyes along its blue-and-white design. "You're very much like your mother. Like, look at you at work. How well you put everyone and everything into its place."

"What do you mean?"

"How you lead all these parallel lives in tandem. With us, me and your uncle, you have your real family life. But no one at work knows about that. So, there's your work life, with everyone there believing something totally different about your family life. It's like you've put us in one room, and them in another room, but there's only a one-way mirror so we can see, but they can't. And then there's this man, no one at work knows about him, and he doesn't know about us. He's in a room all his own. Your mother does that, too; she's very skilled at putting different aspects of her life in their proper place, and controlling how they interact with each other. With other people, all the different parts of their lives bleed all over the place." Martha tsk-tsked that thought and shook her head. She pulled out another scarf and said, "Your uncle would like this one, don't you think?"

Leticia glanced outside the shop, where Uncle George sat in the car the whole time while the women hopped from store to store.

The two women kept bringing more things to the car. Each time they came back with another bag, he'd say, "Are you girls ready now?"

"Just one more store," they'd promise.

Uncle George would smile, shake his head ruefully, and return to reading his book. By the time they were finished shopping, he had finished his novel. "You ladies can really shop," he observed as they shoved the last bag into the back of the loaded SUV. "Is there anything you didn't buy?"

"Only the things they didn't have," quipped his wife.

On Sunday, Leticia accompanied her aunt and uncle to church for the first time. They had asked her if she wanted to join them every weekend she'd been in New York, and every time, she politely declined. Despite her expectations, she found the sermon to be enjoyable and thought provoking. She spent her whole Sunday feeling contented and peaceful.

PART SIX—FULL CIRCLE

CHAPTER 26

T HE FOLLOWING MONDAY MORNING FOUND a similar atmosphere at work: an air of calm and tranquility had settled over the place. Without Melba's crazy-making presence and the stress of trying to land the big BALI account, everyone seemed happier and more congenial. Leticia felt lighter, as if she had at long last shucked a heavy load.

She went to her workstation and perfected her usual winter disrobe, although she was down to just a coat and scarf. She just wasn't feeling the cold as much anymore. Maybe she had started to adapt.

She prepared her computer and waited and waited for Evanne to arrive, to see if she'd get a pastry.

She was not disappointed. Evanne bustled up to her and laid a custard doughnut on Leticia's desk.

"Is this a good sex doughnut, or an I-like-you doughnut?"

"It is definitely an I-like-you doughnut," Evanne laughed. "After all that food on Friday, I was too pooped to pop. C'mon! Follow me; I want to show you something!" Evanne was grinning like crazy. She grabbed Leticia's arm and pulled her up from the desk. "Wait till you see; wait till you see!" she said gleefully.

Leticia laughed. "Okay, okay! What is it?"

"Wait, wait." Evanne pulled Leticia back, toward the newly fumigated restroom. When they entered, the room smelled faintly antiseptic, with just the barest trace of an unpleasant odor.

Leticia crinkled her nose. "They didn't get rid of the smell totally."

"Never mind that, Leticia! Wait till you see!"

Evanne stood in front of the bathroom mirror and looked at her friendly eagerly.

"Okay, so show me! What is it?"

Evanne was wigless again, but this time her hair was a little longer.

"Tony used his clippers and evened it out for me." Leticia then noticed Evanne had a natural effervescent smile. Evanne beamed.

"Know anyone that wants to buy some exotic wigs?" Evanne laughed.

As she did so, Leticia gasped. "Oh my God!" she exclaimed.

"I know! I know!"

"I can't believe it grew so *fast!*"

Evanne ran her fingers through it. "Feel!" she said.

Leticia shyly stroked along the hair. It felt soft. "Congratulations, Evanne!"

Evanne's eyes were shining with tears. "I never thought I'd see my hair again, not like this. Hopefully, I'm going to have a full head of hair back in no time. No more wigs!"

"I thought you loved the wigs," Leticia laughed.

"They're fun, but I much prefer my real hair." Evanne winked at Leticia. "And Tony loves it. I may have been too pooped to pop this weekend, but there wasn't any lack of trying on his part."

Leticia laughed. "I'm so happy for you, Evanne. If anyone deserved to be beautiful on the outside, it's you, because you're such a beautiful person on the inside. I wish I were just half so nice."

Evanne wrapped Leticia in a tight hug. "Oh, you are! You're the one who brought me the tea. I don't forget! My hair never grew back right after the cancer went away, and I tried *everything*; oh, girl, you don't know the things I tried. Until your tea. I don't know what was in it, and I don't want to know. Just thank you!"

"You're welcome! You're so welcome!"

Evanne laughed again, wiping her eyes on her hand. "Wait until the office sees me with my real hair!"

"No one will be able to take their eyes off you. You're beautiful!"

"Thanks to you. But enough about me! How are you? Did you go to church this weekend?"

"Not this weekend," Leticia answered around a little custard that dribbled out of the corner of her mouth. She wiped it away.

"Did you hear from toothy?"

"Nope, didn't call, still waiting on those dentures."

As they walked to get their coffee, everyone they passed stop to stare at Evanne, who seemed pleased but otherwise ignored everyone.

Whispers followed them, and with each one, Evanne's grin got wider and wider.

"Evanne!" said Pete on his way back from the break room. "You have more hair than you did Friday!"

"And it's beautiful!" said another worker as she stopped.

In fact, a small crowd gathered around Evanne as she and Leticia poured their coffee; everyone was shocked to learn that she had real hair and was wearing it to work!

Evanne commented to her friend, "Leticia, this morning as I walked into the office, I felt different. I felt as if a dark cloud has lifted and been replaced with beaming sunshine."

"Me, too! The whole office feels different today."

"Maybe they fumigated the office this weekend and pumped some love in the air," Evanne joked. "Nah, we just didn't realize what an emotional black hole that woman was."

No need to name the woman.

"You know how some people just suck all the happiness and joy out of a room? Well, that woman did it for the whole office. And now we're getting back to the way things *should* be."

"I hope you're right!"

Leticia returned to her cubicle to find a sticky note from Frances asking her to see Mr. Foles at 10:00 a.m. today. For once, Leticia was not nervous at all, and right on time, she dashed over to Frances's area.

"Hello, sunshine."

Leticia smiled.

"Did you enjoy Friday?" asked the matronly assistant.

"Oh, yes! I loved it! Also, thank you for the coat. That is all I talked about at the rooming house this entire weekend. I even called Mrs. Shelton. She is the only person in my district in Jamaica that has a phone, and she relayed a message to my mother for me. I was hoping this would help my mother to take her mind off her own pains. Frances, I have never seen so many types of foods and meats in my entire life!"

"Wonderful! Well, Mr. Foles is ready for you now." She opened the door to the private office for Leticia and stepped back to let the young woman in. Frances then closed the door to return to her desk.

To her surprise, Paul was also in the meeting.

"Good morning, Leticia," Mr. Foles greeted her.

"Hello, there, Leticia," Paul said with his usual charming smile, and just the hint of a blush. He laughed. "It's okay, Leticia; you can sit down."

"How is your mother?" Mr. Foles asked.

"Sir, she is getting better by the day. I called a neighbor this weekend and left her a message to tell her about the wonderful celebration on Friday. I was hoping the good news would help some pain to go away."

The two gentleman smiled along with Leticia.

"She is walking," the Jamaican continued, "but just a few steps at a time. She was pretty banged up, you understand." The two men nodded sympathetically. "It's going to take time for her to get back to her regular self."

"Of course."

Leticia went on to detail the conditions back home. "Everything else is still the same. She's with Aunt Peggy and Uncle JoJo. And sister Fala from her church is still taking the produce to the market for us."

"I am not surprised at the help your family is getting," said Mr. Foles. "It is apparent that you are good people."

Leticia smiled demurely. "Thank you, sir."

"Here is the news, Leticia. One, here's your paycheck. Two, as of Friday evening, Melba is no longer with Lexhouse Advertising."

"Sir!"

"She tendered her resignation Friday. She came in on Saturday to meet with me and human resources. She took all of her personal effects and returned all company properties that were in her possession."

"I didn't even notice that her office was cleaned out!"

"Yes. Three, going forward, you will report to Henry Ross, who will be filling the position vacated by Melba," Mr. Foles said.

"Oh! Well, he'll be good in the position," Leticia said neutrally. She didn't know Henry that well. Other than the occasional leer, he mostly ignored her.

"We'd like you to help him transition into the role. You have a better idea than anyone else here what Melba's workload looked like. I'm sure he'll appreciate your help."

"Of course. I'm happy to help, sir."

"Good, good. And one last thing," Mr. Foles interjected. "I understand that you were told you're a file clerk. I also understand that you were, well, performing duties at Melba's instruction as though you were her personal assistant or secretary. I just want to clarify. You are nobody's assistant, and you are not a file clerk. Your official title has always been document control specialist. You are no longer going to be asked to perform any duties that don't pertain to your position."

"Oh, good," Leticia murmured.

Mr. Foles nodded. "I think I speak for everybody when I say we are very pleased with your performance. You have demonstrated a lot of initiative, drive, and perseverance. You met with challenges and met them head on. Eventually, once you've accumulated more experience, we would not mind seeing you sitting in Melba's office, because in a tight spot, you were able to come through. Continue to work as hard as you can, especially with your attitude. Those are exactly the qualities we want in our account executives."

"Then we'd be working as peers," Paul commented.

Leticia nodded.

"Paul," Mr. Foles said, "if you could please excuse us for a moment."

"Of course, sir." Paul stood and spoke softly to Leticia. "Congratulations."

Was that a tremor she detected in his voice? Now that Melba was gone, would his feelings change …?

Once he had closed the door behind him, Mr. Foles turned back to Leticia and said, "Now, Leticia, I understand you had a very upsetting encounter with Melba."

Leticia nodded slowly, wide eyed.

"Yes. HR would like to speak with you further about that incident. We hadn't realized Melba's condition had become so … well. The well-being of our employees is always the top of our priority list, you realize."

"Of course, sir."

"We would never knowingly ask employees to put themselves in harm's way."

"I know that, sir."

"Good! You're a valued employee here, and we want to take care of you. Did you require any medical care after Melba's assault?"

"No, sir."

"Good, good."

"Is Melba okay, sir? I mean, I was so shocked by what she did ..."

"We all were, Leticia! I'm afraid I don't have any information about her mental or physical state. She called in and accused you of attacking her, but you more than most know the value of Melba's word these days. When I saw her Saturday, she was bundled in her coat and didn't look any different to me. When I think back on how seriously I took her false accusations against you—stealing money and the like—I'm ashamed to admit how thoroughly she fooled me with her insinuations and half truths and lies."

"Me, too, sir; me, too. And I worked with her every day!"

When Leticia stepped out of the office, she was positively glowing. Frances grinned at her and came over to give her a congratulatory hug. "The new assignment? You deserve it, sweetie!" Frances said. "And putting up with that woman. You won't believe what she said—" Frances looked around to see if anyone was listening. Then she took Leticia by the elbow and pulled the Jamaican closer to Frances's own desk. Mr. Foles's assistant whispered, "You know how it is. The whole office will know this by noon anyway. Melba didn't resign at first, you know."

"She didn't?"

"She called to accuse you of attacking her."

"Mr. Foles said!"

"Don't you worry; Mr. Foles never believed her. She's like the boy who cried wolf. She used up whatever credibility she had a long time ago. Besides, she was talking like a madwoman, from what I overheard. She said you used voodoo against her!" Frances shook her head. "What nonsense."

"Voodoo comes from Haiti," Leticia said.

"Does it?"

"She accused me of sabotaging her?" Crocodile tears welled up in Leticia's eyes. "I only ever tried to be nice to her. My papa told me to come here, lie low, keep my head down, just learn everything I could about New York and business." A big fat tear streaked down Leticia's cheek. "That's all I was trying to do. I was as nice to her as I could be."

"I know, Leticia. Everyone here knows," Frances said. She patted Leticia's arm. "Don't you worry about anything. Mr. Foles is going to fix everything all right. You've been nothing but a joy since you've been here."

Leticia ventured a small smile. "Thank you," she said. "Everyone here has been so nice to me. Well, everyone except—"

"No need to name names. We all know who that is. And she's not here anymore. It's a new day at Lexhouse!"

The rest of the day continued as perfectly as the beginning. She played all her CDs, but only her favorite songs and sang along with them. At lunch, she started to tell Evanne the news, but Evanne beat her to the punch.

"I always make a point to know what is going on wherever I work!" Evanne said with a sneaky grin.

"Leticia, you are a good friend, but I just have to ask you one thing. These men you are always meeting: they are always crippled or scared or marred. What is up with that?"

"Oh, Evanne, just laugh it off. I made all that up."

"You—! Really? Even Toothy?"

"Yes, even Toothy."

Evanne was quiet for a long moment. Then she just shook her head and laughed. "Yeah, those stories were pretty out there. Don't worry, girl; I don't judge. I'm the last person to judge! Everyone has a secret; yours is meeting nonexistent men." Evanne laughed again. "You are still my friend. Leticia, you know that you are the only person that never asked me about my hair and wigs."

"I figured if there is something you wanted for me to know, you would tell me."

Evanne nodded. "That's why I was willing to tell you about the cancer. And see what happened? I told Tony that night, 'I can trust Leticia. She's good people.' And see, Leticia? You prove it; you bring me back some good ole Jamaican medicine that gives me back my hair. That's what faith means to me; I take life one day at a time and fill it with the best of everything. Thank God I am now cancer free. That is a big reason why I love Tony; he was with me the entire time. So, my dear Jamaican friend, we all only have one life to live, and I am going to live it."

Both ladies got up and just hugged each other as if they were the only two people left in this world.

After lunch, they stopped by Melba's old office. It was empty except for brand-new furniture, and it was so clean it practically sparkled. Henry was unpacking boxes.

"One day you might be sitting in there," Evanne whispered into Leticia's ears.

Leticia just laughed.

Later, as she was leaving, she heard Paul call her name. Startled, she turned and found him jogging up to her. Like her, he was heading out; he was wearing his coat and carrying a case.

"Going home?" he asked.

"Yes, sir."

"I deserve that, don't I?" he said amiably. He opened the door for her. "Can I walk with you?"

"Yes ... Paul."

He chuckled. "That's better. I owe you an apology. I let Melba get to me too much the other day. I'm sorry how I reacted. It wasn't my best moment. I just thought, well, I knew Melba was already giving you a hard time. I didn't want to give her any more ammunition. Against you or against me."

They paused at the elevator in the hall. Paul hit the "down" button.

Oh! thought Leticia. *So part of the reason he backed off was to protect me?*

"And so I think I inadvertently ended up snubbing you. And I could smack myself for it now." He looked at her expectantly. "Do you think you can forgive me?"

"I don't know," she hedged. Paul looked so crestfallen she was torn between laughing and reaching out to give him a big hug.

The elevator dinged, and the doors slid open. The pair stepped on, and the doors shut behind them. They were alone. Paul was watching his feet, all semblance of a smile faded away.

"I don't know," she said again. "Maybe I should 'focus on work right now.'"

The elevator lurched into downward motion.

Paul groaned. "I wish I could take every word back. But I understand, Leticia, I really do. I ... well, I wanted to ask for a second chance, but I don't deserve it."

"That's true," she said teasingly. She reached out and hit the button to make the elevator stop.

Paul looked at the display of elevator buttons, and then at Leticia, his brow furrowed questioningly. Leticia took one of his hands in hers. "That's true, but that doesn't mean I wouldn't give you one."

It took a minute to sink in, before a slow smile spread over Paul's face. His blue eyes filled with a light that had dimmed. Leticia reached up and traced the edge of his strong jaw, his short stubble rough under her fingertip. His took that hand in his own, leaned forward, and locked his lips on hers.

* * *

After she got home that evening, Leticia immediately called Aunt Martha into her room. "Auntie, the woman quit, and Paul kissed me again!"

Martha screamed with joy, and soon, the two women were jumping up and down and clapping hands. Uncle George wandered into the room. "Wha's da racket?"

"Leticia's awful boss left the company, and her boyfriend—"

"Auntie!"

"—kissed her again!"

Uncle George laughed and hugged Leticia congratulations. "That calls for a drink!"

"Sure do!"

"Let's make up a new drink. We'll call it the Melba Punch." Leticia laughed. The trio moved out into the kitchen, and Uncle George started pulling out some liquor bottles. "Gotta start with some rum."

"What'd they say?" Aunt Martha asked. "What was the reason why she left?"

"I don't know, Auntie; they just told me she resigned, and they're having me report to Henry now."

"Oh, Henry? Do I know that name? Have you mentioned him?"

Leticia shook her head. "He used to work for Paul. He's been promoted."

"Him and not you?"

Leticia shrugged. "He's been there longer."

"Well, sweetheart, your day is coming!"

"And some juice," Uncle George muttered.

"Yes, Uncle," Leticia agreed. "Prune juice! That's perfect for the Melba Punch."

"But no," Aunt Martha protested. "This is a celebratory drink. It should be the Mama Dassa Punch!"

"Mama Dassa? Who is Mamma Dassa?" Uncle George interrupted.

The two women burst out laughing.

"You know what Mama Dassa told me?" Leticia asked. "She said her solution would make Melba twitch. And it did, Auntie! It made her *twitch twitch*."

"The Mama Dassa Twitch, then!" Aunt Martha declared.

Uncle George finished fussing with the drink. He poured three jiggers. They clinked glasses, and the women said, "To Mama Dassa!"

"Who's Mama Dassa?" Uncle George asked after taking a sip.

Leticia and Martha just laughed again. Then Aunt Martha said, "Leticia, let's call your mother now."

They got Mira Patrick on the phone and shared the news. Leticia told her aunt and her mother everything that had happened, unembellished and unchanged.

Her mother had a long laugh. "Yes," she said. "Mama Dassa once again."

"Yes, Mama. Twitch twitch!"

All three women laughed.

CHAPTER 27

T HE NEXT MORNING, LETICIA FOUND a small bag under her desk. After removing the contents, she realized it was from Paul. Her heart jumped. A gift already. She secretly took the bag into the bathroom and entered a stall. As she pulled the contents from the bag, she was surprised to see a brand new cell phone, with a note attached. "This is so I can communicate with you. Don't worry; the cost will be on me. My phone number is already programmed for you. Call that number anytime. Plus, a lady needs a cell phone in this time and age. Never know when an emergency will happen." Leticia beamed from left to right. This was the best she had ever felt since moving to New York.

"Wow, he really cares," she whispered to herself. She was happy; she could not tell anyone at work. And she could not wait to tell Aunt Martha. She called Aunt Martha from the bathroom.

"I told you, my child: what is for you will always be for you, so enjoy!"

Leticia hurried to her workspace to put her gift in her handbag. She was beaming.

Evanne stopped by and insisted they go to see Melba's old office after getting themselves some coffee. Henry Ross was unpacking boxes and trying to settle in. Absorbed in his efforts, the portly fellow didn't look up.

"Hello, Henry," Leticia said.

Henry looked up. "Oh, hello!" He smiled, more of a leer, at Leticia. Then his gaze shifted to Evanne. His smile faded, and he nodded at her.

"Still smells like crap in here," Evanne said cheerfully.

Henry nodded. He looked perplexed, as if he wasn't sure if he should be offended or not.

"Mr. Foles asked me to help you transition into your new role," Leticia said formally.

"Of course, of course. I asked for you to be my assistant."

"I'm not anybody's assistant," Leticia reminded him. Was it something about this office that made people think about her that way? "I'm a document control specialist. I'm reporting to you, but not as your assistant."

"Well, either way, I'll be working closely with you." This was not said in a strictly professional manner. Leticia smiled uncertainly.

Evanne whispered, "Working *on* you is more like it."

Henry's sharp gaze moved to Evanne. "What was that?"

"I saaaid, 'Working *on* Leticia is more like it.'"

"Evanne!" Leticia exclaimed, scandalized.

But Evanne just waved her objection aside. "Really, Henry Ross, don't go getting above yourself just because you went and got yourself a promotion. We're all equals here."

Henry looked affronted but again awkward and unsure how to respond. "I need to ask Leticia some questions about the work Melba left behind," he said stiffly. There was a short pause, and then he added, "Alone."

"Well, you behave yourself, Henry Ross. Don't forget what happened to Leticia's last boss who didn't play nice!" With that, Evanne winked at Leticia and strode off.

"Finally," Henry said under his breath.

Leticia stepped into the office. "How can I help you, Henry?"

Henry didn't make eye contact. "I've been so busy unpacking I haven't eaten today. Go get me a muffin, cupcake, will you?"

"Um, okay. Did you want a muffin and a cupcake both, or just one or the other?"

Henry looked up at her and then rolled his eyes. "Oh, Lord. You always seemed so nice and demure. Evanne's rubbing off on you, and not in a good way. Not allowed to call you 'cupcake,' is that it? I'd like a *muffin*, sweetheart."

Leticia paused again, put off by his manner. It wasn't exactly new; he had a tendency to say inappropriate things, but this was taking it to a new level. She would have been happy to get him a muffin as a nice gesture, but he was being a jackass about it. Was this office really cursed or something? "Actually, I'm pretty busy. Mr. Foles asked me to help you get caught up with Melba's work, but if you don't need me for that, I really should get back to work."

Henry pursed his lips and then walked over to her. Leticia shied away, and Henry closed the office door. "Look, Mr. Foles already told you that you have to help me. So there are two ways this can go. We get along." Henry took a step toward Leticia. This time she didn't back off, and he came uncomfortably close to her personal space. "Or we don't get along. In the first case, we'll both be happy. In the second, I guarantee you'll be unhappier than me." Henry smiled at Leticia. His front teeth seemed awfully prominent, and one was slightly angled.

Leticia didn't smile back. Seriously, what was it with her and all these witchy people? Her mind's eye went right to her purse. Even though the sticks were meant for Melba, Leticia thought they might work on Henry, too. Melba was gone, but Mama Dassa's sticks weren't. They were sitting right in her purse in a little plastic baggy, ready and waiting, like a loaded gun.

At that, Leticia smiled brightly. "Would you like coffee with that muffin, sir?"

THE END